Praise for John Rechy a̲

"Fresh, beautiful, totally courageou̲ ̲ ̲ ̲ ̲
Rechy doesn't fit into categories. He transcends them. His individ̲
is unique, perfect, loving and strong."   —Carolyn See

"An elegy of a lost era."   —*Arts & Understanding*

"With his ground-breaking *City of Night* in 1963, Rechy wrote the manual for
gay representation in contemporary literature. . . . With his latest, *The Coming
of the Night*, the author comes full circle. . . . [His] style has a lyricism and
emotional content that belies its simplicity."   —*Flaunt*

"A rhapsody of odd, quirky, hilarious people trying to find meaning and
chaos in Southern California . . . The ending to the novel is frenetic, sweaty,
almost religious."   —*El Paso Times*

"What he has given us for more than thirty years is a wonderful and terrifying gift. . . . He has given us life and literature."   —Michael Bronski

"Rechy creates a stark, stinging, and anxious atmosphere in which desire
makes people do awful things, and lust commingles with promiscuity, ob-
session, self-hatred, depression, and narcissism."   —*Library Journal*

"[He] is one of the heroic figures of contemporary American life . . . a touch-
stone of moral integrity and artistic innovation."   —Edmund White

"Rechy doesn't skimp on plot, character or action, and the ingenious ending takes an unanticipated but thoroughly logical turn. In its gritty evoca-
tion of time and place, the novel goes beyond its narrow subject matter,
reaching for a broader and deeper understanding of an era."
                                                      —*Publishers Weekly*

"His tone rings absolutely true, is absolutely his own, and he has the kind of
discipline which allows him a rare and beautiful recklessness. He tells the
truth, and tells it with such passion that we are forced to share in the life he
conveys. This is a most humbling and liberating achievement."
                                                          —James Baldwin

ALSO BY JOHN RECHY

Novels:
City of Night
Numbers
This Day's Death
The Vampires
The Fourth Angel
Rushes
Bodies and Souls
Marilyn's Daughter
The Miraculous Day of Amalia Gómez
Our Lady of Babylon

Nonfiction:
The Sexual Outlaw: A Documentary

Plays:
Rushes
Tigers Wild
Momma as She Became—But Not as She Was (one-act)

The Coming of the Night

A NOVEL BY

John Rechy

Grove Press
New York

Copyright © 1999 by John Rechy

The author wishes to express his thanks to Paul Zone of Man2Man for permission to quote from the copyrighted songs "Hard Hitting Love" and "Who Knows What Evil?" written by Paul Zone and Miki Zone.

Published simultaneously in Canada
Printed in the United States of America

FIRST PAPERBACK EDITION

Library of Congress Cataloging-in-Publication Data

Rechy, John.
    The coming of the night : a novel / by John Rechy.
        p.   cm.
    ISBN 0-8021-3742-3   (pbk.)
    I. Title.
PS3568.E28C66   1999
813'.54—dc21   99-22538
                                                    CIP

Design by Laura Hammond Hough

Grove Press
841 Broadway
New York, NY 10003

00 01 02 03   10 9 8 7 6 5 4 3 2 1

For my brother Roberto,

and my sister Blanche

And for the memory of my brother Yvan,

and of my sister Olga

I would like to thank Melanie Gill for her graciousness during the writing of this book, and Michael Earl Snyder for his invaluable creative observations, suggestions, and encouragement, from the inception of this novel to its completion.

J.R.

Rage, rage against the dying of the light.

—Dylan Thomas

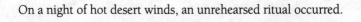

On a night of hot desert winds, an unrehearsed ritual occurred.

J.R., Los Angeles, 1999

Saturday
Summer
1981

One

The park in West Hollywood is small, attractive, no more than two blocks square. In the morning, parents roam about with their children, who often stop to play in sandy areas. Other strollers, alone or in couples, walk their dogs. Still others wander along flower hedges or sit on benches under trees, some of which sprout Japanese orchids. A scattering of palm trees among ficus and pines reminds that this is Southern California.

Today, Saturday, there is an added reminder that this is the City of Lost Angels. A Sant'Ana is blowing. Each hot arid season, these winds—known as "devil winds" because of their destructiveness—invite fires. They spread flames that twist this way or that, depending on the whim of fierce currents.

Jesse
MORNING

Jesse—"the kid"—woke with one thought on his mind. Today he would do something wild to celebrate one glorious year of being gay—and it *was* great to be gay and young and good-looking and *hot*. Of course, his designation of "one year" was not exact. He had been gay from the time he became aware of sex—early—and he had turned twenty-two three days ago, but the celebration he planned came from the fact that he had been able to go into gay bars only for that long. Not that he'd been idle before that. He had had his share of sexual encounters. This special day, his strategy formed, he would charge himself up from morning to earlier night. He would not come until deepest night, and then he would be the hottest ever.

Wild!

In his bedroom in his neat apartment in a court of units surrounding a pool in West Hollywood, Jesse became hard thinking about the prospect. He sat on the edge of his bed wearing only white briefs, now being punched by his aroused cock.

Depending on how he dressed, combed his hair, he could look eighteen, if he wanted. Often, in bars, he would be asked for identification. He was very good-looking—and, even better than that, spectacularly "cute," a description he welcomed, along with being called "Kid Jesse." That made him sound like a young outlaw, although, someone once pointed out, he must be confusing Billy the Kid with Jesse James.

Still boyish, but not in the least bit "fem," he was neither tall nor short. His blue eyes were rendered clearer by dark eyelashes, and his streaked blond hair was just long enough to allow an occasional strand to fall over his forehead. Thank God femmish long hair was going out of style among gay guys. Checking himself out in the mirror of a bar, he knew he looked sensational.

An expert gymnast in school, he did not work out with weights, like other gay men were doing. He ran, biked, swam. That kept his body tight, fabulously defined. He ate only good healthful food, didn't do drugs, and he slept a full eight hours each night, except, of course, when, real late, the cruising just kept getting better. He had a natural glow that courted a perfect tan in summer—now. The tan accentuated glistening hairs that coated his legs, which he showed off by wearing shorts as long as the weather allowed, into the beginning of winter, and even during winter in Southern California.

He was usually alone. By choice. Sure he had friends, lots of them, lots of invitations to parties, but that often put him in a bad situation. Guys he was not attracted to were attracted to him. Those he did have sex with wanted to get together again, and he preferred variety.

There was another reason for his choice to be a loner. He didn't want guys he went with to know more about him than they needed to know, and that was that he was hot. All *he* required of his sex partners was that they be lusty—he liked that word—and want what he wanted.

Existing only as you appeared to be—that was another great thing possible in the gay world of cruising. You didn't have to waste time talking, except to make arrangements about getting together. He loved being a terrific fantasy figure. So why mix things up with identities that didn't matter? Yes, he'd figured life out—gay life, there was no other.

Jesse welcomed the perspiration that had moistened his shorts and outlined his cock—and especially, he knew as he stood, his buttocks, indenting the crack. He touched himself there and closed his eyes—imagining.

He forced himself not to think now about tonight. He didn't want to ruin his plan by getting too aroused alone. That would be a waste. Ugh.

What had triggered this huge desire?

It wasn't unusual for him to feel horny, especially on weekends. Had his plan originated last weekend when he met two hunky guys and went home with them? He had been fucked by both, several times. They took turns entering him, assuming a wonderful rhythm, a couple of thrusts, and then it was the other's turn for a few more thrusts. There had been hardly a moment that he didn't have a cock in him, and the brief seconds without added even more sensation when they ended. The two guys had lain back, prone, face up, legs spread, butt against butt, cocks pressed together to form one doubled erection, and he'd lowered himself over it, tantalizing the two guys into believing he would attempt to take them both into him—and he thought about it—but he just remained there, two straining cock-heads quivering at his ass, titillating the downy hairs there. He pushed himself into one of the cocks and then immediately into the other and both guys came in him—wow!—but when he left their house, he felt lustier—and went with another guy and kept wishing for two.

There was also this to account for the sexual demand he welcomed. The day itself—the impression from last night had been confirmed—was ready for celebration, heated with those winds that were supposed to arouse tensions, and—he'd heard this—violence, but who wanted that? Whatever the truth, Jesse knew that the Sant'Anas charged the night with sexual fever.

And sex was everywhere!

There were hunky guys on every corner. You didn't even have to go home with a guy, if you didn't want to. There were cruisy places all over where you could make out, right there, all hours—bars, baths, even some streets—and you could move from one person to another, have several at the same time. Not that he wouldn't *ever* want to go home with one guy again. Sure, that was fine, having sex several times with one person—or two—but there was a time for that, and a time when you needed more.

Music—that's what would start this magical day on its way. He riffled among his collection of albums. Van Halen—which song? "Everybody Wants Some." True, and more than some. "Loss of Control." Yes!

The agitated strum of a guitar, a howl or a siren, laughter—a bomb or a roaring motorcycle. His sweat-stained briefs pasted to his body, he gyrated to the record's opening explosion. Who needed control?

Without altering his fast rhythm, he let the next song play out its funky tune, about—what else?—love, love turning tragic.

Tragic? Who needed tragic.

He stopped the record abruptly. He needed something else to set this special day on its way—the song he'd danced to, and shouted out phrases from, when it first came out last year, the beginning of the eighties, the beginning of his life. The song's words had seemed to announce the vista opening before him—of bars, sex, dancing, sex, great times, sex, partying, sex, great sex, sex— *Ugh* for straight music, with all those sappy songs. The stuff they played in gay bars *said* something, really *told* it, knew what it was *all* about. He found the album, the song he was looking for, Kool and the Gang and "Celebration." All *right*!

Although he hadn't heard the record in a long time, his body responded from memory, swaying into the rhythm before the alerting beat started, announcing a long-lasting party that had just begun.

He tossed himself into the drumming pulse, which electrified his young body, connected him to invisible partners, lots of them, *lots!*— all fusing within the same current surging between them, among them, through them, commanding their bodies in reckless synchrony. His head, arms, hands, hips thrashed—exhilarated. Perspiration dampened every limb, his growing excitement contoured on the white shorts.

Wow! That was enough of a charge, for now. He turned off the stereo.

When tonight ended, right before dawn, he would have the best orgasm of his life, so far, because it would contain all those he would withhold throughout the day. He had to plan everything, to make it all possible—and it sure was possible.

He stood up and looked out at the pool. A man was lounging there. From here all Jesse could see were his long bare legs. The man stood up, to oil himself. From the back, he looked fine—broad shoulders, tapered waist, dark hair. Masculine, so far. Sometimes you couldn't tell until they started talking and, ugh, what a surprise. Safe to assume, too, with that bikini he was wearing, that the man was gay. Gay guys weren't afraid to wear brief trunks. Straight guys wanted to cover themselves up and most of them should. Did the man have a mustache? Jesse didn't much care for mustaches—they made guys look like cops. Still, so many gay men were sporting them that you couldn't avoid them. Just wait, though, soon the fad would pass, and the only ones left with bushy mouths *would* be cops.

How old was the man?

Jesse went with no one over thirty, although sometimes he couldn't be sure because good-looking gay men in shape often appeared younger than they were. He preferred guys *slightly* older than him, because he liked being "the young one"—the kid. Old guys depressed him. Old guys who *really* depressed him—why didn't they stop cruising, who'd want them?—were the ones who looked old but dressed like kids, brief shorts over sagging butts—ugh—and then there were the old guys with grizzly stubble, decked out in the same leather stuff they wore ages ago, as if *that* would keep them young. He winced when he saw them. Sometimes they even acted *fem*.

The man by the pool turned in Jesse's direction.

O-*kay!* Make him his first "conquest" in preparation for this night that would be like no other? He could hardly wait for the coming of the night.

But he would, and that would make the sweaty night even hotter. And *wild!*

Buzz, Toro, and Linda
MORNING

Buzz tried to leave the house before his mother could detect his absence. That way he wouldn't have to listen to her bitching about his staying out of trouble. He was, after all, almost eighteen, and he knew more than she did about all kinds of shit. These hot winds excited him, made him feel mean.

When, in a few minutes, he joined his friends, Toro and Boo and Fredo, he'd talk them into getting some booze, picking up some street chicks, maybe gettin' a little rough. Toro—he called himself that because of his bullhead and because, he boasted, he had a cock like one, a cock he constantly groped—was only nineteen but because of his size he could buy liquor, easy. Boo was tiny, but you'd better never tell him that—tiny and tough, with tattoos crawling over his skinny arms. Fredo—"the crazy one" because he shaved his head daily and never did anything first but always went along with what anyone suggested—constantly scratched his shaved head. He, Buzz, was the "sexy one," the one who approached girls—punkies, druggies—on Hollywood Boulevard. He had a vague "Valley" drawl and a sleepy look.

Now he sat on the far side of the steps that his mother called "the porch." He would hide until Toro came by. Toro drove a hot Chevy convertible he spent hours on, keeping it bitchin'.

Buzz hated this ugly city, one of several outside Los Angeles in the San Fernando Valley, tract houses, stucco houses, mobile homes that never moved, auto-part garages. Along the blocks, skeletons of cars squatted permanently on yards of weeds and dirt, hoods up, bodies propped on bricks. Once he had seen a photograph of the City in the fifties, and it had looked just like it did now. "White trash" and "rednecks"—that's what they called the guys from this part of the Valley, including even Mexican dudes, tough dudes—*not* fuckin' immigrants!—who lived here and hung out with white guys. He didn't mind the designation "redneck." It gave him and his friends a ready reputation for being tough.

He heard the Chevy approaching—blasts of Judas Priest shooting into the air from Toro's tape deck—before he saw the shiny car swerving to avoid a huge tumbleweed, several tangled together, that crashed, bursting into splinters, against the window of a Carl's Jr. take-out.

Still hunched by one side of the house to sneak away, Buzz prepared a wide smile to greet Toro. That might help when he explained that he and Fredo and Boo hadn't been able to score the shit they had planned to bag up loose and sell at a good profit to those dumb punkies in Hollywood. "Gee, Toro," he had rehearsed last night with Boo and Fredo, "when we took a taste from those niggers, it was dummy shit—even for punkies—and the niggers tried to go AWOL on us, but we messed them up—they turned out to be suckers, man. So—" Here he would spread out his hands. Empty hands, wide smile. Then he'd give back Toro's investment.

"Wassup?"

Christ, even in this wind, Toro had the top of his Chevy down—and he already had a chick with him. His girl?—the one he talked about but they had never met?

"Wassup?" Buzz answered back, shouting, as they always had to, over the stereo—and, today, the wind—while he sized up the girl next to Toro, where *he* usually sat, in front.

"Linda," Toro introduced the girl.

Without answering, she cocked her head toward the music. "I like this one." While Toro bounced his head to the machine-gunning sounds, she repeated random words. "Crushed—rage—" She turned to Buzz and said, "Hi."

Dark, a sexy bitch, Buzz evaluated Linda, wearing a brief tight top to show off her tits—look at those fuckers tryin' to shove out, and look at her skirt so tiny you wouldn't have to lift much to see her cunt. Fuckin' bitch. He'd like to shove it into her so hard she'd scream.

Transferring to Linda the smile he had prepared for his explanation to Toro about last night's deal, Buzz hopped into the front seat, his thigh pressed against hers.

"Hey, don't crowd me, man!" Linda protested.

Buzz pushed his leg tighter against hers.

"Yeah, man, don't crowd us," Toro said, nodding toward the back seat.

What the fuck! Angry, Buzz jumped to the back. Fuckin' bitch, she wouldn't be acting so close with Toro if she knew how easy it was gonna be to fake him out about last night and the niggers. Buzz restored his smile at that thought, and waited to speak the memorized words to Toro.

"Hey, Buzz—," Linda started, lowering the stereo.

"Hey, man," Buzz objected, "turn the fuckin' sounds *up*—I like that part." He waited for Toro to agree. He always played this tape at a blast. Now he continued to nod his head to the lowered sounds.

Linda didn't respond to Buzz's order. "Huccome you smile so much, Buzz—man?" she asked him. Then she raised the volume again.

Fuckin' cunt. She had just wanted to make sure he'd hear her. Well, so what? "How about this, Linda?" He pulled at his lips with two fingers and twisted his smile into a mean smirk.

Father Norris
MORNING

Father Norris had awakened, as he always did on weekends, into the awareness that, very soon, he would be hearing confessions—more than on weekdays, when only *beatas*—old rigidly religious Mexican women who lived in the neighborhood about lower Sunset Boulevard in the section known as Echo Park, populated mostly by Hispanics—confessed insignificant sins as if they were giant transgressions. Father Norris was convinced that many priests enjoyed hearing sins and passing harsh judgment. Father Terso, old and irritable, was known for the severity of his penances, and some *beatas* searched him out at confession for that. Father Norris had seen younger confessors pretend not to be aware that the old priest's booth was available, in order to avoid confessing to him. Father Norris tried to be understanding, and that made him lenient in the penances he awarded. Often he wished that he could absorb the sins of those who confessed, absorb them and thus purify the sinner through his own acts of contrition.

Now, in his confessional, he waited, with his missal, for the next confessor to recite a litany of minor sins. He removed his rimmed glasses. No one would see him without them here. He did not need them, and wore them only in an attempt to thwart the designation he did not welcome—"the handsome young priest." For a period in his life, he had dieted strictly, to make himself so thin that he would be unattractive, but that only added to the intensity of his moody looks. He tried eating, to gain unsightly weight, but the added food nauseated him, and he stopped, still lean, still handsome. Not that anything could obstruct his devotion to purity. From the first moment in his early life when he had seen the body of Christ wrenching with pain and love on His crucifix, he had known that he would devote his life to Him, serve only Him, love only Him, small token for His extreme sacrifice. Daily, he knelt praying before the crucifix at the altar. Daily he renewed his dedication to serve the tortured figure, "I will be faithful to You, to Your calling, I shall strive to be worthy of You, Your grace and Your love."

"I have to speak to *him*." Father Norris heard a woman's voice, Spanish-accented, talking too loudly into the usual quiet of the church. "But I was here first," another woman objected in Spanish. "I know, but—"

Why the urgency? He was the only one hearing confessions now—Father Terso preferred to hear them during the earliest part of the morning, "when confessors are closest to their most grievous sins." Father Norris cocked his head toward the small screen that would separate him from the woman who would now be kneeling in the adjoining cubicle.

"Father Norris!" The voice, clearly that of the woman who had demanded to go ahead of the other, rose in urgency.

It was not usual to address a priest by his name during confession, and certainly not in that commanding tone. Was she the woman he had seen outside the rectory? She had seemed to be about to approach him when he hurried past her, a strange, sorrowful—ominous—woman wearing a black coat, or shawl, in this heat. Was she in mourning? he'd wondered.

"Bless me, Father," the woman in the confessional rushed her recitation in accented English.

She had not finished the invocation. Bless me, Father, for I have sinned. So he said, "What are your sins?"

"Help my son."

"You can't confess for another."

"He's a *maricon*—"

Father Norris knew the designation—a *maricon,* a "queer."

"—and he's been arrested for prostitution—"

Father Norris leaned back, away from the words—and then forward.

"He's out now and back on the same streets."

"How do you know that?"

"I went there, to that street, that Santa Monica Boulevard. He was there, he's always there. He saw me, he ran away. When I returned later, he was getting into a car with an older man, Father."

Father Norris almost stood to leave the confessional, to confront the woman, tell her that hers was not a confession, that he would not listen to this terrible story, tell her that he—

"His name is Angel, Father." She pronounced the name in Spanish—*Ahn*-hel.

"*Ahn*-hel," Father Norris repeated the name. "How old is—Ahn-hel?"

"Eighteen."

An eighteen-year-old prostitute. How was that possible?

"Some of the others on that street, the ones who have been there the longest, they're already corrupt, young but corrupt—but not him, Father. Not yet."

"The young can be knowledgeable beyond their years," Father Norris mouthed words. "Have you extended to him spiritually?"

The woman's voice lowered. "With all my soul. I've seen the power in your eyes, Father, I've seen with what love you kneel before our martyred Lord, I've heard your sermons, I've watched you for very long. I *know* you. Today I gathered the courage to turn to you."

Father Norris listened only to words now. He had seen Hispanic boys about the rectory. Ahn-hel—even in his mind he pronounced the name as she had—would have dark hair, yellowish eyes. And a sad smile.

"Is that what he looks like?"

"What?"

He had thought aloud.

"He's very handsome, Father. Beautiful, sad eyes. Very sad."

"If you bring him to me, of course I'll—"

"No, Father! Listen! He won't come!"

"But I cannot—" He prepared words to deny the outrageous demand the woman was about to make.

The woman's next words were such a quiet whisper that he wasn't sure that was what she had spoken. So he repeated what he had heard. "—naked?"

"—yes, he has a naked Christ tattooed on his back."

A young man was walking the perverse streets of the City, selling his body, which had a tattoo of Our Lord— "Our Lord is stripped of His clothes, of course. He was flogged—" His voice had grown automatic.

"You don't understand. The tattooed Christ is *entirely* naked—*everything* is revealed."

Father Norris closed his eyes. The air conditioner must have stopped. He could not hear its whir, heard only the howls of wind rising—and then a harsh scratching at the small window above his cubicle, which was uncovered at the top. He looked up. A piece of a dry palm frond entangled with debris had been thrust against the window. The snarled mass quivered as if attempting to claw its way in. Then it stopped its desperate trembling and remained there. Father Norris watched it in horrified fascination.

"Find my son! He's waiting for you."

Za-Za and the Cast of *Frontal Assault*
MORNING

"May we gather in the cabana, *s'il vous plaît*?" The voice addressed six handsome men milling about a lavish pool, all naked except for one wearing cutoffs, tank top, and engineer boots. The grounds of the mansion in the hills were bordered by balusters on which were mounted alabaster Greek gods and goddesses. Large trees and high walls thwarted the Sant'Ana, which thrust forth only in nervous attacks.

Za-Za LaGrande, preeminent director of gay pornography, wore a white chiffon blouse, stylish black shoes—short-heeled to foil a stumble—and pleated loose slacks meant to disguise laborious buttocks over heavy legs. Round face swept with orangy blush, false eyelashes weighted down with mascara, red-waxed lips wilting in the heat, orange wig secured, the director, a man in drag, had just spoken in his—her, she preferred the feminine designation—most authoritative voice, her director's voice.

It exhilarated her to direct in drag. Drag asserted that it was a queen, a *drag* queen—*notez bien*—who shaped the fantasies about "studs" and for the "studs" who imitated her filmed images, the very "studs" who would otherwise deride her as "a fat queen," not even allow her in the bars they might frequent. Of course, those who saw her movies knew her only as "Z.Z.," a mysterious appellation that aroused conjecture about her identity, reputed to be, a porn critic wrote, that of a "*man's man.*" Ha!

The squadron of nude men—the man in cutoffs lingering behind—followed her into an elaborate dressing room with upholstered benches. She had told her cast only that they would be filming—"and you must strip quickly, *au naturel*"—in the mansion of "a powerful Hollywood mogul" she discreetly called Mr. Smythe, "with a y and an e."

Feeling distressingly like a coach pep-talking his players in the locker room, Za-Za announced, "We're here to rehearse for a film titled *Frontal Assault.*"

"How do you rehearse fucking and sucking?" Tony Piazza, a dark broody beauty, spoke out everyone's confusion. A twenty-three-year-old Italian with eyes innocent and knowing, he possessed a sensational round butt so famous his fans claimed they could recognize it even if a shot did not reveal the small kangaroo tattooed on his right buttock.

"With a vacuum," Jim Bond, another of Za-Za's stable, offered. He was a not-quite-tall young man with a tendency toward stockiness if he missed a few workouts.

"Think of it as a command performance," Za-Za instructed.

"For the big queen," snickered Sal Domingo. He had masses of dark curls—and buttocks which, some said, rivaled Tony Piazza's, bruitings that had incited a frosty competition between the two men.

Decorum intact, Za-Za went on to explain, "Mr. Smythe wants to enact a lifelong *fantaisie*"—she loved to pepper her speech with French picked up during a night course at a community college—"to see a private performance—he calls it a 'rehearsal'—for which he will pay *beaucoup d'argent,* and for which he has *écrit* a script—"

"Huh?" Dak Boxer offered. Hairy sinewy body heavily tattooed, he specialized in looking mean.

"—yes, he has *written* a script, and he has invited a few wealthy guests for this 'audition,'" Za-Za moved on intrepidly.

"Sugar daddies," said Lars Helmut, except that he pronounced that "chugger dahddies." Square-jawed, with a dumb face, he appeared all the more muscular because his body was shaved except for one shock of hair at his groin.

"*Vraiment, trésor.*" It was true that in addition to being a director of "erotic films," Za-Za was an "entrepreneur" for gay male clients who were smitten with one or another of her "models"—to whom she always gave new names to add panache. The "erotic film" business had reached a tenuous peak—only a smattering of theaters in large cities exhibited porn. Although the industry was abuzz with predictions that video cassette recorders would soon usher in a golden age, now only a select number of gay performers deemed "stars" made money. Most hustled their bodies.

None of that concerned Za-Za now. The source of her enthusiasm was that this "rehearsal" would allow her to leap into "the world of true cinema"—because, despite all the buttocks and cocks she had scrunched behind a camera to record, she was, *vraiment, trésor,* a real *artiste.* All she lacked was the weight of a studio behind her—Mr. Smythe's studio—for her monumental debut. She had already written the script for her epic, *A Message from Out There.* The film would be "a kind of *Last Year at Marienbad* but with *real* ghosts and in bright color," she was prepared to tell Mr. Smythe.

"Now here's a little treat to get you into your roles." From the depths of her pleated slacks, she brought out a cellophane packet and a tiny spoon she had admired at Knott's Berry Farm, and she passed both among the expectant performers.

Rex Steed—the man in cutoffs, "the blond God of porn"—didn't use the spoon. He dipped a finger. Obviously to call attention to himself, he had remained partially clothed. Extravagantly handsome, he was one of a handful of "models" who might be called a "star." He was reputed to pack "ten inches plus"—difficult to verify since photographers learned to shoot from angles that enlarged even modest endowment. Although he was not one of her performers, Mr. Smythe had demanded his presence. "I want to see Rex Steed fuck Tony Piazza's ass."

Ah, Tony Piazza! Za-Za's longing eyes stared at him, as they often did. Catching her hot looks, Tony Piazza assumed an extra-sexy pose. Always tantalizing me, Za-Za fumed. That fabulous ungrateful shit I plucked out of the streets when he was peddling his ass for quarters, and I catapulted him into stardom, like Von Sternberg did Dietrich. Oh, what she wouldn't do to have his fat cock up her ass. But he only *got* fucked, *never* fucked, only sucked, never got sucked. Of course, it was true that without her power as a director she would never be able to approach *any* of these men. Sex was limited to her giving them blow jobs during "auditions." While she puffed and huffed on her knees, they'd close their eyes. If she dared demand to be fucked, the fabulous cocks, even when they pretended to want to squeeze in, stayed so soft she never even felt them. But, oh, if Tony Piazza would deign to fuck, to *put* it in, then God would intercede, guide him into her, and he and she—

Summoning all her dignity, she marched past him and out of the "cabana," followed by her entourage.

Atop a grand veranda mantled with bougainvillea, the great Hollywood mogul sat on a high chair as if he were the Pope. He was a man of about sixty, impeccably dressed in jacket and tie, even in the rising heat. Flanking him, in lesser seats, were four of his friends—"talent scouts." They, too, wore jackets—required?—though no ties. Mr. Smythe had insisted on distancing himself and his friends from the "rehearsal"— "to retain a sense of fantasy." On small tables before the spectators were binoculars. Mr. Smythe's manor, Za-Za thought as she surveyed his domain and mimed ecstatic appreciation for him to note, seemed arrogantly to look away from lesser mansions in these hills—

One of which was burning!

"Thank you for hiring me, darlin'." It was Wes Young, who had just arrived.

"How could I ignore your fabulous uncut cock?" Za-Za had a special fondness for Wes Young because he had been one of her first "stars" and had remained "faithful" when others had tried to lure him away. He had craggy good looks, a lanky body. Today, his wind-rumpled hair exposed his thinning pate. He claimed to be thirty-five. Za-Za noticed the Erase under his eyes, glazed from the coke he snorted for breakfast. He was the only player Mr. Smythe had not specifically asked for. He had merely stated that he wanted "a dark stud with a fabulous uncut cock, lots of skin."

Wes Young pecked her cheek and moved on to the "cabana" to undress. Mr. Smythe's binoculars followed him.

Had Wes Young begun hanging out at the Spotlight, the sleaziest hustling bar in town? After that, where? Za-Za did not let herself wonder what happened to her "actors" when their short reigns ended.

Now she located herself so that Mr. Smythe might note her concentration on his script. When he first discussed this *fantaisie* with her, he had emphasized, "There shall be no deviation from my script. But the finale is yours. *Étonnez-moi.*" He had gone on to explain that those were the instructions—"Astonish me!"—that Diaghilev had given Cocteau when Cocteau was commissioned to do the book for a ballet. As if she hadn't known that famous *riposte*! Indeed, her debut film would be tinged with unobtrusive *surréalisme* that would evoke the sublime Cocteau, except that *her* statues would move their *mouths*, not their eyes. But, now, *trésor*, how could she top what Mr. Smythe was demanding in his script? Art couldn't match the epic of sex occurring everywhere, every day, in the liberated gay world. Pornography could only attempt to mirror it.

"*Faire* close *attention*! Tops over here, and bottoms over there," Za-Za followed Mr. Smythe's directions.

The roles of top-penetrator and bottom-penatratee were neither strictly adhered to in porn—nor in reality. Bottoms might bravely top if called upon to do so, while tops more frequently bottomed. Tony Piazza had acquired legendary status by *always* being a "bottom," and Rex Steed had achieved the level of Olympian hero as a rigorous "top." He insisted that he was "one hundred percent hetero." He would neither suck, nor be fucked—nor even kiss. That made him even more desirable in some quarters—the unattainable stud who deigned to lend his highly restricted presence to the world of gay porn, which he visited only because of huge demand.

Tony Piazza, Sal Domingo, and Jim Bond responded as proud bottoms to Za-Za's direction. Dak Boxer, Lars Helmut, Wes Young—and, taking his time, Rex Steed—sauntered together as tops.

"Vat is da story?" Lars Helmut wanted to know, as if he had just become conscious.

"Boy meets boy, boy sucks boy, boy meets other boy, other boy fucks boy," Jim Bond offered. High-fiving each other, everyone laughed except Rex Steed.

"Contain yourselves, girls," Za-Za warned.

"What the fuck did you call me?" It was a growl from Rex Steed.

Oh, oh. She couldn't afford to have him walk out. "Now, girls— and Mr. Steed, the famous stud," she revised.

"And what about *me*?" demanded Dak Boxer.

"Yeah, vat ya call *us*?" Lars Helmut added to the menace.

"I said, now girls *and* fabulous studs," Za-Za adjusted.

"Uh, Za-Za, bottoms aren't girls, ya know?" Tony Piazza joined the protest.

"All right, all right, *controlez-vous,* studs and studettes!" The last word flew out. She cleared her throat. "The story is this, *trésors.* Marine Sergeant Dick has secretly taken a room in a fabulous motel for the weekend. Sergeant Dick is played by Mr. Lars Helmut."

Rex Steed turned a fierce scowl on her.

"*You,* Mr. Steed, are playing the sergeant's *straight* lover," Za-Za assuaged.

Rex Steed relaxed. Eyeing the gallery at the top of the veranda, he removed his tank top, slowly. From his perch, Mr. Smythe toasted the bared chest with a glass of the iced tea an imperturbable maid had passed around the veranda.

"And who the fuck am I?" Dak Boxer demanded.

"You have a better part, later," Za-Za tried to whisper to him.

"Oh, yah?" Lars Helmut protested.

"Not a better part, just a *different* part." Za-Za resumed with Mr. Smythe's directions, "What Sergeant Dick doesn't know is that his straight lover, who was supposed to go out of town on business, has decided to join him in the motel."

"How does the straight lover know where the hidden sergeant is?" Sal Domingo queried.

"And how can he be his lover if he's so goddamned straight?" Jim Bond aimed at Rex Steed.

Za-Za continued intrepidly, "Now Tony Piazza is—"

"—the great-looking bellboy," Tony Piazza already knew.

"Yes, but there's another bellboy—" Za-Za placated Sal Domingo's glower.

Huck Sawyer—freckle-cheeked, sandy-haired—rushed in, led by the oblivious maid. "I'm sorry I'm late. I had to go back for my briefs." He jumped out of his clothes, leaving on Jockey shorts, his trademark. He kept them on in all his movies, having them pulled down only to the crests of his buttocks when he was being fucked. He came by rubbing his hands on the briefs so that cum smeared on them. That transformed him into a shy country boy.

Za-Za waved him away. Her eyebrows soared as she read into the script.

CLOSEUP. TONY PIAZZA'S ass, puckering.

CLOSEUP. REX STEED'S cock, throbbing.

EXTREME CLOSEUP. REX STEED'S mighty cock probing TONY PIAZZA'S pleading ass.

TONY PIAZZA

(moaning)
Ahhh. Yeah, stud, fuck me! Fuck me!

REX STEED

(in husky voice)
Yeah, I'll fuck the fuck out of your fuckin' ass.

Extreme closeup? Pleading ass? Fuck the fuck—? All part of Mr. Smythe's elaborate *fantaisie*, Za-Za soothed her anxiety.

Or did he intend to film this?

She shook that consideration away with a poke at her wig. Still, she might learn the correct form of a script, for *A Message from Out There,* in which she would employ overlapping dialogue, like Robert Altman, except that you wouldn't be able to hear *anyone.* "Ready for your entrance, Mr. Steed?"

"Ready." Rex Steed unveiled the edge of his golden fleece. He directed a wry smile at Tony Piazza. "Remember. No kissin'. But I'll fuck your ass like you've never had it."

"Oooh." Tony Piazza wiggled his celebrated butt. "Do that, stud, you *do* that."

Jim Bond approved the exchange with a high five between his legs.

Oh, oh. Something unscripted might happen. These crazy winds stirred everything— Za-Za glanced toward the not-so-distant hills— including fire.

Thomas Watkins
MORNING

In his robe and pajamas, lightweight for summer and somewhat large for his fit, fortyish-year-old body, Thomas Watkins sipped his coffee and looked out the window—a glass wall—of his beautiful home at the top of Laurel Canyon. Today, though, the wind seemed to be agitating the vista of trees and flowers almost vengefully.

"Is your coffee warm enough, my dear?" he asked the handsome young man who had just joined him, wearing his own robe.

"Yes, thank you. Are you enjoying the great view your home provides of the Canyon, Thomas?" The young man extended his hand for the older man to clasp in both of his.

"*Our* home. We share everything."

"Oh, yes, Thomas"—he kissed the older man on the lips—"our love of ballet, great literature, and, of course, the Divine Maria. Thank you for leading me to Proust's *Overture.* I look forward to spending a year of my life reading the whole novel, with your guidance."

"Thank you, my dear."

"We have an isle of civility here, Thomas—away from the barbarities of the Reagan Administration."

"Indeed we do, my love."

"Before I met you, Thomas, all I could think of was polishing my car—"

"But, my dear, that, too, was charming. Now where would you like us to go this evening? They say that British film *Chariots of Fire* is quite moving."

"Let's spend a quiet evening. I think they're showing *Camille* on Z Channel. I always cry when Garbo—"

"My beloved, you're too young to cry—"

"Tears of joy?"

"Ah, well, *those* should never stop, especially when they're shared."

"We've shared everything from the lucky time when you drove past my house and I was polishing my car and I waved to you and you stopped. But what we share most is our love."

"Yes"—Thomas closed his eyes—"especially our love." He sighed, over the strains of the glorious voice of La Divina soaring with Puccini and Tosca through his fabulous new stereophonic set—

Vissi d'arte, vissi d'amore—

Thomas opened his eyes, and the young man of his imagination was gone from the impeccably decorated home.

Thomas Watkins was alone, envisioning that someone special was sitting with him—yes, the young man who lived down the Canyon—and that they were about to enjoy a light brunch, he and this handsome young man who was capable of seeing beyond appearance. Not that there was anything wrong with his appearance—despite the fact that Herbert, that terrifying man who dared to call himself his friend, referred to him as "pleasantly plain"—it was simply that he was not "a great beauty." He wasn't old, barely forty-seven—younger than Herbert anyway—and certainly he looked younger than his age. He might have added a few pounds in the last year, but at his height, five foot, eleven inches, he surely wasn't heavy. The few extra pounds added presence.

Thomas held his coffee at his lips, waiting for a special cherished moment of La Divina as La Bohème—

Sì, mi chiamano Mimi—there!

If the bell rang, he wouldn't answer it, because it would be that hateful Herbert. He might never have moved here, beautiful as the house and the Canyon were, if he had known that that man lived up the road from him, and that he felt he could pop in whenever he wanted, announcing that he knew "Tom"—Thomas hated having his name truncated—would be alone, and then assaulting him with all kinds of lurid stories about his purported sexual conquests.

Of course, Thomas would acknowledge about himself, he did have a reputation for being "a good listener." At the only gay bar he frequented, a cozy, quiet one, he enjoyed the confidence of young men lamenting broken affairs or exulting in new ones. So many of those young men had a propensity for shabby affairs, he often noted to himself. With them, he commiserated and congratulated. What he didn't like was that if someone attractive entered the bar, they would glide away from him, sometimes blowing him a kiss of gratitude for listening.

Certainly, he had other friends, men, women, cultured friends who had him over for dinner, or he would have them, or they went out, to the opera, the ballet. All were unattractive.

The wind screeched, flinging palm fronds onto his small balcony, heaving them about so that they scratched at his window as if demanding to be let in.

Thomas hated these Sant'Ana days, especially the nights. That was when everyone—especially that despicable Herbert—claimed to have the most sex. Well, *he* wouldn't go out on such a violent day, not even for a drink at his bar—the only subdued bar left in the City—not one of those loud places with trashy music and men without shirts leaning over a pool table in vulgar attitudes. So much vulgarity in the gay world now, wasn't there? Why, even in his bar a few of the younger men carried small brown bottles of chemicals they said they sniffed from for added stimulation during sex, as if sex was no longer enough.

No, he would not have a scotch yet, not until, oh, perhaps two o'clock, or maybe, since it was Saturday, one o'clock. Just a touch of this fine Chivas Regal—

The doorbell rang, forcing him to swallow the drink he would have enjoyed sipping. It had to be that horrifying Herbert at the door, who else? With La Divina soaring ever higher, there would be no ambiguity about his being home. Of course, he could pretend he didn't hear him because of her—or that he'd gone out and left the recording on.

What if it wasn't Herbert? What if it *was* that young man down the road, always washing or working on his car in his baggy beach trunks— he must live with his family, sophisticated, cultured liberals, of course. Every time Thomas drove past—slowly because, precisely there, the road curved—the boy—young man—would look at him for steady seconds, and he'd begun to smile, and, most recently, he'd held out his hand in an uncertain wave, clearly shy. Perhaps today, he had emboldened himself to come over and—

Thomas went to his door and peered through the peephole.

"It's Herbert, Tom!"

It was impossible for Thomas to be rude. He was courteous to his own detriment, everyone said so. "Herbert, I was just—"

"Oh, don't apologize, Tom, I could hear that woman shrieking and knew you were here by yourself."

There it was—four in a row and he hadn't been here but two seconds—calling him "Tom," calling La Divina "that woman," referring to her celestial voice as "shrieking," and assuming that he would be alone. Here he had been picturing himself having morning coffee with a beautiful lover, and whom should he actually be going to have it with? Herbert Lavet, the "friend" he detested more than anyone else in the world.

"Oh, Herbert, please come in, of course."

"Thanks."

Herbert Lavet was an unattractive man of fifty. It angered Thomas that he kept referring to men "our age" although he'd never told the man how old he was. Nothing could be more incongruous than the sublime strains of La Divina's "*Vissi d'arte, vissi d'amore*"—now refilling the air with grandeur—and coarse, terrible Herbert, who would soon—Thomas girded—make another remark about the Great Diva.

"Another friend of mine, our age—"

Thomas shut his eyes. Then, resigned, he led Herbert into the room he had just occupied with his imaginary lover.

"—is also an opera queen, and every time I—"

"I have told you many times that I am *not* an opera queen. I enjoy—yes, I love—opera."

Herbert squirmed his broad hips onto a chair, waiting for Thomas to pour him a cup. "And the ballet, right—?"

Here it came, along with that despicable laughter. Thomas heard it in his mind before it erupted out of Herbert. Ha-aaa, ha-aaa, ha! "Yes, you know I love to go to the ballet."

"A crotch watcher," Herbert said before the monstrous laughter burst out of him. "That's what I call a friend of mine who takes binoculars to look at all the stuffed crotches. Ha-aaa, ha-aaa, ha. Me, I prefer *real* men, not those mincy fairies on tiptoes."

"I take," Thomas measured his words and held his cup steady because his hands were about to tremble, the wind increasing his edginess, "*opera glasses* with me so I can delight in catching the nuance of an intricate *pas.*"

"Whatever. Um—hot coffee on such a hot day." Herbert blew into his cup. "Love these hot, windy days that give you a constant hard-on."

Now it would begin, his ghastly recounting of purported sexual encounters. "I don't like these windy hot days. They make me nervous, especially when I have to go out—" He was preparing an escape.

"I love them because that's when I make out best. Last night, when the winds were kicking up, I met this one number outside that all-night sex-book store on lower Sunset. He was six foot two, but, like Mae West said, I'm not interested in the two inches. Ha-aaa, ha-aaa, ha!"

There he went. So unattractive and heavy-set—*and* fifty—yet bragging about his great conquests and appreciating himself so much—and oh, the way he laughed—Thomas could hear that laughter for hours after he left. Thomas tightened his lips, feeling that a rude insult would fly out of his mouth beyond his control. The wind shoved against the window.

"And, hon," Herbert proceeded as expected, "that number was *hung*—" He spread his hands almost a foot. "I had to gag, and then he motioned his buddy over, and *he* was even more gorgeous—and *bigger*—well, I wanted to *faint* when I saw it, and the three of us—"

The window rattled. Thomas looked out and saw tangled weeds sweeping down the Canyon. He stood up, knowing he would now say words thought a million times, never before spoken. "Herbert, I must tell you that I don't believe your stories about your great conquests."

Herbert's expression did not change. "Because I'm a troll?"

Thomas winced at the unexpected reply. He hated that word, "troll." He knew that it was used on posted signs restricting entry into certain gay bathhouses. Fliers for such places—warning "TFF" to stay away—were often passed out, sometimes tacked onto light poles, in gay neighborhoods. Thomas regretted having unintentionally introduced such an unpleasant subject. "I'm sorry, I—" He sat down, pouring himself more coffee although he did not want more.

"Listen, Thomas." Herbert's voice was ominously serious. "You know why you don't make out? Because men our age—"

"I am not your age."

"—men our age have to face certain things if we want to go on in the gay world, and I do."

Thomas did not want to hear any more. The recording had ended. There was only the insistent sound of the wind, and the sound of Herbert's voice, almost somber.

"*I* accept those things, Thomas, the three curses in the gay world—unattractive, old, and fat. I've been spared the fourth curse, the curse of a small dick, but that's not a blessing for me because no one notices." He leaned toward Thomas.

Thomas retreated from him. He wanted to protest any possible implications in Herbert's words, but his mouth was too dry to speak.

"So I go where none of that matters."

"I don't want to hear, I really—"

"There's a tunnel a few blocks away from two gay bars in Silverlake, near the sex-book store. The tunnel connects Sunset Boulevard above to a street below. It has a long, angular flight of stairs. It's dark at night, almost pitch-black, and it stinks, dank with the odor of dried cum and piss."

Thomas stood up, trembling.

"If you want to see who'll go in the tunnel, you wait outside in the streetlight and then you follow. If not, you go in and squat and you wait until, out of the darkness, a cock will push itself into your open mouth."

"Herbert, I *really* don't—"

"Or I pay for it—like I did those two last night. You know why? Because I *have* to. But I make out, Thomas." Herbert stood, facing Thomas. "And you don't."

Thomas's words came out as gasps. "I will never pay anyone for sex—and I will never be a mouth in the dark!"

Orville
MORNING

Orville usually slept soundly. Not last night. He had been wakened several times by the Sant'Ana, which had started like a beckoning whisper, after midnight. Intermittent surges of wind became so strong that he got up and closed the windows, but the room became unbearably hot. Locating his body on his own perspiration on the mattress so that that would cool him for moments, he managed to fall asleep and slept late.

Now he stretched on the bed. Like most gay men, he slept naked. Most often, he woke with a hard-on, like now. He looked at his dark body on white sheets, his black body—chocolate-brown *and* good-looking. Yes, black was beautiful. It was true that black people had natural muscular bodies that white people had to work out to achieve, like his.

Handsome, tall, twenty-seven years old, Orville had no trouble making out—well, no more than anyone else did, considering all the games gay men played while cruising, trying to read each other's silent—confusing—signals. He knew, of course, that some white guys went only with black guys. He'd laugh when he heard the familiar saying, "Once you go black, you'll never go back." *He* did not feel that anyone went with *him* because he was black.

He had become used to white people in bars addressing him as "man." He even bantered back, using "man" in every sentence until the other person caught on—some didn't—and stopped. He laughed when someone expressed surprise at his decorated house in the good area of Silverlake. The living room and dining area were done in mostly black and white and beige, with huge blow-ups of great thirties and forties movie stars—women—only the faces detailed from classic photographs by Hurrell. Once he'd been asked if he was housesitting. That was so stupid it didn't bother him. He didn't mind when, at the beach—and why the hell shouldn't he cruise and show off on the beach and "sunbathe" like other guys just because his skin was already dark?—someone would claim to wish they had a "natural tan" like his. Maybe they did.

Waiting for his cock to soften, Orville got out of bed. He turned on the stereo in his living room. The record he'd listened to last night was still there—Frank Sinatra's Greatest Hits. Damn if he'd apologize for liking Frank Sinatra, especially "Strangers in the Night," playing now.

That was a gay song if he'd ever heard one, about strangers glancing at each other, hoping to get together, hoping for more. It was a favorite song of his, romantic, mellow. People thought that if you were black you had to like loud rock, and jazz. Sure he did, but not always. When others were with him, he'd play popular stuff, like Prince or the Police. Not that weird Devo, nor any of that stuff that sounded like an explosion. The cable station they were promoting all day on radio and television—that MTV—was pushing those new sounds. New Wave, they called it.

It would be a sexy night! These winds stirred desire. He felt it now, the invitation to a fantastic night ahead.

Back in his bedroom, he dressed in cruising clothes—jeans, cowboy boots by Tony Lama—not too many white people knew about black cowboys—a shirt unbuttoned to mid-chest. He never wore undershorts when cruising. Sexier without.

The wind was turning angry. These winds were like that. You'd think they were over, everything would be calm, and then they'd whip at the City—and stop, just like that, as if throttled—and then they would rise even more vengefully, as if they had been waiting. Sure, those winds created hot cruising, but they also stirred tensions. He'd read that gay-bashings went up during these hot spells, pulling ratty punks out for

that purpose. A friend of his had been mauled in an attack outside a
bar recently.

Maybe he'd only go out early, have a few beers, play pool, talk with
friends—he deliberated as the wind yowled, straining at the windows.
He was popular, had many friends, all white but not out of choice. He
didn't go to all-black bars, but that wasn't because he wasn't attracted
to good-looking black guys like himself. It was just that there were more
white bars, several nearby.

Perhaps he'd go to the Studio Club tonight, avoid bar-hopping.
People said the popular dance bar in West Hollywood didn't admit black
people, but he never had any trouble getting in. He'd go dancing early,
leave soon, bring someone home, make out, then watch TV—skip the
late-hour franticness always possible on these hot nights.

Maybe he wouldn't go out at all tonight.

For now, he'd just take a ride in his pickup—his new Dodge Ram,
great name!—why did guys insist on calling it a "truck"? He would just
go along with the day. Before he walked out, he put on, at an angle, his
new cowboy hat.

Paul and Stanley
MORNING

"I'm going to San Francisco today, got some business," Stanley told Paul,
his lover during the last five years.

Paul didn't bother to ask what business he had in San Francisco
on Saturday. He was used to the euphemism, which they both accepted.
"Business" meant that Stanley—"named after Stanley Kowalski," he used
to claim until one of their friends said, "Now *there's* a macho queen for
you"—would go to San Francisco for a weekend of sex, keeping his
word to Paul that he'd never make it with anyone else while they were
in the same city. Paul had known, earlier, that Stanley's "business" was
coming up. He had seen him—not that Stanley bothered to hide what
he was doing, he didn't, he was, as he had promised Paul long ago,
"always open" about what he did—had seen him packing his "macho
gear," including some leather. He claimed he wasn't really "into leather,"

but you had to wear the right uniform in the South of Market bars, "the best cruise turf," or they wouldn't let you in.

They had been together since Paul turned twenty-five and Stanley was thirty-one. Soon after they met, they rented a house in the beach city of Venice, built, they both loved to explain to their friends, by a rich man attempting to re-create Venice, Italy. Instead, he found oil. Paul's friends—they became Stanley's only slowly—often told him that *he* was better-looking than Stanley. Paul denied it. "I have regular features, and Stanley is sexy," he'd correct. Overhearing the remarks once, Stanley said, "Yeah, but you're good-looking, too, Paul, and kinda sexy in a clean-cut way." He'd wink. "Otherwise I wouldn't still be with you."

Their unique "arrangement" had begun during their very first year together. Paul wanted to be "faithful," and Stanley wanted an "open relationship." "No reason why we can't both have our choices," Stanley had said. When his "nights off" started to threaten the relationship— Paul telling him that on those nights he couldn't sleep imagining him in the same city with someone else—Stanley said, "If that's what's bothering you, I'll never do it again. Our love means more to me than anything else. Can't you just face that, and that I'm a slutty whore?" He said that with a helpless smile.

He kept his word. He didn't have "nights off" in the City, but he began going away on "business"—during weekdays at first, then Fridays, and then whole weekends. Paul pretended to believe the subterfuge, but soon the matter became open.

What made all this possible, for Paul, was that when they were together, they went out to movies, ball games, watched television, slept in the same bed, took short vacations to Mammoth—both skied, Paul better than Stanley, but, as Stanley pointed out, *he* rode a motorcycle better. They had different tastes in music. Paul got used to Stanley's and never told him that it had surprised him to learn that he loved Judy Garland and Barbra Streisand, whereas he himself preferred New Wave, which he eventually played only when Stanley was away. Sex remained good between them, at times very good, although, of course, it did not occur nearly as often and it was not like at first when they could spend a whole day and night coming over and over.

Now, after having cleared the breakfast table—they had long ago assigned each other respective household chores, equal—Stanley stretched his long body, wiped perspiration from his brow, and said, "Goddamn, it's hot. It's going to be one of those sexy nights." He seemed almost to regret that he would be out of town.

"Then why don't you stay?" Paul offered. With me, he stopped himself from saying.

Stanley shook his head in regret. "I got my ticket, babe. Or else, wow, yeah." He was wearing a sleeveless lumberjack shirt, which he opened lower now, revealing the dark hair on his chest.

"Maybe *I'll* go out tonight, and cruise," Paul said. He had spoken those words!

Stanley frowned—and then quickly he smiled, cocked his head.

He's so fucking confident I won't, Paul knew, wanting me to keep my side of it, be "faithful" to him. Paul looked away from him, out the window.

The wind was whipping up sand from the shore, smirching the glass panes in gray splotches. Still, the heat would bring a lot of people out to the beach.

Stanley stood up, raised Paul by the shoulders. "Do it if you want, babe. Go out and cruise—whatever."

That squint Paul had thought was so sexy—had it changed? Now Stanley looked mean.

"Before I go, kiss me?" Stanley said.

No! But Paul did, their lips hot on each other's. Stanley pushed his tongue into Paul's mouth. Paul opened his lips to receive it. Stanley's hands traveled down, opening their flies, bringing both cocks out, both hardening, slightly moist, sliding his fingers up and down both cocks, hot, sticky. Stanley withdrew his lips, held Paul by the neck, rubbing it at first and then pressuring it downward, down along his chest, moist tongue on moist chest, down, until he had brought Paul's mouth to his crotch. Paul took Stanley's cock into his throat. He worked himself up, feeling a flood of urgency and desire.

"Go ahead and come, yeah, take that cock deep, deeper, yeah, all the way—down, *deep*, let me fuck your throat—yeah, do it, deep-throat me, do it." Stanley arched back and thrust forward. "Shoot with me, babe, cummon! Ah, ah, ahhh—take it, stay *down*, yeah—ah!"

Paul came into his own hand, his body jerking.

Stanley withdrew.

Paul, still kneeling, looked up at him, questioning.

"I couldn't come, babe. I tried." Stanley shook his head. "It's too hot to come, I guess. When I get back, I'll be even hotter for you."

Paul stood up, words ready to accuse, demand—bastard, son of a bitch, fucking shit, you never intended to come, and you pretended you did, just to make sure I came! You think that'll keep me satisfied, you fucking bastard!

Stanley kissed him, sealing his words, kissing him for long seconds, until Paul responded.

Nick
MORNING

"How much?"

"Fifty bucks."

"Shit."

"Thirty."

"Twenty."

"Twenty-five—if you got a place nearby and it won't take long."

"Around the corner, five minutes away, and that's all it'll take."

Nick looked about Santa Monica Boulevard, that stretch taken over by male hustlers, especially at night and on weekends, a stretch of a few blocks, vacant squat buildings, auto dealers, liquor stores, fast-food eateries shoved crudely into storefronts, a few brave trees.

Just noon, and almost every corner was claimed by hustlers taking advantage of these weird winds that brought everybody out. But there were only a few johns circling the blocks, probably others waiting for the hot night to come, Nick figured. In the brief period he'd been on the streets, he'd seen guys—who'd been here before he turned up—waiting, real long, to be picked up. Not him. Nineteen years old, with a hard body darkened by the sun, and natural carved ridges on his stomach, he was tough and boyish at the same time. One of the old guys who had picked him up had told him he was "real butch." He had liked that and had considered calling himself that, "Butch," except that no one asked his name. Fuck, no one ever asked anything about him except about his dick and what he did with it. Sometimes johns acted like he'd been born on the fuckin' street. Well, fuck it, man, everybody was looking for sex all the time, and he was selling, liked gettin' paid for it, liked to hold the crushed bills in his hand. Sometimes he'd go to sleep gripping the money he'd made.

Nick had evaluated the tight situation on the street. Too, he believed this guy because he knew johns often rented a motel room off Sunset minutes away. He'd learned some did that because they were married, in town only to pick up a hustler. "Okay. Twenty-five bucks—for just a few minutes."

He got into the car.

"—to fuck you."

Nick hadn't been listening until those words echoed. "You want to fuck me?"

"Yeah, stick my dick up your tight ass. You know howda squeeze, right?"

"I'm not gay, man." Nick felt insulted when this occurred. Other hustlers on the street said they never got fucked, either. But he'd seen some of them going with men *he'd* turned down because they wanted to fuck.

"Sure, sure, you're not gay," said the man, heavy, sweating. "Doing it for the money, huh?"

"Right."

"You suck?"

"Not that either." Shit, man, what the fuck?

"Don't kiss, right?"

"Right."

"How about letting me fuck your ass with my tongue?"

"You can *rim* me, yeah."

"How big is your dick?"

"No one ever complained."

"Let me see."

"Are you a cop?"

"Hell, no, are you?"

"Fuck, no."

"If you're not, you'll show me your dick and then we can take care of business right here in the car. A few minutes. Twenty-five bucks. There's lots of other hustlers on the streets." Sweat specked his face, stained his collar.

"How do I know you're not a cop?" Nick had learned early about dangers.

"Like this." The man opened Nick's fly and took out his dick. "Real nice, ah-ha, yeah, real nice, *real* nice—"

"Hey, man!" Nick saw that the guy was pulling himself off—must've already had his pants open.

"Ahh!" The man's body jolted. Wiping his pants, he rubbed off the sticky moisture on his hands.

"Motherfucker!" Nick realized what had happened.

"Get outta my car, you little shit whore!"

"Hey, cocksucker, you better pay me or I'll tell all the guys on the street about you and we'll kick your fat ass—"

The man started the car. "Okay, okay, here—" He fumbled for his wallet. "Cops! Behind us!"

Nick pulled his fly together, grabbed for the door, held it slightly open.

The man pushed him out.

Nick clung to the door, and let go when the man sped off.

No cops.

Nick felt a rush of anger, almost as if it were contained in the heated wind that jostled him. He reached down for a rock, a stick, anything. He found a board and flung it in the direction of the fuckin' car. The wind intercepted the board, hurling it back, and the car sped away.

Nick took off his shirt, wiping the perspiration he'd worked up from running and from the anger that lodged like vomit in his stomach.

Clint
NOON

Clint got off the airplane at LAX and felt a blast of heat as he walked through the tunnel that led into the crowded waiting room. The pilot had announced a Sant'Ana condition before they landed. Clint had been prepared, but not for the intensity of the stagnant heat that crouched in the passageway. As he entered the air-conditioned waiting area, he felt a chill that warred uncomfortably with the temperature.

He was a handsome, sensual man in his early forties, with dark hair, thick eyebrows over dark eyes—and a lean frame that allowed his walk a subtle swagger, a masculine gracefulness. Like most gay men who dedicated strict time to their looks, their bodies, knowing that age is an enemy in their world, he looked younger than his years. Although he decried the cruel banishment of the old from sexual turf, he was determined to survive there. He was a desirable "top man," but, like most others, he did not adhere to one role, often reciprocating in all sex acts—an easy shift.

On the airplane, he had reread Camus's *The Stranger*. On a blank page of it he had written, *The randomness of destiny*. Now, on his way to the baggage-claim area, he opened the book to the same page. Laughing at his lofty thought, he paused to draw a heavy inked line through his own words. Then he thought, How similar Meursault is to Sydney Carton, both in pursuit of their destinies. *It was the best of times, it was the worst of times.*

The wait for luggage—he had brought only one suitcase—was always interminable. Today it was especially so because everyone was edgy from the heat and the sound of the screeching wind they would soon be surrendering to.

Either having managed to prod in on a blade of wind and through sliding doors, or having been dropped there, scattered sheets of a newspaper fanned out on the floor. Clint glanced down at the lead story. The City might have to be sprayed with aerial pesticide to combat the spreading infestation of a destructive breed of medflies that had been found in— He leaned down to stare more closely at a large photograph on the spread page. It depicted three Mexican children, about six or

seven years old, stooped low, picking strawberries—"the devil's fruit,"
the accompanying story read, "so-called because of the excruciating
labor involved in its harvesting."

VOYAGER RACING FOR LOOK AT SATURN

Under that headline was a large photograph. Swirls of smeared
white light—the planet's rings—smudged a deep, unperturbed darkness. When he straightened up again, the page itself—blurring—assumed a discordant unity in his mind, fragments of words and images
melding into incoherence. A rush of heat blasted through an open glass
door and against the cooled artificial air. Caught in the two extremes,
heat and cold, he felt dizzy. A ring of darkness threatened to enclose
his vision. He shook his head, and the moment was over.

As he waited outside for the shuttle that would take him to the
parking area where he would pick up the rental car he had reserved,
Clint detected the singed odor of ashes. Familiar with the City he had
lived in years ago—he thought of it often as the last shore before night
fell—he looked beyond for the glow that would signal fire. The horizon was not yet singed.

In the rented two-door Mustang—once inside, he snorted two
pinches of the cocaine he had brought with him—he sped on the freeway to his hotel in Hollywood. The sound of the wind drowned even
the hum of the air conditioner. He welcomed the wind sweeping away
the debris of the City. If, like that, he could sweep away last weekend—

He turned on the radio, hoping for a classical station. If he could
have, he would choose Bartok's "Music for Strings, Percussion, and
Celesta"—not entirely remote since this was the 100th anniversary of the
composer's birth—but the dark strains of that favorite work would only
have entrenched his mood. He roamed through the spectrum of stations,
pausing at Blondie's "Call Me," which he had danced to at discos, last
year. The music slipped into his mind the image of sweat-gleaming bodies contorting, knifed by strobes of colored lights, flesh sliding on flesh,
dancing—no, struggling— That image pushed back into the shadows
of crumbling piers he had roamed in New York last weekend, skeletal
warehouses, butcher trucks abandoned to the night, orgy rooms—

Blood—

When? Whose? Where? A man bleeding— Lying on a dance floor? Among contorted bodies? On rubbish—? In the piers—? No, in— Only the impression of redness and blood persisted, tainting his mind, until he focused his attention on the jumble of sounds from the radio—

"—yesterday's hits, and tomorrow's—and here's Queen's 'Under Pressure'—"

The song's agitated bass line, like a persistent undercurrent, and its words about a final dance, a final chance—made him tenser. He turned off the radio.

He drove off the freeway onto Sunset Boulevard, along its strip of pop-art advertisements for Las Vegas extravaganzas, records, rock concerts. When he reached the slight hill to the Château Marmont, where he would stay, he looked back, beyond ubiquitous palm trees resisting blasts of wind. Now the horizon was flushed red with distant fire. What irony that something that calamitous could look so beautiful.

Ernie
MORNING

Ernie lay in his bed in his Hollywood Apartment—he always slept late on Saturdays, right?—an apartment he intended to move out of but which was okay—and he studied his cock.

Twenty-nine years old, he liked to wake up to the sight of his muscular, weight-pumped body, nude on rumpled white sheets.

His cock was average.

Larger than average, he amended. He had read in a men's fitness magazine that the average cock was five inches—and his was over that, by half an inch, at least, and the fact that he wasn't all that tall, five feet six, made it look even bigger. He did worry at times that the magazine had been referring to cock size when it was soft. Of course it *hadn't*. So he could put that out of his mind.

For all his muscles, Ernie didn't consider himself a "muscleman"— too odd-looking, like that spooky Lars Helmut in porn.

"Hey, Lars, huccome you have to hold your arms way out and walk funny?"

"Coz my lats get in da way and my thighs bump each odder."

"Yeah, well, how do you like *this*?" And Ernie would pose before him, showing the symmetry of *his* muscular body.

"Yah—I vish I looked like dat."

"Too late, guy."

So Ernie preferred to regard himself as a "bodybuilder."

Hey! He knew what he would do. Have sex. Gay guys knew where to go at any hour of the day to get it. After he worked out at the gym—shiny pumped bodies all around, sometimes some good cruising there—he might take in a porn movie at that theater on Sunset in Silverlake. He liked to join the real action along the dark rows while he pretended he was making it with the guys on the screen. He was proud that porn was a part of gay life. Straight people felt dirty about it. Not gay guys. Gay people wouldn't hesitate to elect a hunky porn star president. Didn't some gay guys live their lives like they were in a porn movie?

None of that solved the present problem—he was horny right now. Too horny to set up the projector for one of his super-8 sex flicks, especially since, a couple of times before, he'd become so excited at the prospect that he'd come before he'd looped the film.

His hand on his stiffening cock, he closed his eyes and ran through the scenes of some of the movies he'd watched recently. What scene, what scene? He rejected anything with Rex Steed, dead meat with all his I'm-straight-don't-kiss bullshit.

"Ernie, I used to think I was straight, until I saw you."

"Yeah, Rex? Well, hey, tough shit, because you don't turn *me* on, guy."

Ernie chose to recall a favorite scene from *Drill Deep* with Wes Young, a favorite of his. The movie had been directed by Z.Z.—obviously a real macho guy himself, bound to have big muscles because only a *real* macho could know, that smack-on, what men wanted from men, right?

In that movie—Ernie saw it vividly in his mind again—Wes Young, a construction worker, has gone home with Sal Domingo or Tony

Piazza—Ernie couldn't tell them apart. Wes urges Tony—definitely Tony Piazza—to rim his ass, lick his balls, and suck his big cock, *now*, yeah, yeah!

Ernie looked down at his cock, comparing it with Wes's in the movie. Wes's was longer. But not all that much longer, guy.

Tony Piazza—no, Sal Domingo—follows Wes's instructions to a "T," rimming, licking, sucking—

Ernie opened his eyes, to stop the sexy recollection, but they fell on his own tensed body, and—too late—his cum spurted out. A bad shoot, like he hadn't really come. But that would only make him hornier later, and soon, right?

He got up, stretched. He turned on the radio to the station that still played great disco hits, and guess what was playing? Linda Clifford! One of his favorites that really said it, "Shoot Your Best Shot"—and that's what he always tried to do, right?

For such a muscular guy, he sure could dance, Ernie complimented himself as he twisted about to the music, his larger than average cock bopping. This would make a good scene in a movie, right?—maybe doing it with his briefs on at first? He'd be good at one of those nude-dancing places that were happening around town. Hey, everything was sexy nowadays. He'd come out dressed as—a fireman! He'd keep on his cap and floppy boots, and this one hunky guy in the audience would take his own clothes off, a bodybuilder like him, and—

He almost shot, and it would have been another bad shoot. He sat down, to cool off. They said disco was on the way out. Never! Not in gay bars. New Wave taking over? Bullshit.

He wouldn't want this to get out, with his muscular image, but every now and then he *did* like a good old-fashioned musical—he had two recordings of *Gypsy*. He didn't keep the albums out, though—who would?—because that would make people think he was a musical-comedy queen, which he wasn't.

He stood up, threw out his hands, and belted out—

"Look at Rose!"

He stopped, nervous.

What if that old queen in the apartment down the way from his heard him? She'd spread it around, right? She'd run into him at *Evita* in the Music Center, and smiled a knowing smile, and, then, the next time he passed her apartment, and he was flexing and without a shirt so she'd eat her heart out, she played the campiest number from it on her stereo so that he had to swagger past her window to the strains of "Don't Cry for Me, Argentina."

Hey, he liked sports, too, right? With a group of his friends, he'd watched the Raiders whup up the Eagles in the Super Bowl. They'd drunk some beers, had dips 'n' chips, and punched at each other in celebration when the Raiders scored. Was he a baseball fan? Hadn't the baseball strike sent him into a funk? Fuckin' baseball players—he wouldn't forgive them, striking like that and always groping themselves on the field. Boxing didn't do much for him—droopy trunks on those beat-up guys—but like everyone else he was waiting to see what Muhammad Ali did. You had to admire that old guy, still sluggin'. A credit to his race, right?

The cooling perspiration felt good on his body. He wouldn't have any trouble making out, no, sir. He never did. Almost never. Well— It still amazed him that at times he could go to a bar, and everyone— almost everyone—would look at him, even comment on his body— and then nobody would approach. Those times, going home alone after all the attention, Ernie marveled at the gay world, all its odd games. Safe to say that no one ever avoided rejection. It was just part of it.

Size queens!

Ernie lay back in his bed, holding his cock, semi-hard again. He hated size queens, those guys who asked how big your dick was. One guy had once said, "You've got a great bod, but I don't know a single bodybuilder who's not—" He had held his thumb and his index finger real close together. There was another guy who had told him, "I don't mind that you're not hung because I go for big muscles like yours." Even though the guy was into one of his favorite scenes—body worship—Ernie couldn't keep his hard-on, especially since the son of a bitch kept saying, "Relax, that's okay, really."

Did most bodybuilders have small dicks? Muscles didn't shrink your cock, right? Maybe steroids did, but he didn't take that stuff. He had nothing to worry about because he was bigger than average.

The radio station was playing a song he didn't like about some kind of war. Great beat, sure, odd group—Kano—lousy words. Hey, the wars were over for gay people.

The wind coaxed Ernie's attention. He stood up and looked out the window. Those eery winds were attacking palm trees, tearing off fronds, which lay scattered about the street as if they were wounded.

Mitch and Heather
Morning

Mitch pushed himself into her, focusing his attention on how sexy she was, auburn hair, milky breasts ready for licking, sucking, flat stomach flaring into the curves of her hips, light brush of reddish hair at the parting, moist lips eager for cock—*his* cock—inside her, naked legs.

"You're hurting me. You're forcing yourself."

"I'm not, goddammit, I want you."

Heather eased away from under him. "*I* don't want to."

"Just say that, but don't blame me."

"Okay. *I* don't want to. Not that way."

Mitch fell back on the bed, his head turned away from her. Earlier in the week, this had almost happened, but at the last moment urgency had flushed his cock and hardened it.

They had known each other for almost three months. She twenty-five, he three years older, two attractive people, with athletic bodies, they both liked "healthy food." When Pat Benatar's "Fire and Ice" came on, they would both reach for the volume control to turn up the sound. They loved sexy foreign movies and had recently seen *Spetters* but were equally "grossed out by that one scene." Both had started reading, but had not yet finished, *The White Hotel.* "You gotta really think about it," he had told her, and she had agreed. After they saw *For Your Eyes Only* and he commented on the array of beautiful women in bikinis, she said she could hardly wait to see that new Tarzan in *Tarzan, the Ape Man.*

They jogged regularly along the beach, past vibrant young men and women skating, running, biking. On the sand, they would lie side by side, surrounded by other sensual figures on a stretch of beach that appealed to attractive young people. At times, playfully, without arousing each other's jealousy—an easy banter between them—he and Heather would comment on the attractiveness of those about them, she finding fault with the women he pointed out, and he dismissing the men she admired.

Earlier this morning, on the beach—already crowded because of the heat—Heather had startled him by asking in a serious tone, "Who are you looking at?"

"That girl—she's got a terrific bod, but not as sexy as yours," he said, with their usual playfulness.

Heather removed her sunglasses. "She's gorgeous."

Glancing in their direction, the woman, dark hair bunched behind her, stretched her bronzed body, covered only by three tiny triangles of a white bikini. Next to her, a man removed his sunglasses and followed her gaze toward them.

"The guy next to her's not bad either," Heather said—not the usual light tone.

Mitch stood up. The Sant'Ana, rising, was unnerving him, had begun to unnerve him earlier, sand whipping about, gliding along the beach, the water agitated as it swept onshore toward him. "It's getting too windy and hot," he said. "Let's leave."

Now as they lay in her bedroom, in her duplex in West Los Angeles, he listened to the intermittent gasps of wind outside, and rage and bewilderment at the earlier failure gathered at his groin. He twisted over her, pushing his tongue into her mouth. His hands clasped her breasts, held her rigid nipples to his mouth, moistening them, biting. He mounted her, shoving as his cock refused to respond. She eased him away.

"Goddammit," he said, "I'm ready now, but you're not helping."

"You're damn right I'm not, not when you're trying—just trying—to rape me." She wrenched away from him and stood up.

"What the hell's the matter with you today?" he demanded. "It started on the beach."

"Yeah, when you kept staring at that guy."

"That guy?" He shook his head in disbelief at her words. "Christ, I saw him only because he was with that great-looking woman."

"He wasn't with her, Mitch. Just near her. He's been around before. He was looking at you and you were looking at him. He followed you when you went to the rest room earlier."

"Jesuschrist! I didn't even see him there. So what if we both had to piss at the same time? What the fuck are you trying to do? You blamed me earlier for not making it, and then you admitted *you* didn't want to, and just now you wouldn't even try to respond. Maybe *you* were staring at that woman. I've seen *you* looking at lots of girls on the beach. Maybe that's why we can't fuck anymore—why *you* don't want to."

Dave
MORNING

You'll turn into someone that I choose,
Look in the mirror and be surprised—

Dave did, in the bedroom of his house on the crest of pretty Mount Washington, up from the Eagle Rock section of downtown Los Angeles. He touched the cultivated dark stubble on his angular face, lingered on the scar he had given himself on his cheek. Over the sounds of Man 2 Man pumping—*hard,* dude—into his bedroom—he had speakers even here, in his garage—he heard the panting of the Sant'Ana, doubling the sensation of this sexy day as he looped his fingers over his beltless jeans, lowering them to the edge of the dark triangle of hair that inverted the one on his bare chest.

You'll see a person you won't recognize—
I'll always be a mystery, a figure in the night,
a thought of your own fantasy—

He did an about face away from the mirror and stood over his newest acquisitions, brand-new replacements and additions, picked up first thing this morning and now laid out on his bed like a body without a face. Fitted black chaps open at the crotch, black leather cap with an inclined visor, shiny black leather vest—tailored—handcuffs, black bike boots, black leather gloves, lots of close-knit chains, and, to loop over his black belt, a heavy key ring—looped on the left side to proclaim he was a top man, the one in command, a hot master, dude.

> *They can live their lives their own way—*
> *Let the rest of the world ignore us—*
> *Life's too short, and that's a fact—*

Yeah!

He slung one of the chains over his neck and let it dangle over his chest. He was ready for *action,* rough gay action, no vanilla sex for him!

> *I'll always be out running wild—*

Looking at his new outfit—more than a thousand dollars' worth, dude—made his cock throb under his jeans, ripped carefully near the groin. Smell the new leather! He rubbed the boots on his stubbled cheek. He put them on. He opened the top button of his jeans so that a few dark hairs peeked out. He located the cap almost over his eyes, so he'd peer out in a fuck-you attitude. He turned around to see his reflection in the full-length mirror of his bedroom.

Oh, yeah! Tough dude!

At thirty-five, Dave wasn't handsome. He was better than that, *much* better—who wanted to be a pretty boy?—he was masculine and sexy. Best of all, he looked *tough*—like a gay *man* should look—wiry body, lean face always slightly unshaved, his dark hair beginning to recede—and *damn* if that didn't make him look sexier, rougher, meaner. He twisted his arm to display his large tattoo in the mirror, a griffin. He touched the scar on his cheek. That scar affirmed his toughness. He had brought a sharp knife in a jagged line from his lower cheek to his chin, under his lips, until he drew enough blood to make the scar permanent.

He planted his booted feet apart. His cock bulged under his Levi's and almost pushed out at the rip. The odor of leather overwhelmed him.

Leather, and its world, dude, the world of S & M—that was where the new gay frontier was, *true* liberation.

You see me in the midnight air,
I'm not looking for someone to care—

L.A. was behind the times, new times comin'. New York and San Francisco—heavy stuff there, dude. The Bulldog Baths! Real jail cells! The Toilet Room! Get down pig style. The Mineshaft! Piss-tubs, fuck-slings—
Time for L.A. to grow up, learn what it was *all* about, new sensations, not for sissies, dude, give it like a man, take it like a man, yeah—all willing, trust, ultimate trust, the trust of masculine brothers—*proud gay men!*—totally liberated, everything allowed, heighten all senses, expose the body to all sensations, pain and pleasure, search for limits, discover none—

Hard-hitting love,
  the kind that's hard to crack,
Hard-hitting love
  that pulls no punches back—

From his pocket, Dave took out an ampule of amyl nitrite, popped it, and shoved it into his nose to inhale as long as he could. The chemical vaporescence raced to his brain, encircling him in an encroaching darkness that gradually opened, leaving only a powerful craving lodged in his groin.
New Wave—yeah! New sounds that tapped into gay currents, gay *man* currents—and, dude, gay men were the only *real* men now—and he was connected to those currents, ridin' waves of new sensations that were sweeping the gay world, his world—and he was on the crest of it all—

Follow me and you will see
There's excitement right outside—

He picked up his belt, smelled it, licked it from the buckle to its tip. He heard the wind's howling outside, and he thrust into its howl lines he repeated—

Don't forget who's in control,
You can lose your very own soul—

He swung the belt at an invisible eager slave.

You're the one to burn my fire—
To satisfy my own desire—
Make me feel wild and free—
Hard-hitting love—

Yeah!

Two

You can enter the park in West Hollywood from San Vicente Boulevard and walk in along or behind bleachers that form an L about the baseball field. Impromptu games occur on that field, seldom scheduled. From an adjacent court, the thump-thumping of a basketball is almost constant during the day, at times into evening. Young men join games in progress or wait for them to end so they may start their own. Within this pretty park, regular strollers glance at the players or move on along its many walks. Others remain on benches, reading, having a soft drink, a snack, or just resting.

These regular activities are altered, somewhat, during the Sant'Ana winds. Then, like today, everything seems astir.

Jesse
AFTERNOON

In his apartment, Jesse outfitted himself in the uniform of many gay men in West Hollywood, snug shorts, to show off his legs and round butt, a tight tank top, to show off his swimmer's torso and his slim waist, and Reeboks, without socks, to bring it all together.

Proud to be gay and sexy!

Older people—people over thirty—still had all those guilts about being gay. Guilty about what? he'd like to ask them. He wouldn't change being gay for anything in the world. He didn't *have* to march in the Gay Pride Parade to show *he* was proud. He did go, though, to cruise among all those showy guys without shirts, marching or watching. He always drew lots of admiring looks himself, and extended a lot. He wasn't what people called an activist. *He* showed his pride by being gay every moment of his life. What better way?

What was so special about being heterosexual? He had noticed that, very often, attractive heterosexual men didn't do much for themselves, let themselves get out of shape, wore baggy clothes. Gay men of the same age cared, went to the gym, stayed trim, healthy.

Best of all, at twenty-two—and, here, Jesse decided to wear his faded denim cutoffs, cut short, rather than the khaki shorts he had first pulled out—he had his whole life before him, the part of it that mattered. When he turned twenty-nine, he planned to die, just die. Growing old was kind of like dying, maybe worse because you were aware of growing old—making out less and less until you couldn't make out anymore.

Jesse couldn't imagine—and he would walk away from that sort of depressing talk—a time, not so far back according to older people—when just being in a gay bar exposed you to a vice raid and you could get busted for same-sex dancing. That old stuff was over, battles—he'd heard about them, who hadn't?—fought and won. Now everything was possible—you could dance all night with different guys at a dance bar, shirts off, pants lowered to the hips, assuming all kinds of sexy positions—wow!—and you'd be cruising all the time. Being gay allowed you freedoms others didn't have. Sure you had to be careful about crazies and muggers on the streets, and there were still vice arrests—but you could always call a gay lawyer, a *cute* one, and, chances were, he'd get you out of the stupid mess. The clap, you didn't even consider—except that you couldn't cruise for a few days—double ugh—and that was bad enough. The only problem—but get *this* for a problem!—was that sometimes you couldn't make out with everyone you wanted. SO MANY MEN, SO LITTLE TIME—he had a T-shirt that said that.

Jesse's attention was drawn back to the pool when he heard water splashing. The man sunbathing was still there.

When Jesse strolled out, wind whipped his hair about, giving him an even sexier look. Wow, would you look at that sky? Swept clear blue. But was there a hint of smoke in the air?

The man had now located himself in an area sheltered by swaying branches, the sun slipping past and spilling on the lounge chair where he stretched. The only others about the pool were a couple with two children, and an older guy in loose shorts—ugh—obviously straight. Others in the court had probably gone to the beach to cool off.

As Jesse walked past him, the man removed his sunglasses. Jesse returned his look. The man was about twenty-five—maybe twenty-seven, no older—and hot.

The man's eyes steadied on Jesse's firm buttocks, snug groin. Then he looked up, smiled. "Hi."

"Hot, huh?" Jesse said.

"_Very_ hot." The man looked Jesse up and down.

Jesse sat on a lounging chair next to him, exhibiting his blond, tanned legs.

The man touched his own crotch, outlining the bulge there.

Nice, Jesse evaluated. Another thing about gay people, they liked to show a bulge at the crotch, even when there wasn't that much to show. Well, he was no size queen, but he wouldn't turn down a shortish fat one. A _tiny_ one, that was another matter altogether. Although his preference was being fucked, he was glad he had a more than adequate cock. People often wanted to suck him, and he'd let them, dutifully, but eventually—and without any difficulty—he'd maneuver to get his choice.

Jesse touched the man's cock over the bikini, outlining it as it grew larger. The edge of his balls pushed out. Jesse waved with his free hand at the couple splashing with their children.

They waved back.

The man next to Jesse leaned back, stretching, reaching out to touch Jesse's buttocks. Jesse raised his butt, allowing the man's hand to probe under the short denim cutoffs, locating the parting, fingers poised there attempting—but the cloth resisted—to push one finger in. That felt hot! Jesse removed his own hand from the man's crotch, and the man's from his butt, and he stood up. "You gonna be around later tonight?"

"No," the man reacted to the coming rejection. He turned away in forced indifference.

Another instinct among gay men, keen reaction to the first hint of rejection, Jesse knew. He hadn't intended to convey that to this guy.

"Too bad, because I'd really like to get together with you, but I don't have enough time."

The man stood up and dove into the pool.

As Jesse moved out of the court and into the windy streets, he wondered whether the man would have understood if he'd explained that he had just now begun this day's trip, beginning to collect sexiness for late tonight, and that he must remain pure for this special night.

Buzz, Toro, Linda, Boo, and Fredo
AFTERNOON

"Crazy wind's messing my hair," said Linda to Toro. "Maybe you oughtta put up the top."

"I like the crazy wind," Buzz said as they drove in Toro's Chevy to pick up Boo in another drudgy city in the Valley. "The devil winds are supposed to make you crazy."

"So what do they do for you?" Linda asked.

Buzz wasn't sure if she'd insulted him.

Boo was waiting for them at Taco Bell. He hopped in without opening the door. He was seventeen, but he looked younger although he had a sideways glance that made him seem experienced, but maybe that was so because he had all those tattoos on his skinny arms, all jumbled. A cross on his hand looked more like something smashed. A guy had drawn it on him with spit and ink and a knife, when they were in Juv.

"That's Boo," Toro said to Linda.

"Hi, little man."

"Don't you never call me little," Boo growled. "I ain't little."

"Cool, man," Toro ordered. "She didn't mean nothing."

"Okay, but don't never—," Boo said.

"I just meant you're cute," Linda shrugged, then smiled.

Buzz knew how much Boo hated to be called little. He had called him that, once, and without warning Boo had punched him. Buzz would have returned the punch except that Toro interceded.

When they reached Fredo's "house" in a trailer park, Fredo was calling back into the open door, "I don't know when I'll fuckin' be back. When you see me, you'll fuckin' know." A man's voice called out, "You son of bitch don't fuckin' talk to your mother like that."

A woman's voice called out, "*Vé con Dios, mijo.*"

"Shit, she wants me to go with God." Fredo shook his head. Then he made a sign of the cross, touched the crucifix he wore about his neck. He was swarthy, dark. A big nineteen years old, he cultivated a twisted look to challenge anyone who gave him attitude. He had begun wearing boots with heavy reinforced toes and heels—like the "skinnies"—to go along with his shaved head.

He acknowledged Linda with his twisted look.

"I like your haircut, guy, Linda said.

"Keeps me cool." Fredo exchanged looks with Buzz and Boo.

"Wassup with you guys?" Toro asked. "You fuckin' flirtin' with each other?"

That broke Linda up.

"Fuck, nuthin's wrong," Buzz said.

"Nuthin'," Boo and Fredo echoed.

"You believe them, Toro?" Linda said absently, as if she hadn't really heard what had been said. She pushed her hair back, held it, safe from the wind only for moments.

"Sure, I believe them, man," Toro said. "They're my boys, ain't you, guys?"

"Word, man," Buzz spoke out. He frowned when he saw Linda adjust something under her short skirt. Carrying what in her pants? Buzz didn't know why, but he had a hard-on. The Sant'Ana—that was it. No, it was Linda and that short skirt creeping up her legs. That and his anger at her.

"Why they call you Boo?" Linda asked him.

"Cause I don't even have to go, Boo! to scare no one."

Linda pretended to shiver, "Oooh, bad boy, *big* bad boy."

Buzz thought, Yeah, she's tough, but we're tougher. Would Toro stand with her or them, if it came to that?

"Where's the shit?" Toro asked casually.

Now Buzz could utter the prepared words. "The niggers were try-ing to pass off dummy shit—but we caught it."

"Fuckin' niggers, man," Boo joined. "Thought they could fake us. Us!"

"Tried to shake us up for the bread." Fredo shook his head. "But we messed them up bad."

"Where's my money?" Toro's tone did not change.

Buzz was ready. He brought out of his pocket the money Toro had donated for last night's deal. "Here." *Now* there could be no question about what had gone down.

Linda counted the money. "Hey, Toro, guess what? These guys gave you an extra ten dollars, man. How'd that happen?"

Buzz frowned. "Huh?" He had counted the money, twice, to get it exact.

Father Norris
AFTERNOON

He knelt before the altar in the church.

After the pleading Hispanic woman had left, he had remained in his confessional, listened to the words of other confessors, just words. He asked no question to clarify sins, spoke words, blessed the confes-sors, meted out penance, the same each time.

When confessions were over, he remained inside the church, pray-ing in a pew. Then he walked past the railing before the altar and knelt staring up at the crucified figure of Christ that looked down at him, the tortured but still adoring body violated, bleeding, bared, almost bared. *He,* our Divine Savior—He, that same figure in agony, was tat-tooed on the back of a young man roaming perverse streets. What message have You sent me through that woman, Lord? What is Your bidding?

Father Norris crossed himself, stood up. His eyes unmoving on the crucified body, he recited from the prayers of holy communion, making them his. "Never permit me to be separated from You. Let not the partaking of Your Body, O Lord Jesus Christ, which I, though un-worthy, presume to receive, turn to my judgment and condemnation."

Aloud, he pled, "Help me, beloved Lord, to be ever faithful to Your love. Guide me to You by whatever path You choose."

Za-Za and the Cast of *Frontal Assault*
AFTERNOON

With growing attention, for Mr. Smythe to detect through his steady binoculars, Za-Za studied his script from the beginning now. "An inspired script!" she shouted toward the veranda. But for these moments, Mr. Smythe seemed to be holding his focus on Wes Young. Was Mr. Smythe a foreskin queen?

> LONG SHOT. Sergeant LARS HELMUT, lounging pool-side at the motel, naked as the day he was born, lifts telephone—no necessity for prop—and calls for a drink.

> PANNING SHOT. Sergeant HELMUT stretches his unbelievable limbs, semi–hard-on just beginning.

> CLOSEUP. Sergeant HELMUT's semi–hard-on, growing.

> ENTER. Gorgeous bellboy TONY PIAZZA, in ragged trunks that show the famous kangaroo on his ass.

Za-Za motioned anxiously to Tony Piazza to find trunks some-where, not difficult since several had been strewn about. When he started to put on a pair—not ragged—she rushed at him, yanked them away, struggling with them until she had managed to bite and tear a huge chunk out of them. "There!"

"Wrong side if you want my tattoo to show," Tony Piazza said.

"There!" She bit another chunk, threw the trunks at him, and read on as the performers awaited their entrances. Apart, Rex Steed remained steadfast in his cutoffs.

TONY PIAZZA
Here's your beer, sir. Would you like anything else?

LARS HELMUT
Yah, sug my dig, eat my balls.

TONY PIAZZA
Sir, Management has trained us to please our guests, but I
don't—

LARS HELMUT forces TONY PIAZZA's head over his formidable cock.
With the other hand he rips off TONY PIAZZA's ragged trunks.

EXTREME CLOSEUP. TONY PIAZZA's ass quivering, puckering,
quivering.

REVEAL. On another lounging chair, JIM BOND, naked as a jay
bird, is jerking off while watching them.

JIM BOND
(softly *only* at first)
Oooh, oooohh.

LARS HELMUT
(to TONY PIAZZA)
Yah, I wanna fug your ass, fug your ass wid da kangaroo
tattoo.

Za-Za's gaze was pulled toward the torturing sight of Tony Piazza's
delectable fat cock—wasted, wasted, because it should be *in* something,
preferably her ass. She felt a goosing sensation at her buttocks, but
nothing outside it was creating it.

REVEAL. Straight Lover, played by spectacular REX STEED. He is
so startled by what he sees that he drops his pants—

Now *there* was a stage direction she might find a way to adapt into an *hommage* to Mr. Smythe in her groundbreaking *A Message from Out There*. Za-Za read on.

> CLOSEUP. The head of LARS HELMUT's cock, a glistening dot on
> its tip, ready to enter TONY PIAZZA's vibrating ass.

>   REX STEED
> What the hell is goin' on here?

Enough! "Action!" Za-Za shouted.

The performers in the first scene moved into their roles, bottoms preparing themselves with lubricant, Tony Piazza upstaging them by using only spit. With his sergeant's cap on, Lars Helmut flexed his muscles and lounged. Tony Piazza brought him the beer. Trunks yanked off, Tony Piazza deep-throated Lars Helmut and licked his balls, until Lars Helmut pronounced his desire to "fug" him and Tony Piazza bent over—

"Here's where you enter and drop your pants, Mr. Steed," Za-Za followed the pivotal cue.

With intense concentration, Rex Steed opened a second button on his cutoffs, another, about to introduce his "ten inches plus."

On the veranda, five pairs of binoculars steadied.

The cutoffs fell.

More like eight inches, Za-Za evaluated. But *pas mal*.

While Wes Young and Dak Boxer idled by the pool and Huck Sawyer hopped about nervously in his famous briefs and Sal Domingo looked away from it all, Bellboy Tony Piazza stopped a quarrel from erupting between Sergeant Lars Helmut and his Straight Lover Rex Steed by dropping to his knees and sucking Rex Steed's cock. Rex Steed followed the script, verbatim.

>   REX STEED
> Ummm, ummmmm, yeah, yeah, suck that ten-incher-plus.

>   TONY PIAZZA
> Please, please, I want your big dick in my tight asshole,
> please, big stud.

"Yeah, I'll shove it way in, fuck the fuck out of your fuckin' ass," Rex Steed delivered his lines exactly as rehearsed.

"Yeah, stud, yeah." Tony Piazza bent down, offering his buttocks. His head poking out between his spread legs, he smiled over at Jim Bond, who stopped "sugging" Lars Helmut long enough to answer, in kind, Tony Piazza's signal, fingers shaped into an "okay."

Something beyond Mr. Smythe's precise directions was going on between those two sluts, Za-Za knew.

Tony Piazza raised his ass.

Rex Steed aimed.

Tony Piazza tightened his ass.

Rex Steed poked.

Tony Piazza squeezed his ass.

Rex Steed's cock slipped up and sideways on Tony Piazza's buttocks.

"Cummon, stud, push that eight-incher in—" Tony Piazza adjusted.

"*Ten*-incher—uh—plus," Rex Steed attempted to correct.

"—push that eight-inch pole up my ass," Tony Piazza retained his expert's assessment. "Cummon, just like you promised, straight stud."

They were seriously deviating from Mr. Smythe's script! Za-Za stood frozen in horror. Rex Steed was beginning to sweat—so unseemly for the blond beauty—thrusting, shoving clumsily, trying to penetrate the famous ass.

"What's the matter, stud?" Tony Piazza looked back and up at Rex Steed with innocent heavy-lidded eyes.

Za-Za wished she had shut her ears, that she had never heard Jim Bond, stopping his chomping on Lars Helmut's balls, say, "Maybe we'll have to let someone else be the straight lover."

Dak Boxer and Wes Young volunteered, cocks and balls in hand.

"Stay where you are!" Za-Za ordered them.

"Oh, look," said Huck Sawyer. He had rushed to the edge of the garden. He stood on tiptoes. He was pointing to the hill next to them. "A fire!"

An arc of flames and smoke, surreal, glowing orange, was pointing, distantly, toward Mr. Smythe's mansion.

Sal Domingo rushed over to look, leaning over the balusters next to Huck Sawyer. There was the distant sound of sirens.

On the veranda, Mr. Smythe stood up and shouted, "Proceed with my script!"

Detecting an acrid sting of smoke that portended sparks that might set her wig afire, Za-Za watched in horror as Rex Steed, sweating, still attempted—only attempted—to fuck the fuck out of Tony Piazza's locked ass.

Thomas Watkins
AFTERNOON

Invigorated by a touch of scotch, Thomas Watkins drove down the narrow roads of Laurel Canyon in his Cadillac—he bought a new one every few years. People said Cadillacs belonged to an "old time," that only old people drove them. Not true. A Cadillac was the most elegant car. Thomas drove it proudly, enjoying its spacious luxury.

Herbert had left soon after the unsettling talk earlier, had left the way he always left, as if he had said nothing disturbing. Thomas often thought that he came over only to upset him. Otherwise, how to account for the fact that he always did?

Now he was going— He'd decide later. He simply had to leave the house after the unpleasant interlude with Herbert.

The young man down the road wasn't there. Naturally not, on this windy, dusty day. Still, Thomas felt cheated. He always looked forward to the boy's cheerful greeting as he passed by.

He drove past the Hollywood Bowl—so many lovely orchestral evenings spent there listening to beautiful music under stars and palm trees, cherished evenings with friends, but shared with no one special, never anyone special—and into Hollywood Boulevard.

How wonderful this splendidly gaudy street had once been, with shops and curios and Orange Julius stands. Now it was dying. Once-grand theaters that had hosted great premieres, boarded permanently. The Egyptian Theater with its bronze statues and art nouveau ceiling, a burst of gold—forlorn now, its abandoned lobby unswept.

Look at that fuchsia pornography store—so crude—with those grotesque rubber manikins, one of a woman, the other of a man, both with gaping holes—*holes!*—for mouths, figures looking like unfinished giant puppets. Only once—out of curiosity—he'd gone into that cavernous sex magazine store on Melrose and had been accosted by displays of chemical inhalants, giant dildos with all kinds of attachments, contraptions— What *did* they do with all those things? Was *that* what had rushed out of the closet?

He drove past a surly group of young men and girls idling before a stained outdoor food stand. Why did they *want* to look unclean? He certainly was not an enemy of young people. Look at his affection for that young man down the road near his house. He *did* resent the "new gays," as they called themselves, who denounced as "repressed" everything that had occurred before them.

Did they know that the behavior they derided and even judged had been demanded in those times of outrageous pressures? "Vice" roundups of bars, routine! A bullhorn blasting its command, "All queers march out in single file!" Show identification while you stood in the glare of headlights. When they demanded to know if you were queer, answer, No, or they'd arrest you. Still, a voice out of the crowd would inevitably shout back at the cops something like, "Oh, ladies, you're too much," and a derisive chant of "Oh, Mary!" would go up among the captives—and right here in the City of Angels, gay men fought police raiding a popular bar, *years* before that protest in New York everyone talked about. He himself had said to an officer, "Don't push me!" The officer had been so stunned he released him. Thomas smiled at the treasured memory.

He was driving past what had once been a fabulous dance emporium, now a congregation hall for some demented fundamentalist religion.

Those times! "Soliciting"—a crime. Entrapment—rampant. Men ordered to register for life as "sex offenders," forbidden to frequent "known gathering places for perverts," police breaking into homes, violent headlines you lived with. "HUNDREDS OF PERVERTS ROUSTED, QUEERS QUESTIONED." Sinners! Neurotics! Criminals!—judgments from pulpits, psychiatrists, the courts. Thomas had slowed toward Hollywood and Vine. Only Musso & Frank's Grill remained. Other great Hollywood restaurants—the Derby!—all gone! Ghosts of Astaire and Rogers—

Did those "new gays" spinning about like giddy tops in discos care
to know that dancing with someone of the same sex was punishable as
"lewd conduct" then? Still, a club in Topanga Canyon boasted a sys-
tem of warning lights. When they flashed, lesbians and gay men
shifted—what a grand adventure!—and danced with each other, laughing at the officers' disappointed faces! How much pleasure—and
camaraderie, yes, *real* kinship—had managed to exist in exile.

Did those arrogant young people know that, only years ago, you
could be sentenced to *life* in prison for consensual sex with another
man? A friend of his destroyed by shock therapy decreed by the courts.
Another friend sobbing on the telephone before he slashed his wrists—

Thomas's hands on his steering wheel had clenched in anger, anger
he had felt then, anger he felt now. And all those pressures attempted
to deplete you, and disallow—

"—the yearnings of the heart," he said aloud.

Yet he and others of his generation had lived through those bar-
baric times—and survived—those who *had* survived—with *style*. Faced
with those same outrages, what would these "new gays" have done?

"Exactly as we did," he answered himself.

The wind had resurged, sweeping sheaths of dust across the City,
pitching tumbleweeds from the desert into the streets, where they shattered, splintering into fragments that joined others and swept away.

Now, they said, everything was fine, no more battles to fight. Oh,
really? What about arrests that continued, muggings, bashings, mur-
der, and hatred still spewing from pulpits, political platforms, and
nightly from the mouths of so-called comedians? Didn't the "new gays"
know—care!—that entrenched "sodomy" laws still existed, dormant,
ready to spring on them, send them to prison? How could they think
they had escaped the tensions when those pressures were part of the
legacy of being gay? Didn't they see that they remained—as his generation and generations before his had been—the most openly despised?
And where, today, was the kinship of exile?

He had neared Barnsdall Park. He never could pass by without
turning up into the circular drive to delight in the splendor of the
Hollyhock House. He did that now, and there it was, one of three homes

built by Frank Lloyd Wright in the City, timeless architecture, old and
futuristic. Oh, thank God for it!—and for the miracle of Monet's "Water
Lilies," La Divina Callas, and for Proust.

He had driven down Sunset, toward downtown, in the area known
as Silverlake, down a side street, another— Where exactly was he? He
slowed his car.

My God, there was the tunnel Herbert had mentioned. A gaping
mouth, dark even at this time of day, opening from the street—
Thomas drove away from this terrible coincidence.

He turned, circled the long blocks—and parked his car, not near,
away. Having driven here—unintentionally—he wanted to see the place
that Herbert claimed as his.

He walked there slowly, past an abandoned lot full of weeds, and,
now, palm fronds shaken loose by the heated winds.

He stood at the mouth of the tunnel, looking up the stairs. He took
one step in, another. The smell of urine assaulted him. Up ahead, at a
landing on the concrete steps, a pale light—no, a shaft of light spilling
from the street itself—created shadows. Actual lights within had been
gouged out, shards of glass pulverized by shoes.

Thomas continued to stand in awe of this terrible place. Now he
was able to see that on the walls of the fetid steps—certainly no one
would use it to cross the street anymore—there were gnarled words,
splotches of paint, carved scrawls. He walked a few steps up.

I WANT A BIG COCK UP MY ASS— Next to that, a crude giant penis had
been etched into the wall.

SUCK MY BIG DICK— A long phallus, bags hanging from it.

Thomas squinted to read.

I WANT BIG HAIRY GUY TO WHIP MY ASS, SHOVE DILDO—

MEET ME 2/30 A.M.—

SHOW HARD FOR BLOW—

Real proposals? Fantasies?

SIT ON MY FACE, I EAT ASS—

YOU DRINK PISS?

EVERYTHING YOU GOT—

Who read these? Who scrawled them?

The rancid odor overwhelmed Thomas. He gagged. He covered his nose and moved farther up into the tunnel. He stood in the shaft of gray light from the street. He heard the rumble of a car above him. He heard the wind, distant, like moans. He heard a noise, scraping, scratching— He froze. The wind had hurled a tangle of weeds and trash from the street down the stairs. There it lay, gnarled, twisted, and—

Someone else was in the tunnel.

Orville
AFTERNOON

There were several gay neighborhood bars in the Silverlake area, a section of Los Angeles that bears spotty signs of better times, especially in spacious houses that perch away from it all on the slant of hills gathered about an artificial—silver—lake. Early Saturday afternoons in these bars, gay men gathered to shoot pool, drink beer, catch up on bar talk— and, of course, to cruise—but serious cruising occurs mostly at night.

When Orville walked out of his house earlier—he always paused to assess his surroundings, gentrified houses on hills dotted with wild flowers—he decided, definitely, that he would avoid the hot-night's cruising, sexy but also frantic if you got caught up in its fever. He would go to a couple of bars nearby, look them over, try to connect early, something mellow.

Holding on to his cowboy hat, he hopped into his pick-up and drove to one bar, had a beer, talked with friends, played a game of pool—no one there who interested him—and then drove away to another bar.

There, cars spilled out of the lot into side streets, everyone stirred by the Sant'Ana. Orville parked his pickup and cocked his hat. The wind tossed it into the street. As he ran to catch up with it, a car drove by, brakes screeching. That was always alarming in this area—lots of punks prowled, harassing gay men. The car had apparently stopped for him to reclaim his hat.

"Ride 'em, cowboy!" Laughter.

Stupid kids, Orville dismissed the group driving away.

He walked into the bar, a heavy cruising bar at night. During the day, it was kept dark like all other gay bars. The flush of light announcing an entering presence always drew evaluating eyes, withdrawn if there was no further interest.

Orville paused at the entrance, his imposing figure a silhouette. From the sound of voices—and laughter, a forced laughter often heard in bars—he could tell there were many more men than usual, and that the more relaxed cruising of weekend afternoons would be replaced by more serious hunting. When his eyes adjusted, he walked in, recognizing a few acquaintances. Although it wasn't a leather bar, there were two or three men in leather. That scene was becoming so prevalent that you'd see leather guys even in dance bars, the silvery studs on their outfits blinking like sequins. Orville was not into leather, but if someone was attractive, he'd go with them, after informing them he wasn't into "S & M."

He decided to sit alone, to signal availability. He waved at a cluster of men he recognized—maybe he had made it with one or another, wasn't exactly sure. They waved back, in tacit understanding of his separation. In sex-hunting places everything else became secondary to a conquest.

An attractive guy was staring at him, about thirty, masculine. "Buy you a beer?" the man asked Orville.

"I'll have one with you, but I'll pay for my own," Orville said. He always liked to assert equality. As they sipped their beers—the shirtless bartender recognized Orville but discreetly kept from more than greeting him—Orville did what had long become automatic for him. He looked for signals that this man was not interested in him because he was black. Even when two men indicated interest in each other in a gay bar, their eyes were constantly searching about, evaluating other possibilities. Orville noticed, with the usual relief this precipitated, that the man's eyes glided away toward attractive white men and then returned to him. Orville moved his leg so that it touched the man's groin. The man's cock was hardening.

"Your place or mine?" the man asked.

"Mine," Orville offered, always proud to show off his home.

Outside, Orville stood deliberately for seconds in the bright glare of the afternoon. The two exchanged directions about where their cars were parked, where they would meet, one to follow the other.

"Nice place," the man complimented Orville's house. They were in the living room. He pointed at the enlarged photographs of glamorous stars. "Those are great."

Not surprised by his home—and he had admired the photographs, easily. Orville noticed that the man's chest was brushed with hairs, just dark enough to show, a turn-on. Plus the guy had slim hips, another turn-on. This would be a *real* good scene, Orville was sure. He would keep his cowboy hat on, his boots, and—

The man took off Orville's hat, placing it on a chair nearby. Then he groped Orville's crotch. "Wow."

Bewildered for only a moment—maybe the wind had tilted the hat precariously and the man had intended only to adjust it—Orville reached for the other's groin. This was just preparation. They'd move into the bedroom, take off each other's clothes. He'd keep the boots on.

The man pushed Orville's hand away. "No, let me." He slid down on his knees, unbuttoning Orville's jeans, pulling off his boots, the pants. As he knelt before Orville's hardening cock, he seemed to be whispering to himself.

What? Muttered words. Orville listened instead to the wind.

The man's mouth opened, sliding Orville's cock into it, sucking hungrily, making urgent, gagging sounds.

Orville reached down, to touch the man's crotch. The man pushed his hand away. "No. Let me. I want to suck your big, bl—"

Orville thrust his cock into the man's throat, throttling the words.

The man pushed his head forward, swallowing the cock, gurgling as if gasping, allowing the cock to slip out, grasping for it with his mouth, swallowing it again. He pulled back and stared up at Orville. "You like to see a white man on his knees sucking your big dick? Yeah, look down at me while I deep-throat your big black cock."

Orville closed his eyes.

"Yeah!" The man was groveling on the floor, running his tongue around Orville's balls, up the length of the cock, interrupting himself only to gasp, "Black cock. I'm sucking off a black stud. Ummmm. Look down at me, black stud—ummm—look at this white man sucking your big black cock. Ummm-ummmm. Yeah! I'm your white cocksucker—sucking black cock."

Orville shoved the man back. Excited, the man crawled toward him.

"Yeah, black stud, yeah, push me away, call me your white queer!"

"That's it, man," Orville said. "Get the fuck out of here!"

Paul
AFTERNOON

"You didn't believe I'd go out and cruise, did you, Stanley?" Sitting on the porch of their house, Paul could hear the wind stir distant waves. "I know why, too, because all along you've taken me for granted. I've been stupid to put up with your bullshit."

"I'm really sorry, Paul. You call the shots now. Nothing's worth losing you. I'm not going to San Francisco, not this weekend, not next. Let's fuck, babe, cummon. I love you. Why else would I have driven back from the airport?"

But he hadn't. Paul sat alone on the screened porch that had charmed him and Stanley when they had leased this house by the beach. He had been sitting there since shortly after Stanley left, imagining that he would turn around at the corner and come back. When time stretched, he imagined him turning off the freeway. Then he imagined him rushing back from the airport.

Would he be able to go out on him? The bars would be charged with sex on this hot, windy day.

Paul had been very active soon after he came out—hunting for sex every night, several encounters in one day. That had been before Stanley. Unlike others who welcomed that life, who wanted only lots of sex, never with the same person twice, Paul was always looking for one person to share his life—friend, companion, lover. During those times of cruising bars and discos and, soon, shadowy parks, dark alleys, spontaneous orgies in garages, it became difficult to enumerate how many people he had made it with, and, even then, he would still be left unsatisfied—and curiously frightened. He would imagine what it would be like to wake up with someone he would get to know, would have breakfast with, go out with, and return home with to have great sex. He did not narrow the possibilities by creating a strict fantasy of what that person would have to be. He would know when he met him.

He did, when he met Stanley at a disco. They kept abandoning other partners to dance with each other. Soon, they were dancing only together, both shirtless, gyrating back, back, and then toward each other, closer, dancing pressed against each other, open mouth on open mouth, flesh on flesh, tongues probing, hard cock against hard cock. And they talked!—outside, between dances, as they stood cooling off on a balcony, talking about themselves and asking about each other, asserting their identities.

There followed "the perfect almost year" that included their moving in together into the small house in Venice. Whether during that time Stanley went with others, Paul would wonder only later. Not then. All he knew, then, was that he was happy, and that he did not miss the world of anonymous sex which had begun to terrify him.

Stanley did miss it. That became clear with sudden absences, quarrels—and it all led to their present arrangement, Paul "faithful," Stanley in what he chose to call "a committed open relationship—and no contacts within the same city."

Paul had, at first, tried to equalize the arrangement. When Stanley was gone, he went to discos, only to discos so that he could tell himself he had "gone dancing." That would turn out to be true. When an agreement was made to go home with someone, he would separate with an excuse—"I just remembered"—and go home, hoping Stanley would be back. But Stanley never came back early, often extended his days away.

That son of a bitch made me come while I blew him and he had no intention of coming—thinking that would pacify me. "This is it, Stanley," Paul said aloud. "No more. I swear it."

Inside, he stood over the turntable where Stanley had left the record he'd played last night, "Judy Garland's Greatest Hits." No question about it, Garland *was* a great performer, but she made Paul nervous with that edge-of-despair note in her voice. Gay people said things had changed a lot, but Garland remained a favorite among many gay men, often a closet favorite. He replaced the Garland record with a favorite of his own, from last year, Geraldine Hunt and "Can't Fake the Feeling."

The telephone rang.

Stanley! He would be calling from San Francisco, to say he was coming back. Maybe he'd just waited at the airport, here, didn't even take the plane, thinking it all out, and now—

"Hello?"

No answer. Hang-up. A wrong number. Oh, no, it *was* Stanley—Paul was sure of it—Stanley, making certain he was still home—Stanley, rushing back to him, at this very moment. Paul lifted the needle from the turntable, to stop the record Stanley wouldn't like. The needle slipped and scratched across the surface.

Nick
AFTERNOON

He'd gotten into three cars—and not a single hustle had worked since that cocksucker jerked himself off in his car. The reason he'd come out earlier than usual was to make extra bucks, maybe rent a motel room for himself tonight, watch TV. Sant'Anas made you weird, man, and if you became frantic on the street, you didn't make out. Where the fuck was all the money today?

"Hustling?" A man had stopped his car at Nick's corner.

"Yeah."

"How much to blow you?"

"Fifty."

"Okay. Get in."

Nick did, and saw, ahead, a guy standing at a corner, an older man. That's how they worked, in two's. A cop picked you up, drove to a corner where another cop stood, both would flash badges, cuff you.

"Changed my mind," Nick said, and jumped out, sure he'd saved himself from being busted.

When he looked back, he saw that the man he had seen at the corner was a woman—the dusty wind and his imagination had converted her into a man.

Goddammit! The guy hadn't been a cop, and look at him taking off with another hustler. Fifty bucks blown away. What the fuck was happenin' today, man?

Furiously as if she was responsible for it all, he searched the block to make sure he *had* seen a woman at the corner. Yeah, there she was— and, man, was she a weirdo, rushing away, then just standing there like she didn't know where to go, and wearing that black coat—in this damn heat—like she was actually cold.

Clint
AFTERNOON

He checked in at the Château Marmont off Sunset, a still fashionable hotel because of its offbeat-starrish clientele. He didn't like gay hotels, he didn't like ghettos. That's how he thought of the pockets of gay men living in New York's West Village, Castro Street in San Francisco, and, increasingly, West Hollywood—there was talk about turning it officially into a city, a "gay city." When he had first come to reside in Los Angeles, he had stayed briefly at this hotel before leasing a house in the Hollywood Hills, later transferring to New York. It had seemed appropriate, on this day, to return to the same hotel.

In the elevator, a woman kept staring at him. He looked away, knowing she was trying to recognize him. "Aren't you—?" she began to ask when they were alone in the elevator.

He shook his head, rejecting identity for now, a life in another world. The world of gay sex hunting thrived on anonymity. It was a world of lives without past, only present. The present began the moment you appeared, available, in cruising turf. Within that anonymous world, he needed to define himself.

At the window of his hotel room—the hotel is built on a slight elevation—he looked down on a palm-fringed pool. The wind crinkled the water as it sliced across it. Beyond, it swept along Sunset Boulevard, the area of stylish shops and cafes, canopies flapping now, tables outside occupied despite the wind. Inside his room, the sound of the wind was muted, absorbed by the hum of the air conditioner.

Hot, sweaty, tired, he took a shower. He remained under the water for long moments, letting it stream down his trained body.

He put on a bathrobe, swallowed a quaalude to bring him down from the coke he had snorted again, and he began to unpack. Responding to an overwhelming weariness that warred with the lingering edginess of the coke, he closed his eyes as if even in that position he would surrender to the exhaustion extending from last weekend. He turned on the television, the sound off. On the screen, wind swept across streets—bending trees, scattering blossoms within clouds of dust, a glowing dusk. There was an abstract beauty within the storm, if it was separated from disaster. He snapped the television off. The screen faded into a lingering pinpoint of light. Then it vanished, the screen blinded by impassive gray.

He lay on the bed. Sunlight carved shadows into the room, creating a premature twilight. What had sent him here was all that he had seen and experienced as if for the first time, last weekend.

NEW YORK
A Week Ago

He worked out early, in his chromy apartment building gym. Then he dressed for the sex-hunt—in jeans, the correct style of lumberjack boots, plaid shirt open. It was a warm New York day full of sun. He welcomed that because this would be his first weekend of cruising familiar areas since he had returned to Manhattan from a sojourn on Fire Island one week ago.

As he had waited then at the station for the train into Manhattan, he had run into a friend who related, in enraged detail, that a friend of his, whom Clint did not know, had been brutalized by a group of

straight punks a few nights ago. The man had left a gay bar in nearby
Sag Harbor and was walking home when five teenage males drove by
the bar shouting, cursing. They seemed to have driven away, but had
stopped, gotten out, and were waiting to ambush the man. They kicked
him with heavy boots, screaming, "Queer! Faggot! Cocksucker!"
Thrashing him with their belts, they shoved him against a garbage bin.
As he lay on trash, they spat on him, and one of them pissed on him.
All this violence had occurred with such swift force that those who had
run out of the bar to help, including Clint's friend, had not been able
to reach the man before the marauders drove off. The man was now in
a hospital, in critical condition, the punks had not been arrested. Other
gay men waiting at the station had reacted to the news, like Clint, with
the usual anger—another outrage on their turbulent horizon.

Back in Manhattan, Clint took the subway from his expensive apartment on the East Side. He intended to get off a few stops before his
destination, to savor the day, and then walk on into the West Village to
cruise familiar streets and bars.

When he stepped out of the subway and into the street, he expected
a splash of sun. The day had altered. Grayish sunlight filtered through
the City's grime and a thickened layer of clouds. That cast on the scene
a muted light which banished shadows, rendering everything stark, as
if a camera had found its focus.

As he walked along the streets—strawy grass sprouted out of cracks
in the concrete—Clint saw the usual bands of gay men, many handsome, many shirtless, exhibiting prepared bodies, exulting in vaunted
freedom, drenching the air in sensuality, this vague army of "lumber-
jacks," "motorcyclists," "cowboys," "leathermen," all in masculine regalia even while they tended to flower stalls, or shopped at chic
boutiques or antique shops.

And yet—

Yet, born ironically out of a detestation of effeminacy—the horror
of being labeled "sissies" had become an aversion to "looking gay"—
this new gay man—and Clint knew he was among them—had become
as identifiably gay as drag queens. When that aversion to being effeminate succeeded, it produced stunning men, supremely arrogant, proudly
sexual, flaunting a unique masculine glamor, their walk a graceful strut.

But the aversion did not always succeed. Among the macho men, there were those who wilted under the uniform—under tension, or when drunk. Then, wind milling gestures, sighs, cries of "Oh, Mary" ambushed the postures. The strut would transgress into a swish, a tensed fist might melt into a drooped hand. The laughter—

Clint heard the familiar laughter as he walked on. He lingered before a group of about six men, all in decorated leather. Today the laughter sounded different to him—a forced, toughened laughter. The same laughter that erupted in crowded bars in deep-night hours? He listened. It was a mirthless laughter. It broke in the middle—a lonesome hollow at its core—retreating as if it had stumbled on a raw bruise. Then it jerked toward forced euphoria. The sound of dubious survival.

On this shadowless afternoon, Clint moved on past dying buildings, toward deserted piers at water's edge, past loitering men in masculine drag. Among them, queens strolled or leaned into cars driven by men looking for "women." "The visual assault of gay theater," a friend of Clint's had once described this vista of costumed men. "Camouflage," Clint had contributed.

To enter the remains of a warehouse, which extended the length of two blocks to the brink of the Hudson River, Clint stooped under an oxidized gate. Fire, vandalism, and marauders had battered the abandoned building. Blackened frames, scorched walls, shards of glass in windows remained. Fire-carved gouges riddled the ceiling, higher than two stories. All was quiet as Clint penetrated the dusk of this giant gutted room he often hunted within.

He walked along floors pocked with holes, littered with broken glass, metal pipes, tangled wires, scrap iron rotting. Truncated stairways led to the bones of other smaller rooms. At the farthest end of the skeletal warehouse, a portion of the wharf had collapsed into oxidized water.

Clint was aware of familiar sounds separating from silence. Many presences were stirring, footsteps disembodied. He heard those noiseless sounds as never before, strange in this decayed structure. Within a small hollow room permeated by the odor of amyl poppers, four men bunched into one contorting form, hands groping, mouths licking, kissing, mouths sucking, random cocks inserted, withdrawn. Clint neared the cluster. A man standing held Clint's cock for a kneeling man to suck. "Suck, pig queer!" the man barked at the squatting man. Clint had heard those words, similar orders, had used them himself, responded to them. They aroused him now. But today they seemed to continue to echo in the burnt-out cavity of this warehouse. He moved away, as if cast adrift by the twilit day.

He walked along charred ruins, in and out of wafting poppers. He passed two men fucking in a burnt-out hollow. A man on the floor licked the inserted cock as it emerged. Lying on rubble, another man moaned, an ampule of inhalant stuck into one nostril. Legs straddling him, two men pissed into his mouth. One of the men standing beckoned Clint to join them.

Had he dozed, only for a moment, pushed into defensive sleep by the clutter of memories? Clint's bathrobe was soaked with perspiration. He removed it. Had the air conditioner in the hotel gone off, if only briefly? Sant'Ana winds toppled electric lines, creating outages. He listened, heard the hum of the air conditioner.

Ernie
AFTERNOON

At the gym nearby, in West Hollywood—large windows faced the street so that those walking or driving by might look in and see terrific bodies—Ernie worked on his pecs first, proud of the flare they created toward his shoulders. Lots of bodybuilders emphasized the lower pecs. In the extreme, that gave the effect of breasts, and if you took steroids, you got "bitch tits," pointy nipples. Ernie didn't do too many shrugs either, not liking the slope that many musclemen developed. Hey, everything was okay if that was your trip, right?—if you wanted to look like a goon. Like that Lars Helmut.

"Hey, Lars, I figured I'd run into you at my gym someday."

"Yah, Ernie, I figured dat, too."

"How d'ya know my name and where I work out?"

"Word gets around about da cute guys."

Someday that would happen—but Ernie would be blunt and tell Lars that he wasn't into huge muscles like his, ugly trapezius muscles that looked like padding under your neck. *His* more moderate "traps" emphasized his wide shoulders.

And made him look shorter.

Hey, his height never bothered him, right? He was now evaluating himself in one of the mirrors that outlined the room, multiplying bodies, not all of them that muscular, several beginners here. He stood on his toes, not so he would look taller—that didn't bother him—but just to stretch his calves, which were good, hard to develop, too.

He wiped sweat and looked around. More gay men were working out now. When he first started, several few years ago, he was exceptional—not among the professionals who hung out in Venice Beach, but on gay turf. Now, every few blocks along Santa Monica Boulevard, chances were you'd see a trained body on a gay guy. Jeez, even some effeminate guys worked out. There they were pumped, while they shrieked, "Go, girl," and wilted like big lilies. Hey, it was okay with him if all gay guys were trying to get into shape now, like a fit army during peacetime.

"How're you doing? I was watching you work out."

The guy who had spoken to him was *right,* yes, good-looking, muscles beginning to shape. About his age, younger.

Ernie flexed, inviting a compliment.

"—and I was wondering if you'd give me some tips. My upper arms—"

"Sure, guy." Ernie loved being asked to be an inspiration. He agreed to show the guy the proper grip with a barbell. "Not too wide, because then you have to swing your body, not good for the biceps, not good for the back, gotta protect your lower back." Yes, he'd go home with him. Lots of people waited until the end of the night, especially on weekends, to make a connection, and sometimes ended up alone. If you made out early, you could relax, and even if you went out again, you'd go to the bars with a different attitude, that you'd already made it, and so you didn't *have* to make it. Besides, people said the "devil winds" stirred bad stuff. So what was wrong with makin' out early, relaxin', maybe watchin' a porn flick together on his projector, spend the night, see each other again, get somethin' going, become lovers. Hey, this guy was *real* cute.

"I can tell *you* know how to work out," the guy said, "cause you got a great bod."

O-kay! That was it. He'd make it, early, settle down for the rest of the day, even if the kid had to leave. He felt—crazy, right?—that this encounter would save him from prowling on this restless night.

"You wanna come over to my place, after we finish working out?" he said casually, as if it didn't really matter.

"Yeah." The guy smiled, smiled. "I gotta tell you, I'm into *big* guys."

"Well, you sure got one here, guy." Ernie tried not to flex too obviously in response to the compliment.

Mitch
AFTERNOON

"I'm sorry, Mitch. I just couldn't face myself. I used you, Mitch."

"You *were* looking at that woman, Heather, I knew it—"

"Yes, the same woman you were looking at. We both wanted her. When you went to the rest room—"

"Are you going to start that up again, Heather?"

"No, listen. When you went to the rest room, she came over—we kind of made a date. Her tanned body excited me, Mitch. I imagined her naked. I imagined her going down on me while I imagined what it would be like to go down on her."

Mitch understood now, but he was still angry. "Goddammit, Heather, you used me, you said *I* followed that guy into the rest room, that *I* was looking at him—"

"Discover yourself before it's too late!"

The words exploded Mitch's imagined encounter with Heather, leaving him staring at the woman who had spoken them.

"Didn't say nothin'. You a psychic, too?" The woman, old, burnt brown by the sun, an orange bandanna wrapped about her forehead, was one of many psychics along the boardwalk of Venice Beach. She sat behind decorated fruit crates and a sign.

PSYCHIC
ALL PROBLMS SOLVED.
DISCOVER YURSLF BEFOR ITS TO LATE!!!!

"No," Mitch told the woman. "I read your sign and I guess I heard it aloud."

"Don't run away. Five bucks and you'll know everything you want to know."

"Nothing to know." Mitch walked away from the beach psychic. He forced his concentration away from Heather's accusation and onto the concrete stretch bordering the beach, a carnival stretch of gaudy shops—he lingered before each—some meant to last only for the day, cardboard boxes and wooden crates adorned with paper, balloons, beads, shiny tinfoil stars. Other shops, more permanent, wedged into old buildings. Posters, cheap jewelry, sunglasses, trashy clothes with false designer labels, a band of black men with improvised instruments, a magician with a bird, a ventriloquist, a clown, derelicts huddled on benches next to astrological charts—and, everywhere, male and female bodies, gliding by on skates, in bathing suits or clothed, idling about or lying, almost exposed, on the beach, ignoring sand slicing by in sheets of wind while agitated waves crashed against the shore.

Mitch reared back. The man Heather had pointed out on the beach earlier—had accused him of staring at—was walking toward him, no longer in trunks, now in shorts and an open shirt. Yes, and this much was true. The guy *had* come into the rest room soon after he'd gone there. What the fuck did the son of a bitch want? Wasn't it enough that he'd caused that scene between him and Heather? Jesus! The woman who had paused at a bracelet shop—that was the woman who'd been with that guy, the woman Heather had been looking at. Mitch braced to confront them both.

Dave
AFTERNOON

He tinkered with his Harley, polished the chrome. Ordinarily he would have done it outside, on the sidewalk, his shirt off, like now, because you never knew who might be driving by and stop, get together, dude. But the dusty wind did not allow that this afternoon. In his garage, he treated the leather seat with special soap, special shine, the odor of leather, of rough sex, so overwhelming that he paused to snort an amyl inhalant and felt such a rush that he rubbed his groin against the leather seat of the bike—

"Get on that fuckin' bike, motherfucker, yeah, shove your face against it. Now pull down your fuckin' pants. *Down!*" The lithe form did.

"Now spread 'em, let me see that hole beggin'. Yeah, motherfucker, you're right, I handcuffed you to the bars. Tighter? You feel that? Yeah, sniff the leather, sniff some amyl. Smell the leather of your master. Yeah, sniff, beg, *beg for it, pig!* You want this belt across your fuckin' ass before I push my cock into your fuckin' hole? Yeah? Yeah? Then *feel* it, you fuckin' shit!"

His cock bore into the begging asshole—so deep it would come close to the leather on the seat of his spectacular machine. He would leave his cock buried, feeling it throb as he smelled the leather. "Beg, motherfucker, I said, beg, you cocksuckin' queer! Beg for my fist up your fuckin' queer ass—"

He stopped rubbing against the machine, and blocked his fantasy of a slave he would work over on it—stopped because in a few more strokes he would have come, dude, and he didn't want to waste that on fantasy.

Three

Many regular visitors choose not to walk on the grass in the park in West Hollywood. They prefer to wander among cleared paths, some of which lead to a lot with parallel bars and other gymnastic props. At times, the equipment there is used by young men showing off as indifferent cars drive along the bordering street. In another small lot nearby, there are a merry-go-round, a slide, a set of swings, and a few benches. Children swirl or play within enclosed pits of sand. Against one extremity of the park are two small buildings, one story, each the size of one large room.

Their location and a clutch of trees and shrubs about them tend to block the wind from that area on Sant'Ana days—today—but, then, the heat lingers, hovers, stays there.

Jesse
AFTERNOON

In his tight cutoffs and tank top Jesse strolled along Santa Monica Boulevard, welcoming the anxious wind that mussed his hair.

West Hollywood!

"Boys' town," some people called it. Whatever they called it, it was the place to live in California—although some claimed that in San Francisco things were even hotter, along Castro Street, and, in New York, the Village. He intended to visit both those cities. All gay men did. For now it was L.A.

He stopped at the French Quarter Cafe to have a green salad, iced tea, some fruit—he didn't care for junk food, what it did to the body.

The French Quarter Cafe had an outdoor section under a colorful awning, red, white, blue. Gay men assembled there, to eat and comment on the men passing by. Jesse had made some good contacts here. Today he sat in the outdoor part—wide awning flapping but holding off the wind—and watched the parade of men. He hoped none of the people he knew would come by to interrupt his special day.

God, there were a lot of beautiful gay men, and they weren't reticent to be sexy and show it off! Watch that guy across the street! He looked almost naked, chest bare, fingers looped over his low jeans, no belt, top button open. Jesse enjoyed "collecting" in his mind sexy types he would like to make it with, hunky guys not near enough to cruise when he saw them, or unavailable, at the time, like with someone else.

Maybe he'd *never* go with only one guy again, he thought, shifting his eyes to the array of men in the restaurant, and then again, alternating, to others walking by, many in shorts, a lot without shirts—and not just because of the increasing windy heat, but because they were aware of looking great in tight jeans, sculpted muscle shirts, tailored Western garb—so many men, so little time. Still, being a long way from thirty, he estimated he could have thousands of encounters.

Smiling at several of the lusty men who had looked at him—you never knew who you'd meet later, when you were ready—he paid and left the restaurant.

On the street now, an old man passed by, paused, looked him up and down, and stopped. Ugh! Jesse discarded him with a look of disgust. He felt insulted when old guys thought they had a chance with him. One old guy had offered him money. Well, he wasn't a whore like those guys down the Boulevard. Why did people let themselves grow old? He sure wouldn't.

Watch. Those two hunky guys approaching him would turn around and look at him. They did. Great! Often, timing went off, like a clumsy dance. You'd look back at someone *after* they'd already looked back at you. Missed connections. Jesse shrugged, but smiled, at the two guys to indicate that nothing was going to happen now—but maybe later, another time?

It was a wonder that gay men connected so often, with all the considerations involved in cruising—like who looked first, who spoke first, who claimed to do what in bed and was it what the other wanted. The last wasn't a problem since most gay men, whatever they claimed, were "flexible." Not Jesse. He liked to suck, sure—who didn't?—and no one complained when he did, but what he loved most was getting fucked. Bottoms, that's what they called guys who liked what he did, Jesse knew. Fine! He was a proud bottom.

He felt in absolute control over so-called "tops." He went crazy when a stud rimmed him before fucking him, and he manipulated his ass to make sure the tongue went *in*. When he had a guy's dick in his ass, *he* drove *him* wild. He contracted, released the cock for a moment, squeezing tighter, holding it locked. When a guy claimed he didn't want to come, that challenged him. Before the guy knew it, he'd be shooting loads of hot cum into his ass. Very often *he* ended up on top, sitting on a guy's cock, controlling the strokes exactly like he wanted them.

So who was in charge?

Ugh. Some drag queens, or transsexuals—you couldn't really tell anymore what they were—walked by. Why didn't they stay on their part of Santa Monica Boulevard, farther east, where they hung around along with the male hustlers—some of whom were hot-looking, but fuck 'em, who needed to pay? One of the two queens, black, looked like a giant, in a green dress slit in front. The other, white, was wearing a huge wig—so stiff with spray that every hair resisted the wind—and a skirt that came just above what would have been her cunt. Was it a cunt already? Jesse wondered. Queens gave everyone a bad name. During the gay parade, they turned up full force, fluttering feathers, posing, blowing kisses. Ugh.

Why would a man want to be effeminate? Jesse couldn't imagine wanting to be a woman. Gay men desired other gay men. He walked past the queens, ignoring them. He returned his attention to the *men* roaming the streets, some not fully committed to cruising yet—but wasn't everyone cruising all the time?

Wild! That guy over there on the corner—Jesse collected him in his mind for a future time. The guy was wearing sweats, but he'd rolled them over his waist a turn or two so you could see a couple of inches of flesh, slim waist, between them and his sleeveless T-shirt. Gay people today sure knew how to turn everything lusty.

Of course, there were some straight people in West Hollywood, a lot of old Jewish people who didn't even seem to see the gay men, or didn't care that they were gay. Not too many lesbians on the streets—they didn't cruise the way gay men did. They had their bars, of course. Most of them coupled.

What would it be like to have only one person? Awful. He had been with guys who intimated the possibility of a "longer connection." He dissuaded them. If someone was *real* good sex, he'd see them again, sure—but not when they started talking about being "faithful." Who'd want to be "faithful" for longer than a day? Yet you constantly heard guys in bars talking about their lovers and claiming they were there only to have a drink, because their lovers were out of town, as if having a lover was the greatest thing in the world. Not for him, thanks.

Wow, was he collecting admiring glances. And look at that hot guy jumping out of his convertible to go into the cleaners—in beach trunks, and nothing else, legs and chest just hairy enough, great tan. The Sant'Ana was sure heating up everyone. It was wild just to walk the streets. Jesse collected more candidates for future times, a man across the street, wearing a white tank top ripped exactly so that his nipples were exposed, and nearby, a great-looking guy in jeans with a large tear on one side so you could see most of his muscular thighs—and, great display, walking along the block without a shirt, a guy in sweats washed and chafed so often that the now-gauzy cloth exhibited a full silhouette of his lower body, the outline of full genitals. *Hot!*

The day augured super for this special night, for what he saw now—right now—as the *real* beginning of his life.

Buzz, Toro, Linda, Boo, and Fredo
AFTERNOON

The Chevy convertible cruised along Valley streets, messy coffee-shops, mini-malls, ugly old buildings, ugly new buildings, as Toro's favorite Judas Priest album blasted the same songs over and over—Toro yelling out their titles—"'The Rage!'" "'Rapid Fire!'"—so that they all had to shout to be heard over the tape and the wind.

Buzz saw Linda touch the edge of her skirt. Again! Hiding what? Making sure *what* was there? Holding some shit of her own? He'd wait for the right time to find out what the bitch was up to.

They passed a blond young man in a Firebird. Toro slowed down, parallel with him. The man in the Firebird looked over.

Buzz stood up in the back of the convertible, the wind forcing him to hold on to the side of the car. "Hey, fag, you wanna blow me?" He clutched his groin.

The blond young man flicked him a finger, and shouted back, "Go blow your mammas, motherfuckers!"—and sped off through a yellow light.

"You gonna let 'im get away with that?" Buzz goaded Toro.

Toro's Chevy ran the red light, halting cars at the intersection. "I don't let no one get away with nothin', man!"

Unless you don't know about it, Buzz wanted to say, but only smiled at Fredo and Boo, both standing up with him in the back of the convertible.

The Firebird swerved onto the freeway at the very last moment. Toro tried to back up, but he almost crashed into the car behind and had to brake. He greeted the blaring honks with stabs of his upraised finger.

Boo was laughing, a harsh laughter. "That faggot left us way behind, man."

"Fuckin' fag did it to us, man," Fredo joined.

"We'll have to make up for that," Buzz said. "Right, Toro? Have to show what bad motherfuckers we are, right?"

"Yeah," Toro said.

They all felt the defeat, anger—and he was prepared to contribute to the tension, and even the wind and the heat were adding more. Great night comin', Buzz thought.

They neared Hollywood, where Cahuenga leaps into Hollywood Boulevard.

"Hey, Linda, what you keep rubbin' your leg for?" Buzz decided to let her know he'd seen her sneaky actions.

"I'm wearing your mamma's panties," Linda said, "and they're too big, keep slipping."

"Oh, yeah? Well—" Buzz couldn't think of anything more to say now, but he would, he would.

"Why don't you take 'em off, Linda?" Boo offered.

"Cause you'd be sniffing 'em," Linda said.

"Give 'em to him, man," Fredo challenged.

Buzz studied Toro for a reaction. Nothing.

Then, "Why *do* you keep rubbing your leg?" Toro asked Linda. "You got an itch down there you haven't told me about?"

Buzz leaned over and padded Toro on the back. All *right*! So Toro was with them, he evaluated. He believed them about last night. Pretty soon, he bet, Toro would frisk the bitch. *They* would frisk her—good and rough—to see what she was hiding. So obvious about it, too, the stupid bitch. Did she think they were dumb?

Linda sheltered her hair from the grasping wind. She threw her head back and laughed.

Father Norris
AFTERNOON

From the chapel, he walked to the rectory. The *beata* who worked on the premises—a Mexican woman who devoted her whole life to ministering to priests—bowed before him, and, in the old tradition, reached to kiss his hand. He pulled away. She looked startled. He raised his hand over her and blessed her.

Then he hurried into his room. Before a crucifix, he removed his collar. He took off the rest of his dark clothes and replaced them with casual clothes. He removed the glasses he did not need.

"In your name, Lord—" He made a sign of the cross, bowed his head, looked up at the crucified figure, staring at it for moments. Then he walked out, in search of Angel.

Za-za and the Cast of *Frontal Assault*
AFTERNOON

Za-Za called to Rex Steed, who was slumped over Tony Piazza, "You want to try again, Mr. Steed—*please*?" She squinted. Tony Piazza was relaxing his famous butt now to let Rex Steed in! Oh, thank you, God.

"Yeah, I'll fuck the fuck out of him," Rex Steed enunciated.

Still bent over, Tony Piazza widened his stance, parted his ass with his hands, wide. "All yours, stud."

Rex Steed worked himself up, pulling at his cock, pulling, pulling. Tony Piazza wiggled his ass. "I'm waitin'."

With the sturdy beginnings of a hard-on, Rex Steed poked at Tony Piazza's ass. Tony Piazza contracted, rejecting the cock curtly. It surrendered, growing limp on the round buttocks.

"A star is worn," Jim Bond said.

What a *désastre,* a rebellion of bitchy studs deviating from Mr. Smythe's script! Za-Za glanced at Mr. Smythe. His binoculars were focused—like a two-barreled gun—on this *fromage. Fromage?*—that meant cheese. *Quel dom*—? Oh, fuck it. What the hell was that awful— terribly beautiful—Tony Piazza thinking?

His buttocks tossed into the wind, Tony Piazza was exploring a strange feeling. All along he had been a bottom, taking other people's cocks, in his mouth, up his ass—and he loved that. But what would it be like to feel *his* cock in somebody's ass? He pushed away the thought. Too bad he had to bring that bitch Rex Steed down a notch, because he wouldn't have minded that blond eight-incher exploring his hole, but he'd had enough of his bullshit about being straight and slumming in gay porn, while he showed off for those rich bitches who'd come to watch. Well, Rex Steed was a fucking whore like the rest of them, and goddamn if *he*—Tony Piazza, star bottom—was going to let the bitch inside *his* ass.

Malheur! If all this was going haywire on the very first page of Mr. Smythe's script, what would be next? Za-Za glanced nervously ahead in the script, hoping for something easier—

During a break in the fucking and sucking—
An *entr'acte!*

—all bottoms lean over the edge of the pool, buck-ass naked, while Dak Boxer, in the pool with only boots on—
In the pool—*with boots?*

—squirts a powerful stream of water—find two water hoses at edge of pool—at their asses, one at a time, the water spraying back after splashing the buttocks, to create a clever fountain effect.

LARS HELMUT, with his own hose, will then join DAK BOXER, and, the water turned off, they will push the nozzle of the hoses into the bare asses, taking turns, one after the other.

Oh, the pervert! Za-Za shook her head. Was everything going wacko? She wasn't hesitant about experimentation—and in her serious films she would interject avant garde elements into conventional approaches, all very *noirish,* creating an existentialist *feel* during the family outing sequence. But what Mr. Smythe was demanding! The water hose—all right. But nozzles? Quickly she reminded herself, "Mine is not to question why, Mine is but to do or die." And die she would if she didn't satisfy Mr. Smythe.

Where were the damn hoses?

A gasp of wind whipped the script out of her hand, scattering the few pages around her. One floated in the pool. She almost fell trying to retrieve them. Wes Young helped her up—so gallantly!— and gathered the pages, diving into the pool to save the last one. Za-Za *felt*—yes, she *felt*—Mr. Smythe's eyes on her as she clutched the dry pages with her teeth to thwart another ambush. She shook the wet page to dry it.

Oh, but the binoculars were trailing Wes Young, who was moving away, dripping—and the water had been unkind to his thinning hair. Was he aware of Mr. Smythe's attention on him? Did they know each other? Some kind of conflict? Please, God, not another unexpected development.

With growing desperation, Rex Steed tried again—aiming carefully at Tony Piazza's ass—which snapped shut again, ejecting the desolate cock, which now plopped over the renowned kangaroo.

This was it! Za-Za rushed over to Tony Piazza, bent down, and whispered, "You know damn well this isn't in the script." Even in this position—precariously because of her wig—and directing her words at his face—upside down and framed by his spread thighs—she lamented, Oh, to have that miraculous cock at my disposal! "So how can you be so *cruel*?"

"I've been taught by masters." From under his legs, Tony Piazza quoted a favorite line of Za-Za's.

The monster, mangling that perfect *riposte* from *The Heiress*. Za-Za straightened herself out from under Tony Piazza's butt.

"Sha-Sha, vie don't I fug da guy? *I* can get in," Lars Helmut offered.

"I can help out," Wes Young offered like the veteran he was.

"Want me to slap Rex Steed's ass, Za-Za?" Dak Boxer suggested.

Tugging nervously at his briefs, Huck Sawyer looked at Dak Boxer with eager eyes.

"*I* can get Rex Steed hard," Sal Domingo asserted. "Obviously he needs *true* inspiration."

Loyal Jim Bond came to Tony Piazza's defense, "Listen, bitch, if Tony Piazza's ass can't get him hard, *nothing* can."

With a cry, almost a sob, Rex Steed propelled his body against Tony Piazza's ass with such force that Tony Piazza fell. "Ouch!" Tony Piazza jumped up and shoved Rex Steed away. Rex Steed landed on the ground, back down, long blond legs straight up.

Dak Boxer's and Lars Helmut's cocks both pointed at Rex Steed's ass.

Oh, dear God, Jesus, and Mary, Za-Za prayed, if You come to my aid, I'll return to the Church, I'll donate all of my earnings from today to Your charities—well, half my earnings. Only please, please make Tony Piazza let Rex Steed in! Was this God's answer? She had glanced away toward the neighboring hill. The fire was coming closer in a kind of zigzag.

But worse still—

Rex Steed was not making any attempt to get up—just lay where he had fallen, his legs way out, his feet propped—firmly—on the ground, his eyes closed. Was he dead? Oh, no, that puckered ass of his was *very* much alive!

And!

Tony Piazza was scrutinizing it!

And!

His beautiful sturdy cock was unequivocally interested!

And, oh, saints, angels, and blessed martyrs—

Mr. Smythe was shouting at her!

John Rechy

Thomas Watkins
AFTERNOON

Thomas remained in the tunnel, frozen, listening to slow footsteps and staring at the dried frond the wind had pushed in. It lay, still shuddering, as if dying, not yet dead. The crunching of trash, nearer—footsteps moving down. Thomas wanted to run out but he couldn't. The footsteps stopped. Thomas saw two shoes, two legs. A man had descended from street level. Only the lower part of him was visible in a muddle of light. Was the man aware of him? Or only that someone else was in the tunnel? The figure advanced, down, two more steps. His pants were open. His penis, exposed, was hard.

Thomas stumbled back down the steps, tearing his hands away from the filthy wall he fell against. He was out of the tunnel. The wind resisted his advancing toward his car, pushing him back toward the tunnel. When he was finally in his automobile, he waited, panting, to restore his breathing.

Thomas drove back to his beautiful home in his new Cadillac. On Sunset Boulevard—

"Young man, what are you doing on this street hitchhiking?"

"Thanks for stopping. Can I get in? Thank you. I wasn't really hitchhiking. I recognized your car and motioned to you. You drive past my house, remember?"

"Of course! You're the young man who waves at me down the Canyon. I've seen you washing your car, but not today."

"I had to pick up some things, and then my car stopped, I was on my way to the parts shop."

"Why, I'll drive you, of course."

"I'm tired of hassling with the car—"

"—and in this terrible hot wind—"

"—yes. You mind if I take off my shirt?"

"Of course not. I'll turn up the air conditioner."

"Thanks, Thomas."

"How do you know my name?"

"The mailman—he says you're really a nice guy. That's a beautiful tape you're playing. It's—"

"Callas, the Divine Voice. 'O mio bambino caro—' Puccini. But how remarkable, I didn't know that young men your age loved opera."

"Sometimes I walk past your house when you're playing that same record, and I stand outside and listen. I wonder, Thomas—could we ride back to your house? I'd like to listen to more of your beautiful music. I'll tend to my car later, it's parked okay."

"Why, of course! This evening I was thinking of going to a movie—"

"I haven't seen Raiders of the Lost Ark. Everyone's talking about it.

"Exactly the film I was intending to see!"

Thomas had reached the mouth of the Canyon. His imagined encounter with the young man who lived down the road from him—and whom he had placed on the street—made him sigh again as he drove past the boy's house and the boy still wasn't there.

In his home at last, Thomas sat in his favorite chair. The obscene messages on the filthy walls seemed still to shout out their horrifying pleadings. To blot them out, he turned on his stereo. The voice of La Divina and the music of Saint-Saëns soothed the horror.

Mon coeur s'ouvre à ta voix—

He looked out his glass wall. Rushing funnels of wind were dredging everything that was dirty along the roads. He drank from his glass. Scotch. Chivas Regal. He drank nothing else.

He wished there was an opera in town, something lyrical, Puccini would be perfect, but Verdi would do. He began humming Musetta's Waltz. Oh, he would eventually go see Sweeney Todd at the Dorothy Chandler Pavilion. Too violent for tonight. That English film that had received such favorable notices, Chariots of—

He saw his reflection in the glass of his picture window. The reflection didn't reveal someone awful. He straightened up. He had more hair than most men his age, and he didn't have to comb it across and down—like Herbert.

Feeling better, he fixed himself another—a small—scotch. How thankful he was for his home, his haven that shut out the ugly, the commonplace, the cruel, especially now that the whole world was rife with violence, and indifference. Teenage killers in gangs. That woman

who dumped her child in the garbage. An attempted assassination on
the Pope, another on the President—that bad supporting player, that
Reagan. No, he was not fond of either of those crude gentlemen. Both
were vulgar. *And* insensitive. Did they care about those poor Mexican
children exploited in the strawberry fields? He had wept when he saw
that picture in the paper recently, the little bodies stooped over pain-
fully. Violence and corruption! *And* insensitivity! Imagine, new revela-
tions about that Agnew man—talk about insensitive and crude!—taking
bribes in the White House. Probation, only probation, for that highway patrolman who admitted molesting those children. Probation!
Think what a gay man would receive if he was found in—found in—
that terrifying tunnel he had just fled.

He refused to remember that fetid place, refused—

Of course—he forced himself to regain normal control of his breathing—within all that was frightening in the world, there was this to hold
on to—

The new translation of Proust's masterpiece! "'*And suddenly the
memory revealed itself. The taste was that of the little piece of madeleine which
on Sunday mornings at Combray—*'" he recited aloud from a favorite
passage.

He sipped his drink, slowly, savoring it and the peace he had created
for himself in this lovely Canyon. A trickle of liquor slipped down the
edge of his lips, surprising him. He wiped it away urgently—so unattractive when that happened. His finger touched his chin—he pulled
it away from the skin there. Why did everything seem to *fall*?

Out of shrieks of the wind, softened inside his haven, the loud roar
of a motorcycle invaded rudely. Without looking out, Thomas knew it
belonged to that ridiculous heavy-set old man—he must be all of sixty—
a few blocks up the Canyon, always covered in leather, no matter how
hot the weather might be, like now.

That leather business distressed Thomas. It was so unpleasant. In
his time there had been the Cinema Bar, where everyone was in leather.
How rigid those men were, then—and they were just as rigid now, terrified of a wrist going limp or a hip swinging out in a swish, but wrists
did go limp and hips did swing out, more often than those posturing

men wanted—or even thought—and, God knew, they didn't *all* ride motorcycles. Volkswagens, *that's* what they rode.

"Leather queens"—that was probably the only one of Herbert's phrases that he appreciated—were everywhere now, strutting around the streets like roosters but cackling like hens. Yes, and those colored handkerchiefs that so many gay men were wearing, to signal their sexual preferences, even hideously distasteful ones. As if there wasn't enough lack of *real* communication among gay men, now they had created a mute vocabulary of—what?—*only* sexual preferences. Hadn't Herbert told him that older people frequented leather bars, that they were called "daddies"—what a terrible designation!—and that some young men preferred them?

Thomas faced his reflection in the window. How would he look in leather?

Ridiculous—that's how.

Did he look his age?

No.

Sometimes, when he used his driver's license to cash a check where they didn't know him, the clerk would look up at him and down at the license, clearly not believing he was as old as indicated, silent about it, too.

He looked at the picture on his license. Not flattering, but whose was? Herbert's—which he had seen once when his wallet fell out and he went to the rest room—looked like the head of a whale.

Thomas freshened his drink before he went to his desk in his study. With his Mont Blanc pen, he practiced writing numbers from zero to nine. With an ink eraser, he scratched out the last two numbers of his date of birth. No one would doubt that he was thirty-five. Let them check his identification—they were notorious for that at that popular bathhouse he'd driven past one night where so many attractive young men lined up to enter.

With his new identification, he sat down to nurse a freshened Chivas Regal for a few moments before he would go—

To see that English film—yes, and to bring, softly, to an end this ghastly day.

Orville
AFTERNOON

Orville had been watching television, idly, since the man he had brought home with him had left. Saturday-afternoon television was mostly for kids. He wished it was World Series time—that would take care of the TV doldrums, but that was still a while away. He preferred basketball, though. He especially liked to watch it on television, in bars. That provided an easy way to make contact with guys who had similar interests. Earlier in the year, he'd met a super guy that way— both were avid Celtics fans. When their team won—defeating the Rockets, whom they had booed together—they agreed to "celebrate." Obviously he would have gone with the guy even if they hadn't had a team in common. The guy was good-looking, slim, with brown hair. They went out a couple of times—dinner, dancing, great sex each time—and then— He still didn't know what happened. He didn't phone the guy, but waited for his call—and the guy didn't call him, probably waiting for *him* to call. The next time they ran into each other, they turned away as if they were strangers. Why did that sort of thing happen so often?—possible intimacy broken so easily, before it was even really explored.

He had been idly shifting channels.

The Sant'Ana was creating havoc in small communities outside Los Angeles, an early-news announcer was saying. The camera panned streets lashed by the wind, tumbleweeds exploding against cars. Even in Hollywood, there were occurring sporadic power outages as a result of felled electrical lines. "In the hills populated by some of the City's most prominent figures," the announcer said breathlessly, "fires have been kept in control. But firemen warn that flames might spread if the wind shifts. Not yet considered threatened but in the area being carefully watched is the mansion of Studio Head Dick Gellman—"

That rich queen who wouldn't admit publicly that he was gay, although everyone knew about his bizarre "private entertainments" with half the male whores in Hollywood.

Orville listened as Anchorwoman Mandy Lange-Jones queried a reporter, "What creates the Santa Ana winds?" "Air currents that collide, then warm air rises and cooler air intercepts it. Before that, seasons of drought have turned brush into tinder, and so— Actually, like with all other natural disasters, a series of random situations creates the hot violent winds." "I'm sure," Mandy Lange-Jones offered, "that the people affected by their destruction don't think of them as random. Maybe that's why they call them devil winds." Tommy Basich, the mustached reporter, agreed. "When these fires rage out of control, they keep on destroying until the devil winds die out."

Orville turned the television off and looked out the window. It wasn't there, the mysterious glow that bathed the City when smoke from many fires converged in the sky and the sun turned into a splash of violent red.

Damn! Even with the air conditioner on, he was sweating. He stood before the cooling unit in his elegant living room until he felt a chill. Maybe he'd just drive over to Griffith Park. There was action all the time in that vast park. No. He'd just sit here and read the new Tom Clancy novel.

Goddamn that son of a bitch bigot he'd brought home—and he'd been so attractive.

Paul
AFTERNOON

The man on the bench kept staring at him as Paul walked along the beach-front walk, staring almost as if he recognized him. Paul had walked here, aimlessly, after he had waited long for the phone to ring again, for it to be Stanley telling him he was returning today. But that hadn't happened.

The man on the bench was handsome, clean-cut, about Stanley's age. Paul pushed the thought of Stanley away. The wind flung his shirt open, and he left it that way, to attract further. He fixed his eyes on the man on the bench and smiled, ready to approach him—except that when he was about to speak to him, the man hopped off the bench, and walked away without looking back.

What the hell?

The wind caught Paul in a hot vortex. He sheltered his eyes from the dust until it drifted away along the sandy streets. The good-looking man had disappeared.

Now Paul was less sure that he would cruise the beach. For one thing, this wasn't exactly gay turf, although in Venice there were no strict boundaries.

Despite the wind, but because of the heat, the beach was crowded. Along walks and on the bordering grass, impromptu bands sprouted, gymnasts tumbled, jugglers performed as men and women in trunks and bathing suits sauntered by, past plumed hats for sale, tinny jewelry, posters of Marilyn Monroe—

The man stood a few feet away as if waiting for him.

Paul caught up, paused, walked ahead, looked back, and then he sat on one of the many benches along the boardwalk. Playing this game of risky cruising—the connection might be severed at any moment— he lingered for the man to signal further encouragement.

He did. He took a few more steps, closer.

Paul was very attracted to him, strange as he was acting. There was something about him that was unlike the usual pickup, not only his unself-conscious good looks. He seemed moody—or sad. Maybe *his* lover was gone for the weekend, maybe they'd broken up. That would create a closeness between them. Okay—he'd skip some steps in this game. "Hi!" he called to the man, and held out his hand—

Damned if the guy didn't turn away! That was enough. To hell with him—too strange. Just as he had known, now he felt guilty to be cruis-ing, even though Stanley was fucking everyone in San Francisco. Would he have gone with that man?

"Hi." The man was back, extending his hand to Paul.

Now that getting together was really possible, would he be able to? "Hi." Paul took his hand. They shook. "My name's Paul."

"I'm Mitch Sherman."

Paul was perplexed. No one in the gay world gave a last name while cruising."

"Look, man, I came back to explain why I was acting so strange."

"Yeah?"

"I thought you were someone else,"

Oh, shit, one of the top three lines when you decided you'd made a mistake and were about to reject. "I just remembered I have to meet someone—" "Sorry, I thought you were someone else—" He'd forgotten the third line. "Is that why you kept walking back?"

"Yes, no, I mean—look, man, I just had a quarrel with my girlfriend—"

Paul couldn't believe he was hearing those words. This guy was telling him he was straight. Not that bullshit, especially on the day he was determined to show Stanley he *could*—and would—live without him. "Oh, shit," he said aloud.

"Look, man, I'm telling you," the man said. "I found out only today that my girl's a dyke—"

"You mean a lesbian, right?" Paul and Stanley had several lesbian friends, mostly couples, good, easy relationships.

"Yeah. She's a lesbian. We'd started having problems, and I didn't know why. Then she—"

"You want to find out what lesbians do in bed, huh?" The last thing he needed was some guy's story about breaking up with his girlfriend.

"Oh, hell, that's not all of it. See, I knew you were trying to come on to me, and I wanted to let you know that I'm not gay—"

"*You* were cruising me!" Depression nagged.

"No, I wasn't, man."

"Oh, shit—*man*." The *really* worst thing he needed was a closet case calling him "man" and claiming his girlfriend was a "lez"—and insisting he himself wasn't gay but everyone was always cruising him and he wondered why. Paul jumped off the bench and walked away without glancing back. When a day started wrong, there was no changing it—it continued downward, and this one had already gone *way* down. There was just one thing to do. Go home.

And wait for Stanley.

Nick
AFTERNOON

Not desperate, far from it, but eager to *get goin'*, Nick left his shirt off, like many other hustlers did even on cool nights. He also did this—he opened the top button of his jeans and pushed them real low on his hips. He dangled a lit cigarette loosely from his lips and propped one leg against the wall of a vacated building—he'd seen another hustler standing like that and it looked sexy. An old guy in a new expensive car drove by. Nick signaled to him.

Along the street, other hustlers were abandoning their stands, fast but pretending to be idling away. That meant cops were on the block. Only the few transvestites, or transsexuals—tall figures in makeup and wearing revealing clothes—remained at their posts. Today the cops were rousting masculine hustlers, Nick saw. He dodged off Santa Monica Boulevard, to a side street. The man in the expensive car had stopped near an apartment building ahead. Since the cops were hassling some-one else on the street—Nick saw the steady glow of swirling lights—he could be bold. He walked right up to the car, opened the door brashly, and got in. "Hi," he said to the man.

The man didn't answer. He was looking at Nick with—panic. Then why had he left the passenger door unlocked if he hadn't expected a hustler to get in with him? He had to act quick, whatever was involved because another squad car—the glow of the first one's lights was still fixed away—cruised by. Often cops pulled hustlers and johns out of a car.

"Why don't we take a drive, man?" Nick said.

The man started the car. He drove a block away, to Fountain, along apartment buildings that looked like they belonged in an old movie. On a side street, he stopped, looked at Nick.

Nervous or not, the guy wanted him. Squinting at the smoke from his cigarette, Nick stretched his young stripped torso, and let his hand drop to the waist of his pants, hooking his thumb there, pulling his pants down, to the edge of his pubic hair.

"I don't pay for sex, if that's what you're looking for," the man said. "I was just driving by, and you signaled to me, you jumped into my car, I didn't invite you, please get out."

"Man, I ain't hustling," Nick lied quickly because the man's face was enraged, and you never could tell who was a psycho, "I signaled you and got in cause I *liked* you, man. I—"

"You what?"

"Yeah, because I liked you," Nick lied. All he wanted now was to get the man to drive him back to the Boulevard. This guy was *really* weird, acting like he was surprised by what was happening. What the fuck did he expect on these streets? Jesuschrist, now the guy had put his hands over his face, and his body was shaking—and Jesus fuckin' Christ, he was—

Nick opened the door and hopped out. In exasperation at this *really* weird day, he puffed a cloud of cigarette smoke into the wind, which pushed it against him. Angrily, he threw the cigarette away and put on his shirt because a cop in a cruising squad car had stared pointedly at him.

Jesus fuckin' Christ—that weird guy who'd just picked him up had been *crying*!

Clint
AFTERNOON

Clint heard laughter from the hotel pool. He sat up on the bed. He would get up, and— Fatigue—and pursuing memories—pulled him back down.

NEW YORK
Last Weekend

That late afternoon, when he saw two men pissing on a third groveling in the trash of the piers, and was invited by one of the men standing to join them, he moved toward them as if hypnotized—no, as if to break a spell, no, as if—

The man who had invited him—by now his piss had dwindled to a few drops, while the other's continued in a steady stream—opened Clint's fly, pulled out his cock, held a vial of inhalant to his nose, and growled, "Piss on that fuckin' pig!" and then he flung himself on the floor, opened his own mouth, and aimed Clint's cock at himself. "Piss on *me,* stud, *I'll* be your pig-slave." Clint pushed his cock into the open mouth, stopping the words.

He withdrew before coming, walked away along garbage. He passed more gray shadows of men hunting within deepening evening. He heard the crunch of his footsteps on trash, beer cans. The odor of poppers, urine, musky cum clung. He moved along loosened boards—splinters of glass like sequins—and out of the warehouse, stooping under its oxidized gate, jagged like a guillotine.

Outside, he inhaled. Grime.

The sky darkened, night fell.

Behind a graffiti-smeared tin wall before a truncated wharf, men crouched, others stood, some wandered with their cocks out. Near the edge of oily water, Clint and a man who had followed him sucked each other on the wooden boards without coming.

Distant streetlights cast an ashen orange mist as Clint left the piers, walked to the maze of parked butcher trucks a few blocks away. During the day these trucks hauled denuded carcasses of cattle to wholesale butcher shops across the street. Now, night, in the aisles between the trucks, silhouettes of men waited. Moans emerged from the trucks. Clint jumped into the darkness of one. Hands, mouths, cocks, the stench of poppers—

Back on the street, he faced an apartment building. Wordless graffiti—phallic swirls and arcs—blackened its walls. From a few lighted rooms, naked men signaled with their genitals to those on the streets. Men straggled past like deserters in neutral turf. On stairs descending into a darkened building, a man fucked another.

Feeling pulled along by a trance—no, still trying to break it—Clint walked along the territory of leather bars, street curbs cluttered with garbage. Behind him, the sound of coarsened laughter erupted. There was the assertive sound of booted footsteps. Four men in vitreous leather swaggered along the ragged street. All carried rings of keys looped through thick belts, colored print handkerchiefs in back pockets. They marched toward the Mineshaft, a gray short building. No sign designated its presence next to a wholesale meat company. Steps led up into a dark maw, its entrance.

Recognizing him as one of their breed, the men nodded to Clint, the barest hint of a nod. Clint listened to the sound of their mirthless laughter.

A taxi stopped before the darkened gash of stairs. A leatherman—slouched leather cap, tight chaps, tailored motorcycle jacket, leather gloves, knee-length boots, handcuffs dangling from a thick belt—walked out of the cab. He pulled on a chain. Harnessed by studded collars attached to the chain, two men, young, naked except for leather jockstraps, emerged. As the man in leather pulled at the chain until it was taut, the two nude men crawled on the street. Like fierce subdued dogs, they snapped right and left as if at an invisible torturer.

Fantasy, nothing real.

Within growing shadows in his room, Clint clung to the credo he had lived with in the world he had gazed at that night, last weekend.

Ernie
AFTERNOON

Ernie walked along the streets of West Hollywood with the guy who had asked him for workout tips. They had agreed to take a shower at Ernie's. The guy's name was Andy, and he was real cute and masculine. Ernie was explaining to him why he preferred weights over machines that were now becoming popular. "Cause, hey, you can *feel* the resistance, *see* the weight, right?"

"Right, yeah."

They might get into a posing scene, Ernie planned. That was one of his favorites. Since Andy wasn't really a bodybuilder yet, he'd want to be guided into some poses, assuming them while admiring Ernie's style. Hey, hadn't the guy asserted he was into big muscles? It would all be much better than trying that with some of the bodybuilders who'd manage to crash through their game-playing enough to get together, because, with them, the competition turned in earnest, both guys looking at themselves in the mirror to let the other guy know he wasn't *shit*— wanting to touch each other but damn if either one would go first, a real competition that produced two losers, no sex.

Ernie checked his walk. Some bodybuilders—like that fuckin' Lars Helmut—walked funny, arms way out as if their lats were so wide they interfered with their arms, legs kind of twisted as if their thighs were so huge they were bumping into each other. Ernie let his arms relax a little and he took longer steps.

"What do you do?" Andy asked Ernie.

Ernie said, "I work in a garage. Garage mechanic." That wasn't true,
but it made him sound like a macho stud.

"Wow," Andy said. "I like working on cars."

Oh, oh. Ernie didn't know much about cars. If the guy started talking about engines and—

"But that's not what I meant," Andy said. "I meant what do you do
in bed?"

Ernie preferred a mutual scene, starting out with some good, whole-
some body-worship. He'd lay back in bed, hands behind his head, all
attitude, and let the other guy lick him all over. Then—fair was fair,
right?—he'd return the favor before they got down and sucked each
other in a hot 69, maybe a mutual rim, too, and then he'd ease the guy
over and fuck him and then he'd lie there with his own legs open and
get fucked—total scene, right?

"I—," he started to answer.

Andy interrupted, "I'm into *big* guys."

Ernie puffed up his pecs—a hint of what was to come. He was
getting to like this guy. He'd ask him to stay after sex, make some popcorn, have sex again—he dodged as the wind shoved a palm frond
straight at them before veering into the street, causing a car to brake
—and if this guy slept over, they'd listen to the wind, not be out in it.

He led Andy past a waterless fountain in the courtyard of his building. He pretended to have to bend to tie his shoelace so that if the old
queen in the apartment nearby was looking out—and she always was—
she'd have a chance to see him with this good-looking guy. Eat your
heart out, old bitch. When there was no indication of movement at the
windows of the old queen's apartment, Ernie started to whistle, and
stopped himself when he realized that he was whistling "Don't Cry for
Me, Argentina," the number the bitchy queen loved to taunt him with.
No stirring at the windows. Ernie just moved on.

But there he came, that fucker, swishing down the walk. "Hi,
sweetie," the old queen called out, like they were sisters.

Ernie deepened his voice so low that he could hardly get the words
out, "Hi, man."

Running, he led Andy away into his apartment, not wanting to risk
how the jealous queen might come back at him.

"Nice place," Andy complimented.

"Thanks. A friend decorated it for me." That was a lie, too, not that his place was all that, but, even so, he didn't want Andy to think he was an interior decorator and not a mechanic. He knew a scene could be blown away with less than that.

Now they'd shower, soap each other off, hands lingering over cocks and balls, brushing along the crack of the buttocks, tantalizing—

"*Hey, let's get goin', guy!*"

Ernie removed his shirt. With a sexy nod of his head, he motioned Andy to follow into the bedroom. "You like a mirror scene, after we shower?"

"Uh—"

Naked, Ernie flexed in the mirror, looking great, healthy sweat redrawing his muscles, cock already hardening.

Andy was staring at—

His cock, Ernie realized.

"You said you were big," Andy did not disguise his disappointment. "I told you I was into *big* guys, I made it clear, and I said it again while we were walking here, and you said you—"

"I thought you meant big muscles, and look—" Ernie tried to thwart what was happening. He did his most muscular pose before the mirror.

"I meant big *cocks,*" Andy clarified. "Usually I check guys out in the showers, but you wanted to shower here. So—anyway, we're here, so—" He shrugged, made no move.

"Damn, I suddenly remember!" Ernie grabbed for his clothes. "My lover's coming back this afternoon, from San Francisco."

"Mine, too," Andy said. "Nice meeting you, and thanks for giving me your workout tips."

Jeez, the guy was turning fem right before his eyes. Thank God he'd been saved at the last moment. "Hey, you're welcome," Ernie said.

Then the guy was gone.

Fuckin' size queen!—and a swishy one on top of it all, and skinny, too, thinking he had muscles. Shit.

His clothes still clutched in his hands, Ernie looked at himself in the mirror. Goddammit, look at that bod!

But he knew that now he would need reassurance, to wipe out what had happened with that motherfuckin' skinny, fem, and *real* ugly size queen.

Mitch
AFTERNOON

When he realized that the man walking toward him wasn't the man he had seen earlier with Heather—and that the woman who had paused at an earring stand on the beach walk wasn't with him—Mitch had continued to stare at the man wearing shorts and an open shirt—until he realized the man was not only staring back at him but was about to approach him.

He had walked away, even when the guy had said "Hi" to him and extended his hand. Obviously the guy was trying to come on to him, and that disturbed him. But what was wrong with talking to him? So he came back, extended his own hand in greeting. The guy seemed nice enough, masculine, too—they might have been buddies looking for girls to pick up on the beach. But then they had got all tangled up about the guy claiming *he'd* been cruising him—he hadn't—and jabbing at him for only now realizing Heather was a lesbian.

Christ! He'd caught up with the guy again.

"Now *you're* following me, I'm not," the guy said.

"Look, I—forget what I said." Mitch really wanted to talk to this guy. "Maybe you'd like to come over to my place—man." He smiled for the first time. "It's a long way away, though, but if you—" The guy—what had he told him his name was?—Paul?—was studying him as if to decide what to say next, do next. So Mitch continued to smile his most sincere smile.

For seconds—maybe a minute—the guy seemed to be about to walk away. Then he said, "You want to come to my place? It's only a few blocks away"—still hesitantly as if not yet committed to it.

"Yeah," Mitch agreed. So what if the guy was gay—and desiring him? Gay guys were attracted to straight guys, so what? That didn't mean anything had to happen—and it wouldn't. All he wanted was a guy who would understand how he felt, and this guy looked like he would.

They walked together away from the beach.

Dave
AFTERNOON

Chaps over ripped Levi's, boots almost up to his knees, leather vest wide open on his lightly furred chest, thick studded belt with key ring loaded with keys—on the *left* side, fuckin' proud top man, dude!—studded leather bands hugging his biceps, cap slanted almost over his eyebrows so that he'd have to raise his head and then look *down* at everyone—and an intricate array of silver chains linked about the black leather—Dave, inhaling the smell of leather and what was left of the amyl he had just popped, mounted his polished Harley, gleaming black and *mean*, and rolled out of the garage, followed by the sounds of his favorite group—Man 2 Man—turned up loud—

> *You can't decide if I'm good or bad,*
> *But don't let it drive you mad,*
> *All this time you tried to tell,*
> *You could have sent me straight to hell—*

He arranged his large navy-blue print handkerchief in his left pocket. He preferred the relative ambiguity of dark blue. That signaled a preference for fucking and being sucked, but it also suggested further possibilities. Red, yellow, black handkerchiefs—yeah, and brown, why leave anything out?—came on too strong too soon. How great, this language of sex spoken by studded dog collars, belts, keys, colors, a code that asserted the bond among real men. Love? Shit. Whatever *that* was, it was weak, like sissy sex. Commitment to rites that celebrated manhood, *gay* manhood—there was no other kind—rites pushed close to the edge and then closer—what could unite tough men—and that meant tops *and* bottoms, masters *and* slaves, dude—what could unite tough men closer than that?

Courting the bike's hardness between his thighs, Dave popped a
fresh ampule of amyl and left it in his nose until all its vapor was gone.
The buzz began inside, an implosion, and then it exploded, encircling
him in darkness, which opened into—

Desire, throbbing, hard desire, dude.

Why give yourself a complication
When I can bring you fascination?
Trust me and I'll be your fire—

The flush of the heated wind against his face renewed the rush of
amyl. He pushed down, hard, with one boot, starting the bike.

You'll turn into someone that I choose—
Look in the mirror and be surprised,
You'll see a person you won't recognize—
Trust me, and I'll be your fire,
Don't burn with the heat of desire—

With a growl that he intensified by revving the engine, the motorcycle invaded the streets.

He parked in the lot of the heaviest leather bar in the City, next to
a garage, in an area designated BIKES ONLY. He tore off the tip end of a
cigarette. That way, when he lit it, the smoke would quickly curl toward his eyes and his scar, and he would retain a squint.

A heavy leather drape shielding the door shut out daylight, invited
the atmosphere of night. At first, he couldn't see beyond the reddish
smokiness. He didn't have to see. He knew the bar exactly—stark,
unadorned, the main section separating into smaller sections, even
darker, iron bars creating the impression of cells.

He waited at the entrance until he felt eyes pulling toward him,
expecting a signal back. Not now. He was feelin' out the scene, checkin'
it out. Men, all in variations of studded leather—some wearing jackets
in the Sant'Ana-heated air-conditioning, several shirtless, chests criss-
crossed with harness straps—sat on stools at the long bar, or loitered

about drinking beer, only beer, cigarettes dangling, or hovered over two pool tables—all tough dudes, rough dudes, *real* men—

"Lawd-sake, hon-*nee,* look what just walked in. Look, girls!"

"To *die* for, but I saw him first, Mary—"

Dave wanted to puke when he heard that, coming from a group of men in leather gathered in a corner. The men, four, were all out of shape, stomachs protruding, shoulders sagging. They were drunk—and—fuck this shit—effeminate, hands whirling, leather askew. Why were there so fuckin' many of those guys? Shit, did they think just wearing leather was enough?

As he approached the bar—and the bartender, wearing only leather chaps and boots, had already set out a beer for him, the kind of client leather bars like to display—one of the effeminate men, his leather cap toppling to one side, whistled in admiration.

Dave detoured from the bar and faced him. "Who you whistlin' at?"

"Just admiring you, macho man," the man slurred.

"Light my cigarette," Dave said.

"Yes, *sir!*" the man said. "Looking for a slave, master?"

"Yeah." Dave spread his booted feet and looked down.

The man slid onto his knees.

Dave waited to get full attention. He spat on his own boots. "Shine them with your tongue and my spit," he ordered.

The man licked the glossy boots, hands on the floor like paws. "Master—"

Dave pulled away. "I'm looking for a slave, yeah, but not a fag like you. Lookin' for a *man.*"

The man raised himself uncertainly from the floor. His companions squealed with delight.

Back at the bar, Dave half-leaned against a stool, gloved hand over his groin, his other hand holding the beer at his lips.

A young man, good looks obscured by groggy eyes within dark circles, stood mutely before him. He was wearing a yellow print handkerchief on the right side.

Dave placed his gloved hand on the man's shoulder, coaxing him down. Kneeling, the dazed man looked up at him and opened his mouth. From about the bar, men moved in closer to watch. Dave began to open his fly.

"Yeah, stud, yeah, do it, let the queer drink!" the man who had licked Dave's boots encouraged, voice deepened.

Dave spread his fly open. He swigged from the beer. He let the liquid spill out of his mouth, down his chest, down along his crotch, down along his stiffening cock, into the pleading mouth of the man kneeling before him.

"Pretend you got what you really want," Dave said, moving away, buttoning his fly. Fuck, I could have any one of these fags in the bar, he thought, cocking his cap farther forward. But he didn't want any of them. On this night of fierce hot winds, he was looking for someone special. A slave, yeah, but not just a slave—great-looking, sure—but someone who'd never got into anything real heavy, lookin' for it without even knowin' it. And maybe—the devil winds were *blowin'*, dude!—he'd recruit another top man, maybe from San Francisco or New York, where they really knew how to get *down*. They'd give the slave a night to remember.

Dave drank his beer, and he listened to the music he was sure was being played for him, "Fire and Ice"—yeah, fire *and* ice!

Outside, he felt so fuckin' wild he laughed aloud at nothin' as he mounted his bike.

The coming night was pulsing with excitement—and look, over there, fires were circling the City.

Four

One of the two small buildings located farthest from the streets in the park in West Hollywood is an office, closed early and on weekends. The other is a toolshed, locked when not in use. It adjoins a wire-enclosed field, perhaps once a track field. It is the one section of the park that has been neglected. Only patches of yellow grass grow on it. Between the toolshed and the abandoned field, there is an open passage, a space about eight feet wide, perhaps twenty feet long. You have to know it's there to walk through it.

Today, because the toolshed is sheltered by its location, only the wind's muffled panting, and the heat, alert that this is a Sant'Ana day.

Jesse
AFTERNOON

After feeling out the streets—and finding them lusty—Jesse went to a cruisy bar to charge himself up some more for tonight.

It was early for heavy cruising, even within the created atmosphere of night, but there were more people than usual in the bar—because of the sexy winds? The Pat Benatar song spewing into the smoky air was just right for this special afternoon, saying it about being *hot* and playing with fire. Wow, even the DJ who chose those tapes was in on his celebration. Gay people played with fire, *played* with it, which meant finding more ways to add excitement all the time. If you kept the fire going, you'd never burn out. That happened only when you stopped.

Two men were playing pool. Gay men loved pool tables in bars. It gave them a chance to pose, look even more masculine—and it gave others the chance to admire them while appearing to be entranced by the expert shots.

The men at the pool table had taken off their shirts—typical of players on display. One had rubbed a light film of oil to highlight his chest. Both were showing the outline of their genitals under tight jeans. Now one of the men pretended to spill beer on his jeans, around his crotch, clearly to emphasize his big cock for a guy leaning against the wall. Wild!

Gay guys were supposed to feel guilty about sex. *Straight* men did. Look around this bar. Everyone was here to find sex, and so what? Double *ugh* to being straight. You couldn't pay him enough. Anyone who said it wasn't great to be gay must be a troll—or worse, if there was anything worse than a troll.

The two men playing pool were okay—one was too hairy. Jesse wasn't attracted enough to hang around them or even file them in his mind for another time.

He had gathered remarks—"cute," "to die for," "sexy," "gorgeous," "great buns!" and, what he liked best, "hot kid." But he sat apart at the bar. He asked the bartender for a beer. The bartender was shirtless. He wore a leather arm band across his biceps, with silver studs. Even when the bar was not a leather bar, you saw those menacing costumes. Some guys even dressed as cops. Just fantasy—and as long as it stayed fantasy, what was the problem?

The song on the tape had changed, Gino Vanelli and "Living Inside Myself"—feeling lost— Well, you couldn't count on *every* song joining your celebration. Check out that one guy going out with another. Poured into his jeans so that his leg muscles tensed when he swaggered out, the way they'd strain when he was fucking, and look at how he left his Western shirt open to expose his carved chest. Wow—great pecs. Even the sunglasses he wore—mirrors—were sexy. Jesse added him to his collection of future contacts.

The bartender returned with the beer. They had made it together, but Jesse had no interest in another encounter. Whatever had happened, once was enough. The bartender was asking him if he'd been out of town.

"No," Jesse said, "but I was thinking of going to San Francisco some time soon. Haven't been there."

The bartender seemed not to believe that. "Gotta be kidding."

"I'm still getting off on L.A."

"San Francisco, man," the bartender advised, "gotta go there to believe it, doesn't stop. You can make out *every*where."

The bartender moved away to tend to some new customers. Jesse sipped his beer, absorbing the hot vibes in the place.

"—that new gay illness—"

Two men sat near him. He had overheard the words one had spoken to the other.

With his beer he moved away from them. They seemed so goddamned serious.

Buzz, Toro, Linda, Boo, and Fredo
AFTERNOON

"Hey, Linda, would you wear one of those?" Fredo asked her.

She glanced out the window as they cruised Hollywood Boulevard. She saw what Fredo was giggling about, a pink building with two display windows in which there were lifelike manikins wearing tiny bikinis and lacy things, some covered at the crotch with feathers, like pubic hair, others open there in fancy diamond shapes.

FREDERICK'S OF HOLLYWOOD

"Shit," Linda said.

"Bet she's wearing something like that already," Buzz tested Toro's reaction.

"Let's see," Boo said. His lips barely tilted in what might be a faint grin.

Fredo slapped at Boo playfully. "Yeah, come on, Linda, show us."

"Later, huh, Linda?" Toro didn't look at her.

Linda turned to him as if in surprise. Things were looking good, Buzz thought. Toro was indicating—wasn't he?—that he would go along with them, whatever developed.

Along the Boulevard, gusts of wind lifted newspapers that scattered like birds. Toro's tape seemed even louder when—"Rapid Fire!" he shouted—the wind paused.

Two girls stood on a street corner, outside a hot-dog stand, fifteen, gaunt, skinny, tiny skirts, teased hair different colors. With them was a tall thin teenage boy with jet-black hair pomaded close to his scalp.

"Hey, check those punkies," Fredo said.

"The guy is cute." Linda looked back toward the hot-dog stand, then winked at Toro to make it all right.

"I bet he don't got this." Boo groped himself.

"If it's as small as you are—" Linda interrupted herself with a laugh.

"Bitch! Say that again." Boo leaned over the back seat. "If I rammed it into you, you'd know you been fucked."

"I already know when I've been fucked." Linda put her arm around Toro, who didn't react.

"She's just riffin' on, man," Buzz calmed Boo. No time yet to show anger that might split them.

"Don't sweat it, man," Linda said to Boo. "Everyone knows you're hung like—" She widened her hands.

"You know it," Boo mumbled.

Fredo congratulated Boo with a hand-slap.

"I bet Buzz knows it," Linda said.

"Huh?" Buzz wasn't sure what she had meant. "Shit."

"You wanna see *my* dick?" Fredo taunted Linda.

Toro turned back and said, still calm, "You guys are gonna fuck things up."

"Fuck up what? What you got in mind?" Linda asked Toro.

She was worried. Good. Buzz's cock stiffened.

On a side street, grimy men stood against the walls of a boarded building, selling drugs, pimping for bedraggled women. Two men in drag signaled slow-driving cars, puckering their lips and sucking their fingers.

"Fuckin' queers," Buzz said. "They make me fuckin' mad!"

"What you got against them?" Linda asked.

"They fuck each other in the ass, that's what."

"Yeah," Fredo agreed.

Buzz said, "You a lez, Linda? That why you like queers?" He had to go with it now, or let the bitch think she could get away with shit.

"Ask Toro," Linda dismissed.

"She a lez, Toro?" Buzz pushed on.

"I don' know, man," Toro said.

"What the hell?" Linda said.

"Maybe she'll prove she ain't, to all of us, huh, Linda?" Toro turned to her, smiling.

"What the fuck, man," Linda said.

Buzz and Fredo joined Toro's laughter—and so did Boo, almost. He made a cackling sound.

Now where was all her tough rap? *Now* she was afraid—and there was no question about Toro's allegiance. Buzz felt aroused—really hard—because Linda was afraid.

Father Norris
AFTERNOON

He drove along Santa Monica Boulevard. So many lost young men. Already corrupted? Not Angel! In his mind he pronounced the name over and over as the woman in the confessional had spoken it—"Ahn-hel," not "Ain-gel." Angel—how appropriate.

As he drove by, young men along the street stared, bent, anxious, inviting through car windows. When he had determined that a particular young man could not be Angel—and he would recognize him instantly—Father Norris looked away, although his hand would rise, about to execute a benediction.

Had Angel been picked up by one of the men driving around? How could they add to the corruption of these young souls? How could they separate them further from their spiritual yearnings?

To make a left turn, Father Norris had to stop to allow heavy traffic to proceed along Santa Monica Boulevard. A handsome young man, his shirt open low on a slender, sculpted body, leaned down and forward to peer into his car. Father Norris held his breath. The young man

had dark hair, a spiritual look about him, moody eyes like the woman
had described. His skin was dark— Had the woman in the confessional
told the boy that he would come looking for him? Was that why he
was signaling? No—surely the woman knew that it would be necessary that Angel not recognize him as a priest or he would flee.

The young man stepped off the curb, closer to him, elbows propped
on the window.

"Is your name—Angel?"

"Yeah. Howdya know?"

Za-Za and the Cast of *Frontal Assault*
AFTERNOON

As she dashed toward the steps that led to Mr. Smythe, who continued
to shout at her, Za-Za glanced back to see if Rex Steed's ass was still on
display and those readied cocks were still aiming at it. But the wind
shoved a palm frond before her and threatened her wig and so she
rushed on to her destiny.

Mr. Smythe was standing up. His guests looked like a 3-D audience, Za-Za thought, binoculars glued to their eyes.

"Mr. . . . uh"—she almost called him Smythe—"you want to con-
sult with me?"

What is the meaning of this? Why have you deviated from my script?
Why is Rex Steed lying there with his legs open like a pair of scissors?
Why isn't Tony Piazza being fucked by him? Why are you destroying
my script? Why? Whatever he would say first, he was preparing a state-
ment of doom, doom, doom for her future as an "auteur."

"Why did you bring that man here?"

"Who? What?" Her head was spinning so dizzily that she could
feel the wig creeping over her forehead.

"The old man—"

"Who? Who?"

"Stop that! You sound like an owl. The man you talked to earlier."

"Wes Young?"

"If that's who he is. He's old. I want you to get rid of him, I'll include his full pay, send him away."

Za-Za clutched her heart. "But your instructions were that you wanted another large uncircumcised cock and you left it up to me to—"

"Yes, but not on an old man. Get rid of him. Now go back and take care of things."

Was he blind? Didn't he see how sexy Wes Young was, in a mature way? And didn't he have any sense of priorities? Didn't he see Rex Steed's wide-opened legs, in serious deviation from his script? Whatever! This was definitely not the time to tell him about her astonishing screenplay, to be directed by her, that would usher a new artistic *splendeur* into the world of cinema.

Now, with a heavy heart, of course, she had to face Wes Young. But—on another front—wait a minute! Of course Rex Steed was spreading his legs out. To be rimmed! Yes—and Mr. Smythe had understood that. After all, there was a place in his script where he directed that "two cast members vigorously tongue Rex Steed's blond ass, which puckers and closes, puckers and closes with each lick of a dabbing tongue." Yes, yes, yes! That was it.

She was saved! Now to attend to poor Wes Young, who was waiting for her. He had already put on his pants. Had he become so vulnerable that he could sense a development like this?

"Za-Za, I guess I'm not up for this today. I'd better split."

He knew. "Well, darling, if you must, but the 'rehearsal' will suffer without you."

He smiled. "Thanks. Uh, Za-Za, you suppose you could spare a bag?"

"Of course." She didn't bother to hide this from Mr. Smythe, because he would think she was paying Wes now. From a pocket, she brought out a skinny bag of white powder. This'll get him through, for a day or so, she thought. "Here, and I'll keep your pay for you—"

Wes Young took the cellophane bag, winked at Za-Za, and, still dressing, walked away from the "set."

Very sad, very, Za-Za thought. But, then, no one who came into porn should think he'd last forever, or even more than a few years—and Wes had certainly had a longer career than most. No time to dwell on *tragedie*!

There was the matter of the rehearsal to attend to. So! But before she assumed her director's function, a quiver of her nose pulled her attention toward the horizon. Smoke smoldered within a nest of hills, as if fire was deciding what to destroy next. Those capricious fires were known to be almost human, fighting those who fought them. Enough worrying!

"Scene Three!" she called out. "Ready for Scene Three."

"Which was Scene One?" Huck Sawyer wanted to know, pulling at the seams of his briefs.

Za-Za almost smacked him. Why was he fretting so with his briefs?

"Who got fucked if we're already on Scene Three?" Sal Domingo chimed in.

"No one," Jim Bond emphasized the critical situation.

True—and Rex Steed's legs remained offered up to the hot day—and before Tony Piazza's thoughtful cock. Za-Za saw that with a crushed heart. "Rim his ass, motherfuckers!" she shouted. "*That's* what he wants." Her wig was about to topple. Her feet were killing her. But she couldn't lose her poise.

Huck Sawyer bent obediently before Rex Steed's ass. Almost daintily he dabbed at it with his tongue. Sal Domingo stood scrutinizing the parted legs.

As in Greek tragedy—and she would use elements of Greek drama in her debut film, a chariot to carry *everyone* away, but not to the sun—everything was moving toward *désastre,* Za-Za knew, as Rex Steed's hand reached under his legs and shoved Huck Sawyer away. Huck Sawyer looked at her as if he was about to cry.

"Shee-eet," Tony Piazza imitated Rex Steed's voice, "Rex Steed doesn't want a *tongue* up his ass." He glanced at Za-Za, and winked.

That beautiful monster, torturing me with longing.

Jim Bond surveyed Rex Steed's parted legs.

Impossible, impossible! Za-Za covered her eyes. Jim Bond had gotten a hard-on at the spectacle of Rex Steed's big ass—and it was big. What was happening? The revolt of the bottoms, with Tony Piazza as its leader?

"Fuck me!"

Za-Za clamped her hands to her ears. Too late. She had heard fatal words that could end her career. They had been spoken by none other than Rex Steed—top man extraordinaire, straight stud *legendaire*—and,

THE COMING OF THE NIGHT

oh, *quelle horreur,* Tony Piazza's cock was advancing toward the demanding blond ass—closer, closer, closer.

Thomas Watkins
AFTERNOON

The little bastard! Thomas thought, wiping away tears—of *anger,* he emphasized to himself. He maneuvered back onto Fountain Avenue. The insolent little bastard, thinking I was interested in him, stretching his body like that, letting his pants slide down on his stomach as if that would entice me! Wait until he became a few years older—who'd want him, much less pay for him? Thomas felt a tinge of pleasure within his anger, triumph at his having rejected the hustler who had hopped into his car, *uninvited,* only because he had been driving past, slowly, having taken a wrong street on his way to see the English film.

But wait. Hadn't the boy indicated that he was attracted to him?— yes, right after he'd accused him of wanting to be paid. The boy hadn't asked for anything. Maybe that hadn't been his intention. After all, *he* wasn't an unattractive man, like Herbert.

Thomas turned his Cadillac around at the next block, back onto Santa Monica Boulevard. How could he have been so quick to judge the boy? Of *course* he wasn't hustling.

Off the Boulevard now, he saw the boy. He was standing near some trees and bushes, unbuttoning his pants, as if about to pull out his penis, and he was doing that before a parked car. The driver of that car blinked his lights in signal, and the young man jumped in.

The driver was unattractive, old, perhaps fifty.

Thomas drove away from the terrifying Boulevard.

Orville
AFTERNOON

"It's Bruce—remember me?"

Orville didn't recognize the voice on the telephone. "Oh, yeah, we met—"

"At the Studio Club. We danced and then you came to my place, you gave me your number."

Orville still couldn't remember. He danced with a lot of men he went home with. Of course, he didn't give his number out that much— only to people he really wished would call, at least at the time. Most people didn't call, and he never called—you never knew if the person was going to remember you.

"I've been in San Francisco, that's why I hadn't called before. I was leaving the day after we met, remember?" Bruce was saying.

"Oh, yeah." There were three possibilities. Two of them he really wouldn't care to see again, but the third, the blond guy—he sure would see him again. But how to find out who it was?

"I thought I'd come over, if you're free."

"Sure!" How quickly he said that. He wanted to blot out the earlier encounter, and he hoped it would be with the guy he remembered. If not, he'd make an excuse, say he'd had a call in the interim, had to go out.

He showered, dressed, waited, checked himself out in the mirror. He tried to remember the two men he didn't want. Maybe they had been better than he recalled, or just pretty good but wanting to try again. After all, he had given them his number. What record to play? Yes. "Strangers in the Night."

Too romantic, too soon. Besides, what if it was the wrong guy and he'd think he was suggesting something long-range?—which he wouldn't mind, a terrific lover, but the right one. Better play it safe. He turned the radio on to the station everyone was listening to. That guy in Van Halen was shouting—not singing—"Everybody Wants Some." True. Everybody seemed to be looking—

For what?

When the doorbell rang, he turned the radio off. It was better not to reveal too much about yourself the first times you were with some-body, because everybody had some kind of expectation going. Orville waited a few seconds before he opened the door.

"Hi, Orville," said the blond man.

All right! He was better-looking than he remembered, tall, lanky like a basketball player, with gray eyes, really sexy. As he was apprais-ing Bruce, Bruce was appraising him, approvingly, Orville could tell.

"Can I get you something to drink?"

"Yeah. A beer?"

Orville didn't have beer, he didn't really like beer, drank it only in bars, when it was necessary to look real macho. He preferred bourbon.

"Bourbon?" he offered.

"Sure."

He made two short drinks. They sat on the sofa. Orville reached over to touch Bruce, and Bruce leaned over toward Orville. They kissed—hot kisses—tongues twisting about each other. Their hands explored. Orville took Bruce's cock out, and Bruce took out Orville's. "Why don't we get comfortable?" Orville spoke the familiar words that meant, take our clothes off, go into the bedroom.

"Sure."

In the bedroom, both naked, kissing, legs wrapped about each other, they sniffed from a small brown bottle of poppers the blond guy had with him—probably butyl nitrite, or maybe that ethyl chloride some guys were sniffing in the dance bars. Warm blood surged to their groins, their cocks straining. Dark flesh, white flesh. They maneuvered their bodies so that now Bruce was sucking Orville and Orville was licking Bruce's balls, inching his tongue so that it would dab at the rim of his ass. That made Bruce go farther down on Orville's cock. Now he had it all the way in his throat—and held it there. Orville felt his cock pulsing inside the other's throat, there for incredible moments, long, long, deep, deeper, deep—and then Orville swept his tongue over Bruce's balls, then farther, farther, licking his ass, spreading it, dabbing at the hole, feeling the brush of hairs on the smooth parting flesh, and he probed with his tongue, deeper in, while Bruce released his cock from his throat, only to lunge at it again, swallowing it all.

Orville was about to come in the guy's mouth.

"Not yet," Bruce ordered. "Fuck me."

He lay face down, ass up. Orville straddled him. Looking back at him, Bruce guided Orville's cock in. Orville pushed slowly and waited.

"Go on, that's okay."

Orville entered Bruce fully, stayed there, then pumped in, out, in, almost out, deep in.

Bruce moaned, "Yeah, yeah, fuck me."

Orville couldn't hold it anymore. He shoved against the upraised buttocks and held his cock deep inside Bruce, and came, and came, feeling Bruce's ass tighten and loosen, tighten, squeezing out every drop of his cum.

"Wow!" Bruce rolled over.

Orville reached for Bruce's cock, jerking it off. It was good not to be selfish, to get the other guy off.

Bruce resisted. "I don't want to come."

"No?"

"Uh-uh. I just wanted your cum in my ass."

Orville didn't know entirely why he felt so damned disappointed. Maybe Bruce would stay until he was hot again. He'd love to be fucked by him. He hesitated to ask, not wanting to hear a negative response. "You wanna fuck me?" he heard himself ask.

"Uh—oh. Sure."

Orville was already getting hard again. He lay with his legs open, propped on the bed. Bruce mounted him. It was clear to Orville that the blond guy preferred to be fucked, wasn't doing it right, kind of poking in, getting soft even when he was beginning to slide inside. Orville eased away, still very aroused. On the bed, Bruce, facing him, spread out his legs, Orville held on to his ankles and entered him again in one hard lunge. Bruce came without even touching himself, and Orville came again, in him.

They fell back on the bed. "I hadn't intended to come," Bruce said. "It's just cause you're so hot. I'm kinda drained from San Francisco."

"Lots of action?"

"Yeah, last night, with a couple of guys—but you're the best," he smiled. "Maybe we'll get together again."

"Yeah." Now Orville would ask him if he wanted to hang around, maybe have dinner together.

Bruce was dressing. "I'll sure keep *your* number. Ciao, Orv." He headed toward the door. Orville let him out.

So the guy was going cruising again. So what? Orville asked himself. For him, it had worked out, a terrific scene, he'd come twice, and he'd made the other guy come even though he hadn't wanted to. He lay in bed, and he felt—satisfied—almost satisfied—not quite satisfied— He dozed off to the sound of the urgent winds.

When he woke, he wasn't at all satisfied. The encounter with Bruce was turning depressing—why hadn't he wanted to stay for dinner, make out, hang around, spend the night?—arousing the anger he had felt with the guy before him. Damn! He really didn't feel like going out again. It was good to stay mellow when the day was growing more agitated with these nervous winds.

He'd call friends, two or three, invite them over for dinner, steaks, a baked potato. He had lots of friends, and they often invited him to dinner. He'd made it with some of them, once—not great sex or anything—and then they'd become friends. He dialed the number of a friend who'd just broken up with his lover of three years. He'd welcome an invitation.

"Danny, I'm glad I caught you at home."

"Hi, Orville. Yeah, ever since I split up with Jack, I don't go out much."

"Nursing the blues, huh?" He'd had a lover once—no, twice—one good, one bad. Both kind of bland.

"I guess."

"Listen—wanna come over for dinner? Just you and a couple of guys you already know." That would signal that he wasn't into anything more.

"Great! You couldn't have called at a better time."

After they had arranged the hour, Orville dialed two of his other friends. Not home. He'd call again in a while, and even if only Danny joined him, that would be all right. They'd talk about movies, past tricks, and—

The telephone rang. "Me, Orv—Danny."

"Yes?"

"Listen, I'm sorry. Right after you called, I heard from this guy I've been wanting to hear from. I may have told you about him, remember? We're getting together tonight, so I'll take a rain-check on that steak—okay? I'm sure you understand. A hot date's a hot date, right?"

"Right," Orville said. Goddammit, why did people think *everything* could be canceled—friendship, family, *anything*—when you had something going?

He felt so depressed he didn't bother to call his other friends again. God*damn* them. All they ever thought about was sex.

Paul
AFTERNOON

Paul and the man he had met on the concrete walk braced against the wind—which contained the odor of ashes—as they made their way off the beach and toward Paul's house. Only a piazza, a few buildings with carved columns, and several canals and arched bridges remained of the original plan to re-create the Italian city. A scattering of oil wells like dinosaurs constantly dipped their snouts into fields in the area.

What if, this one time, Stanley had returned? Paul slowed his step.

"Would you rather not go to your place?" the man asked.

Eagerly? Jesus, what was he getting into with this guy. Mitch? Yes. And a last name. What? "No—I mean, yeah, if you want to."

They reached the house with the porch, and they walked in. The wind made the rooms seem even more silent. Determined to go through with it—and the guy was sexy—Paul leaned toward him, holding him by the shoulders, inviting his lips on his own.

The man stiffened. "I—"

Shit. A disaster. Did the guy really consider himself straight, after all the cruising on the beach? Then Paul was overwhelmed by a feeling of sadness, that with this confused man he was sabotaging his own life, with Stanley, whom he loved.

The man sat back on a chair in the living room, the chair Stanley often occupied when he watched television alone. When they were together, they sat on the sofa, Stanley's arm around him.

"I thought maybe we could talk, man," the guy said.

"Talk?" Christ, he was back on that again. "About your lesbian girl-friend? Listen—*man*—that's not why I asked you here."

"I must've made a mistake," the guy said.

"I guess you did."

"I'm sorry, man, really." He paused, looked away, back at him, as if genuinely confused. "You wanna give me head, Paul?—that's your name, right?"

The son of a bitch just wanted a blow job. Fuck, he could pay a whore on Sunset Boulevard to do that. Paul's sadness deepened. He turned the radio on. Sounds.

"Uh, listen, uh, Mitch—that's *your* name, right?—I guess we did get it all wrong, man. I thought—the way you kept cruising *me*—that you wanted to blow *me*."

The man stood up, shaking his head as if to push away what he had just heard. He turned his back on Paul and left.

Paul walked out, to the porch.

A layer of smoke gathered by the Sant'Ana from distant fires was spreading across the sky, singeing everything with an eery orange glow. The sun, like smeared blood, was reflected in shattered waves from the surface of the ocean.

Nick
AFTERNOON

So what if he'd told the guy he was "Ahn—" Whatever name he'd said. Every hustler knew that lots of times johns told you who they wanted you to be, and what—so you always said yes.

Nick was still peering into the car that had stopped for him, sizing the driver up, good-looking, not old either. Shit, some guys preferred hustlers, and this guy was too nervous to be a cop. Nick pushed his pants even lower on his hips and let his shirt open wider. Fuck, man, the guy just kept studying him.

"Please, get in, Angel," the man finally said, and leaned over the passenger side to unlock the door.

Nick jumped in. "What ya lookin' for me for?" he asked, cocky, sure, getting into the role this guy would ask him to play, being someone named Angel for whatever reason he had in mind.

Clint
AFTERNOON

"Only fantasy."

Clint lay, restive, hot. He had spoken those two single words aloud, but others, unspoken, followed—

What did that man feel?—although, immediately after, he wasn't sure which man he had been thinking of, out of those turbulent memories of last weekend.

NEW YORK
Last Weekend

He stared at the leatherman yanking at the chain attached to the iron collars of his two slaves. About to move up the cramped steps with them, the leatherman stopped. He faced Clint.

Does he recognize me from other times here? Clint met the man's stare. Had the man smiled, vaguely?

The leatherman led his slaves into the dark mouth of the Mineshaft.

Clint turned away from the place he knew from countless weekends and many weeknights spent there. He walked along the streets, past blocks of men roaming, waiting. They stood on the steps of buildings or outside bars in clusters, laughing that wounded laughter, or stood alone, on corners, or lingered or pressed against buildings darker than the sky. Some melded into shadows in doorways along crooked streets, others spilled out of male-thronged bars. Some slouched against motorcycles on the curbs of the streets. All waited to connect, creating a vista of dark sensuality extending to the edge of the water.

He went to the Anvil.

Hundreds of men crowded into the huge warehouse converted into a club. The odor of poppers exploded into hammering blasts of music within dark reddish light streaked by cigarette smoke. Pornographic images of engorged organs flashed on the walls from a projector. A short hall led beyond the periphery of darkness into a blackened room. Out of its total darkness there emerged moaning sounds, whimpers, sighs. He knew that inside that darkness a mob of bodies would be writhing and tossing, and within that churning mass tongues and hands and cocks would search invisibly about the darkness, and there would be only sensations. Tonight Clint remained at its mouth, stood in the shaded back of the main hall, where a few bodies roamed among standing figures in preparation for joining the dark maw.

On each of three small improvised platforms about the main room, a naked man, contained in a blotch of light like a gray cage, danced in slowed frenzy to jolts of music and amyl. The bodies arched toward mouths and hands, men gathered before them, watching, groping each other, some sinking down.

In the center of the room, a naked man appeared on a mangy stage. Bathed in oil, his body glowed red within a pool of dark light. Flowing into abrupt rhythms, he contracted his body in spasms, flinging himself on the floor. His head bucking, he crawled toward the booted feet of a man in leather who had moved forward. The naked man halted before the spread legs. He licked the leather-clad thighs, the shiny boots. The man in leather pushed the naked man back. The nude man lay on the floor, face up, torso thrust forth.

The man in leather held a lit candle over the naked body. He tilted the candle. Drops of hot wax dripped on the naked man's chest. The naked man vaulted. Wax dripped lower on his body. He made a hissing sound. The man in leather held the candle over the naked man's cock, which was soft, only his face delirious. Wax like shiny drops of blood dripped onto the exposed groin.

Snarling, the naked man made a sound like a moan, a sound like laughter.

Clint opened his fly, offering his hard cock to a mouth in the dark.

Sun from the windows slashed long triangles of light on the floor of the hotel room.

What did the man feel?

Still, Clint could not identify the single haunting face he was trying to evoke.

Ernie
AFTERNOON

Goddamned size queen! Ernie kept repeating after Andy had left like he couldn't get away quick enough. He remained naked, sitting before the television screen, pointing the control like a gun at the screen. Saturdays were awful television days. He could hardly wait for that new cable channel everyone was talking about, that MTV, with all those cute guys dancing around in tight clothes.

He flicked on the television. Not even a good old movie with Bette Davis, that movie queen old guys loved so much. Lots of stupid talk shows. Who cared about that fucking Jupiter planet? Or Mars, or wherever the hell they were shooting those damn rockets at now. Hey, don't anyone say *he* was against science, but first things first, right? Those scientists couldn't even cure a cold.

Too much to hope for a big special, like when Prince Charles and Lady Diana got married. He'd stayed up into early morning to see the wedding, and damned if he hadn't cried. That old queen—not the English one, the one who lived in the apartment near his—had watched, too, he knew, because he could hear the TV and her sobs. The next day she'd asked him how he'd liked the royal wedding. Of course he'd said, "What royal wedding?"

What he wouldn't give for a rerun right now. Like *Dynasty!* You didn't have to apologize for loving *Dynasty,* because *every* gay guy had watched it at one time or another, even the most macho guys. A favorite gay bar on Santa Monica had held "*Dynasty* nights." Leather guys, cowboys—everybody sat watching and cruising—and whenever that Alexis came on with one of her lines, the guys would yell it out after her, "Dawn't even bothuh!"

Go to the movies? Hey, maybe *Ragtime* was playing. He'd seen it at a preview a friend had invited him to, and he planned on seeing it again, to check out that *real* cute reddish blond kid with a knockout bod, the kid who'd played a photographer by the beach in one scene, and then was in the ballroom scene. Look, it wasn't that he went to movies only to look at cute guys, like some of his friends did. Hey, he didn't have sex in the head, right? But what was wrong with spotting one of your favorite sexy types and having a little fantasy going in Technicolor?

"—two more fires in the hills. No planned evacuation yet. The freeway—" A breathless news bulletin had come on, with that weird anchorwoman, Mandy Lange-Jones, smiling away. "Some are saying this is earthquake weather, too—" Damn if she didn't look even more de-

lighted than usual, at the thought of two disasters at the same time.
Now Mandy Lange-Jones went on to announce a late-evening news "In
Depth Report" on young male hustlers along Santa Monica Boulevard.
"Street-smart young men can earn a thousand dollars a week selling
their young bodies to—"

Ernie clicked her off and waved goodbye with a finger.

He reached for a magazine that pictured muscular men wearing
only boots or cowboy hats, or a leather jacket. He picked his favorite—
a bodybuilding fireman with shiny boots and a helmet. The guy's cock
wasn't even average. Yet look at the attitude on that son of a gun. Get
down and worship me, motherfucker.

"Listen, Ernie, you and me, guy—we'll worship each other's bod,
maybe get into a jockstrap scene, huh, buddy?"

"Sure, guy. Hey, let's *get down and do it!*"

"Hey, Ern, you got a real nice cock—"

"You, too—hey, Lars, I didn't recognize ya at first."

Ernie put down the magazine, banishing his fantasy. Nothing was
working. He was too angry at that skinny size queen.

The afternoon stretched out before him, a blank. Hey! He knew
what he would do. Have sex. Gay people always had that, and they
knew where to go at any hour of the day for it.

In no time, Ernie was dressed and driving his snazzy Volkswagen—
don't call it a bug, his looked sporty, right?—to the porn theater on
lower Sunset Boulevard.

Pulling his tank top low so that his pecs showed, he bought a large
box of popcorn—with lots of liquidy butter—from the concession at-
tendant, who was clearly coming on to him, all hot looks.

If he hadn't been so familiar with this movie house—once an art
deco theater, colored arcs now peeling—he wouldn't have been able to
see a thing except, on the giant screen, what looked like two dinosaurs
about to crush each other. Cocks and asses looked strange in closeup
when you walked in on them, right? He sat down toward the front,
away from clusters of men scattered along the rows.

He ate some popcorn and looked up at the screen. The flick was
directed by Z.Z., his favorite director, king of macho sex, and in the

movie was Huck Sawyer in the famous Jockeys he always wore until
some top—who was this one?—no face shown yet—would flatten him,
yank 'em down, and fuck his round bums—and that was exactly what
was happening. "Ya wannit, ya know ya wannit!" "Yeah, yeah, yeah,
shove it to me!" "Oh, ah, oh!" "I'm shootin', shootin'!" "Shoot your load,
stud, yeah, yeah!" Cum, cum, cum. "Ah, ah!" "Ahhhh!" The end.

Great flick!

Now wouldn't you know it? There was ole Rex Steed in a coming
attraction, twisting his neck to the side to avoid being kissed by the
guy who would be blowing him in a minute. Fuckin' Steed always trying to show he was straight—

"—till I met you, Ern."

"Fuck off, Steed. I don't go for no straight guy."

Time to start cruising, right? With his box of delicious buttery
popcorn, Ernie made his way toward the back of the theater. Now his
eyes could untangle the configurations along the rows, lots of groping
and sucking going on, and, over there, a guy bouncing up and down
on a cock. Ernie walked to the back of the theater, the portion separated from the seats by a railing. A cute guy leaned over the railing with
his pants down while a guy rimmed him. Jesus Christ, the guy doing
the rimming was the guy who sold popcorn at the concession stand!

Ernie abandoned his popcorn on a nearby seat and decided to take
in more of the movie.

He was sitting there encouraging a hard-on when he looked down
to see a face between his legs. The guy must've crawled from under the
row behind him, and there he was on the floor looking up at him. The
guy ran his hands along Ernie's thighs—obviously into muscles, right?
Ernie tensed his quads for the guy to lick, over his jeans, and then—

The guy crawled away, under another row.

Hey, whatever turned you on, right? Ernie looked about. He sure
could use a cock in his mouth. One was waiting on the other side of
the aisle. A tall guy sprawled back, working himself up. Ernie sidled
along two seats, and then another.

A white light swept the theater. Bodies scurried about the rows,
guys jumping up, sitting down, adjusting their clothes. A veteran, Ernie

knew what was happening. A worker in the theater had been warned that vice cops would be coming in. In minutes, the whirling light was gone. Everyone was sitting watching the screen where a guy in the shower was attempting to take two cocks in his mouth. Damned if that made sense, cops busting in on guys doing what was happening right on the big screen!

Ernie left, feeling frustrated—hadn't made it even once. Hey! He'd take a drive to Griffith Park.

In a few minutes, he was in the giant park, acres and acres of natural foresty land in the midst of the City. Sinuous paved drives wound for miles up and around hills. To the sides of the main roads and down intricate paths, branchy trees, tall brush, and tangled vines formed secluded coves and grottos.

Ernie parked his sporty Volkswagen in a lower level of the park and decided to walk up the main drive. He'd already removed his shirt, oiled his muscles—lightly, not heavy like that Lars Helmut, who always looked like he was about to melt.

He walked down an incline, just to feel the cruising out. He heard a rustling that didn't come from the wind, which parted leafy branches to reveal—Five guys—no, six— Doing what? All you could see was flesh. The odor of poppers invaded even the harsh wind. Ernie moved away—he wasn't one of those pushy guys who just busts in on an orgy.

Hey! Look at that guy with the deep tan!

Against the sun, the man—tall, lithe, wearing a cowboy hat he was holding in place with one hand—stood atop a small mound. The guy's free hand was floating over his groin in signal.

Ernie walked up the dirt path, flexing, to the crest of the mound. He halted.

Jesus, the guy was black!

He'd never gone with a black guy. You couldn't say he was prejudiced—that just wasn't for him, nothing wrong with it, right? What would it be like to have a black cock in your mouth, how far could you take it? Or in your ass? Or to push your white cock into a black ass? Black lips wrapped around white cock—white dick, black lips, black cock, white lips, black ass, white cock, black— Why deny he was getting hard? He looked around. He didn't want word to spread that he was into black guys.

Looking back, inviting, the black guy disappeared into a hollow of branches and vines.

Ernie followed.

Mitch
AFTERNOON

That son of a bitch thought *I* wanted to give *him* head! Shit! He'd gone with the guy to talk, just talk, man—but then the guy made an advance right away, like to kiss him, for God's sake—on the lips—and he pulled away, right away. He didn't want to hurt the guy. So what the fuck was wrong with suggesting a head-job? Goddamn Heather! Just because one time—*one time*—he couldn't get hard. Look, he was hard right now.

Back at the beach, Mitch walked on, along the tawdry stretch of glittery shops.

In a small arena, men with giant muscles were working out even with the wind tossing sand at them. The men, in bikinis, were aware of people gaping at them, although they pretended not to notice.

Mitch looked away. All bodybuilders were queer, everyone knew that, and he didn't want to get into another big mess like with that guy earlier, who hadn't looked gay. That guy—he'd been nice, sure, who would deny that?

Two effeminate men were walking to their cars in a lot. A ratty kid rode by on a bicycle and flung the remains of fried chicken at them. "Faggots!" he shouted back as he sped away. "Get off the beach!"

A piece of oily skin hit Mitch. Not wiping it off, he walked onto the sand, past two short palm trees, fronds rustling angrily. He inhaled, prepared to greet the clean scent of water. Instead, his nostrils detected the odor of something burnt but not yet ashes. He walked to the edge of the water.

His hands covering his face, he hunched there.

Dave
AFTERNOON

He swept into West Hollywood, his presence and the growling of his motorcycle alerting all cruisers that he was here! Top leatherman looking for action—

Jeez-us!

Will ya look across the street at that hot kid showing off his ass in those tight denim cutoffs?

Dave revved his engine for attention. The kid looked at him, and he looked back—hard, for only seconds. Then turned away from each other.

Dave made a U-turn and parked his bike outside the cruisy bar the kid must've just left. The kid had walked only a few steps away, lingering but not looking back. Placing an unlit cigarette—tough prop, dude—between his lips, Dave shifted his body about on his bike and sprawled back on the handlebars. He propped one booted foot on a side of the bike and planted the other on the sidewalk. He cocked his cap lower over his eyes, and waited.

Five

Several people, the older ones—and younger ones usually on break—often come to the park in West Hollywood to sit on benches and have their lunch. Almost everyone is careful to collect paper plates, containers, napkins, to discard in one of several trash cans along the paths. Among those who frequent the park, there often develops a camaraderie. The conversations are mainly topical, mostly about local matters. Did you feel the recent tremor? Will it ever rain again? Will West Hollywood become a city?

Is it true that the Sant'Anas augur disasters?

JESSE
AFTERNOON

Let Mr. Macho wait there thinking *he* was going to be knocked over by him. Well, he'd just continue walking away, let the guy get hot over *him*. Jesse had known, as the biker roared by and they looked at each other, that he would come back and park his motorcycle near him—and he did. Now Jesse decided he'd look back, once, before moving on.

Double wow!

It astonished him that his cock reacted. The biker was an older guy, thirty, maybe older. But he was sexy—and knew it—with dark stubble on his face, a wild body. And attitude! For God's sake, the hair on his head was beginning to *thin*! Jesse saw that when the wind jerked the leather cap back and the biker had to hold it, relocating it at a slant.

Despite the guy's age, all of it came together. Jesse allowed himself a few more casual glances. Still, guys decked out like him might be into weird stuff. He didn't mind some rough probing when a guy was fucking him—that felt good—and if the guy was a dirty talker—"I'm gonna fuck the hell outtaya, ya know ya wannit up your fuckin' ass, don'ya? don'ya?"—hot stuff like that. Jesse could get into it.

Heavy stuff turned him off—S & M, huge dildos, belts, chains, handcuffs. Ugh. Still, being got up like the biker didn't mean you were into all that, just rough decoration. It didn't even mean you were a top. Lots of leather guys were bottoms, and others turned bottoms at the right opportunity. The sight of a guy in high leather mincing along like a queen wasn't rare, either. This guy on his bike looked *real*— not *real* real but *fantasy* real, which was much better, like he could *play* a good macho. The navy-blue handkerchief dangling out of his left pocket meant—left or right, which was it? Those signals confused Jesse, and he didn't bother with them on himself. He was almost sure left meant top, and dark-blue signaled being into fucking. Even that could be contradicted when things got going, and the one fucking wanted to be fucked. Where Jesse definitely drew the line was with guys who wore dark-red handkerchiefs. He knew what *that* meant. Ugh. The only thing that belonged up your ass—after a finger or two—was a cock, period.

Jesse realized he had continued to look at the biker, and, no doubt about it, the biker was interested in him, staring at him from under his slouched cap.

Too old, though.

Lusty.

Too old.

Hot.

Old.

Now the man on the motorcycle raised his right arm up, back, stretching or showing off the dark tufts of hair under his arms, or the tattoo of an eagle or something. Jesse didn't like tattoos, but on this guy—

Wild!

Then Jesse noticed that the biker was wearing a black glove on the outstretched hand. Now he lowered that hand, very slowly, then clenched it into a fist, which he raised in one harsh thrust.

Jesse walked away.

Too weird.

Buzz, Toro, Linda, Boo, and Fredo
AFTERNOON

They cruised off Hollywood Boulevard, into a section of decrepit vacated buildings, condemned and boarded, taken over by derelicts who ripped away barricades and signs forbidding entry. Occasionally a portion of a wall would crumble, tossing dust into the wind. Along sidewalks, next to garbage spilling out of bags torn open by the wind, a few men lay, passed out on heaps of rags that flapped about their bodies. Others walked by dazed, on drugs or drunk. On corners, ragged women attempted to hustle, raising their skirts to reveal naked hips. A boy of about ten yelled out his offer of 'ludes.

Toro pounded the steering wheel to rapid-fire blasts from the Judas Priest tape.

Buzz had been trying to figure things out since Toro had seemed to challenge Linda to prove to all of them that she wasn't a lez. Maybe she *wanted* to fuck them all. A fuckin' nympho. He'd prefer it if she didn't want it. Either way, he'd make sure they gave her something she *didn't* want. Like the time he and Boo and Fredo had picked up a skinny ugly druggy, and they felt her up, and then threw her panties away so she'd have to walk back to the street in her tiny skirt. They had followed her, jeering, so other guys would see her.

Even the wind was giving Buzz a rush. It would pause, everything settling, and then it would gust and stir trash around.

Toro turned into an alley. A few derelicts lying on newspapers tried to hide, grabbing at debris. The wind blasted in as if through a tunnel.

Toro parked the Chevy before the remains of a small house on what might have once been a lawn, now a sprawl of debris, liquor bottles, old newspapers, cans, weeds with tiny yellow flowers. Either fire or the rumble of an earthquake had crushed the house. Only portions of some walls remained, their sides swathed with smoke. Jagged edges of gouged windows had trapped fragments of splintery dried brush, which rustled when the wind whipped in.

With a nod of his head, Toro motioned Linda to get out. She did. Too easy? Or afraid not to? Buzz jumped out of the car. Boo and Fredo followed. Through the skeleton of a door, Toro led them into the pulverized house. Buzz, Boo, and Fredo faced Linda. Toro stood halfway between her and them.

Linda glanced at Fredo, then Boo, and then at Buzz. "This where you guys want me to prove I'm not a lez?" She was smiling.

Father Norris
AFTERNOON

Of course Angel would ask him why he was looking for him. He couldn't know, not yet. "Ahn-hel"—Father Norris breathed the name—"I want to see—"

The young man groped his genitals. "This?"

Father Norris glanced away, shaking his head, no.

The young man reached for the door. "Are you a cop?"

Father Norris didn't hear the boy's words. He was hearing his own before he even spoke them. "I want to see your back."

"I don't get fucked," the young man warned.

"I want to see your back."

"My back? See it? Just that?"

"Yes."

"Sure. Money first." He removed his hand from the door.

Father Norris fumbled for his wallet, handing the boy bills. The woman's words this morning in the confessional had alerted him to prepare for whatever might be required. Before Father Norris could say, No!—because this was not the proper place for such an immense revelation—the boy had taken off his shirt, lowered his pants, and twisted his lithe body around. Father Norris braked. The boy's skin was tanned—not brown and—

"Where is it? The tattoo?"

"Huh?" The young man clasped the door handle.

"You're not Angel!" Father Norris wailed.

The young man jumped out.

Father Norris was calm again, entirely controlled, entirely. He had been naive to believe this journey would be uncomplicated. Our Lord's journey had been a harsh one, but at the end of the night of torture, He had attained His goal. And so would he.

Za-Za and the Cast of *Frontal Assault*
AFTERNOON

"Fuck me, fuck me!" Rex Steed couldn't stop shouting those words—his eyes closed, thighs spread, feet pointing to the sky, hands parting his buttocks before a pensive Tony Piazza.

Had Rex Steed gone crazy? Was he possessed?—like in *The Exorcist* just before the demon girl whirls her head around, a scene that Za-Za would pay homage to in her debut film, adding a light touch, of course, like Lubitsch.

"He vants it bad," Lars Helmut observed.

"Somebody better get in his ass," Dak Boxer offered.

"I think he's dead," Jim Bond said. "The strain—"

Mr. Smythe and his guests were standing—watching this spectacle go wildly out of hand.

She must try to bring order out of this chaos, whatever would salvage the opportunity she had counted on to allow her artistic future to blaze. Let's evaluate, *trésor,* she spoke to herself. Rex Steed was asserting his desire *sans equivoque.* Yes, *the* top man in the business—the one who claimed to be Mr. Straight—was asking—pleading, *begging!*—to be fucked, and Tony Piazza—that stunning man of her desires, the most famous bottom in the business—was clearly indicating—there was no mistaking the intention of that upraised cock—that he was willing—eager!—and, God save us all, *able*—to accommodate him. That was the case. What to do?

Inspiration!

She ran over to Tony Piazza, turned him around and smacked his eager cock so forcefully with her hand—ignoring his "Ouch, bitch!"—that it began to deflate immediately, and in an extension of the same movement, she grasped Rex Steed's legs by the ankles, and pulled them *shut*—holding them that way with all her strength and against his resistance.

The binoculars on the veranda swirled.

Tony Piazza grabbed his balls as if in pain. Jim Bond soothed them for him, fanning them with his hand. Huck Sawyer started to run in panic at the turn of events, but he stopped when he couldn't decide where to go. Sal Domingo doubled over with laughter, seizing that opportunity to locate his ass for full display to the veranda. Lars Helmut exchanged mysterious looks with Dak Boxer.

Thrusting out forcefully with his knees, Rex Steed freed himself of Za-Za's clasp and sent her reeling against Tony Piazza, who shoved her farther away, almost into the pool.

On the ground, Za-Za pressed her hands abjectly against her cheeks, attempting to be philosophical about this ghastly saga. She might learn something or other from it for her *newer* wave film, like when Claudette Colbert—

Oh, my God! This was no longer a rebellion. It was a revolution! Among fluttering bougainvillea and delicate lilacs and noble birds of paradise scattered just beyond the pool area—she saw this while she remained, prostrate, on the ground—famous tops Dak Boxer and Lars Helmut were patting each other's asses! And! Jim Bond and Sal Domingo were staring at the two tops as if they were gravely considering how best to join the unexpected proceedings. Poor sandy-thatched Huck Sawyer was the only one doing anything that made sense—running around in bewilderment and tugging at his Jockeys.

Raising herself from the edge of the pool, Za-Za gave a little scream, all that her voice would allow her in response to what she saw now that she was upright.

Tony Piazza had grabbed!

The long blond legs!

By the ankles!

And was spreading them *even* wider!

And now he was leaning over to spit into the parted buttocks and on his own cock in unequivocal preparation—

To—

To—!

Tony Piazza buried his cock in Rex Steed's ass.

Thomas Watkins
AFTERNOON

Just as he promised himself, Thomas drove back to his haven, his serene home, away from that terrifying street with all those corrupted young men. Once inside, he served himself a civilized scotch, only a dab extra so he wouldn't need another.

"Tom—"

"Oh, my God, I didn't see you in the shadows."

"I'm sorry I startled you."

Thomas couldn't restrain his delight. He'd imagined him earlier, hitchhiking, but now there he stood in the familiar baggy trunks, the young man he often saw down the road. "But how did you get in?"

"You left the door open. I rang, then knocked—I guess you didn't hear me—and then the door opened on its own—and so— You don't mind my calling you Tom, do you?"

Thomas preferred his full name, but he wasn't about to intrude on this lovely unexpected encounter. "Of course not. And you're—"

"Lawrence, but everybody calls me Larry."

"Larry." Thomas became very shy, though there was no reason—Larry had come looking for *him* after all those times of smiling and waving at each other—flirting, as it now turned out so clearly. "I've often thought of stopping to talk to *you*, when you're working on your car, but—"

"I kept hoping you would. But that's okay, because here I am—"

But he wasn't, only in Thomas's imagination as he faced the empty shadows where he had envisioned the young man in his baggy trunks. Yet the boy did wave at him all the time—maybe anticipated his passing by? What if he drove down now, slowly? Perhaps the boy would be inside his house, looking out in case he came by, not knowing what to do this Saturday, and maybe he liked English films—that film was, after all, about runners—

From his wide window, Thomas saw palm trees bending as if in protest.

How much of his loneliness—although he wasn't *really* lonely— was a result of the fact that he didn't take chances? That's what that terrible Herbert implied. Oh, the hideous man came right out and *said* it. Was it true?

He went to his bedroom. He had never worn a denim shirt he'd bought impulsively. He tried it on. Slightly tight—because his chest had become broader. To accommodate that, he might leave two buttons open—many gay men did that.

What pants? Everyone wore jeans. He had never owned a pair, finding the material coarse. He did have some black slacks. He slipped them on. Cruising pants were *supposed* to be tight. He had kept the hiking boots he'd bought when he began a regimen of walking. He hadn't liked the men and women in the group he joined. They kept counting every step and then adding "hup." "One-*hup*." "Two-*hup*." "Three-*hup*." They drove him crazy, and he wrote a letter of resignation.

He tucked the pants into the boots he had slipped on. His hair was no problem. Some of it was gone, yes, but not much, and he'd seen very sensual models in fashion magazines who were losing just enough of their hair to emphasize their masculinity. How had that one model worn it? Defiantly back—like this—not like that terrifying Herbert, who combed over his pate the few hairs he had left—awful, awful—but, he, Thomas, was too much of a gentleman to point it out.

Sipping his freshened scotch, Thomas Watkins faced himself in his full-length mirror, standing tall. If Herbert could see him now—

He would laugh.

Orville
AFTERNOON

In a cove of leafy branches and vines, Orville waited for the muscular guy he had been cruising. He'd been able to keep his cowboy hat on easily because the cove rejected the wind, though he did hear its murmur through the twisted limbs of trees—and, now, he heard the crunch of footsteps. The muscular guy entered the cove and stood there. He was even more muscular—a real bodybuilder—than Orville had thought from a distance. His cock hardened in anticipation.

The two men faced each other, fingers cocked into their belt loops, like triggermen in a duel. The muscular guy drew first. He touched Orville's hard cock, groped.

Orville's hand advanced, about to do the same on the muscular guy. He stopped. "I'm not into white guys." The words he had been repeating over and over with no intention of saying them, reciting them only to hear them in his mind, how they might sound, reversing everything—those words shot out of his mouth in fury.

The muscular man rushed out of the cove.

The surge of vindication Orville had felt dissipated, adding more depression to his mood. He had *really* wanted that guy. This often happened when you had a bad encounter, like the earlier one at home with that fucking Bruce. It made you determined to make up for it in any way, even a mean way. So you kept on hunting—and it might all turn hellish, and even then you couldn't stop yourself.

He left the cove. Hearing footsteps, he turned. A black man was cruising him.

Paul
AFTERNOON

"Hello," Paul answered the telephone on the first ring.

"Uh, who—?"

"Stanley, it's Paul. Didn't you recognize me when I answered? I mean, after all, *you're* calling *me*."

"Sure. It's just that you sounded different, and I thought I got the wrong number. Uh—I just called to let you know I'm thinking about you."

This had never happened before—Stanley calling him during one of his trips. Regretting having left? Yes! There was something different about his voice, hesitant, almost breathy. Because he was afraid he'd meant what he'd said this morning. Paul held the telephone close to his ear, closer to Stanley. "I'm thinking about you, too, Stanley. You sure you were thinking about me?" Paul wanted to hear Stanley say that again, and that he was coming back now.

"You know it, babe. I called earlier but you were out. I kept calling from my room. The operator rang me back just now to tell me she'd reached the number—I'd told her it was urgent."

Paul felt even guiltier for having picked up that man on the beach. Thank God nothing had happened or they might have been together when Stanley called. Now everything would change, Paul was sure of it. He'd gambled by threatening Stanley, and the gamble had paid off!

"I'd better go now—"

"No, Stanley, wait, I want to tell you how much I love you." Why wasn't he letting him know what time he'd arrive back?

"Tell me—later—yeah, babe—me, too—later—uh—yeah—great—"

It was as if he'd stopped listening, anxious to put down the phone. Paul was aware that Stanley had covered the mouthpiece, might have whispered something away from it. Why did people think they could disguise that? "You covered the phone." He wished he hadn't said that.

"Just—uh—just holding it against my neck—I'm in bed—relax-ing—callya later."

"Don't hang up, Stanley!" Paul's voice was harsh, commanding.

There was another sound on Stanley's side of the line, a smothered moan—Stanley's—a sound Paul was familiar with, had heard hundreds of times, over the years, this morning. "You're with someone right now, aren't you, Stanley?"

"Hell—no!"

"Someone is blowing you while you're calling me, and you're ac-tually getting off on it."

"You—think I—call—while—," Stanley started. Paul heard Stanley's groaning, muffled, a long moan—"yeah"—that he knew so well.

Paul hung up. Stanley had been concerned—no, his vanity had been concerned—that he would go out on him. So he'd called to make sure he hadn't, had become agitated to find he was out, and then even forgot he'd asked the operator to keep trying the number, and by then he was with someone else. He had dared—

The phone rang again.

Paul's hand reached for it.

He let it ring.

Outside, hot wind dried his tears. He tasted them, salty, mixed with stray ashes. Tonight he would do it finally—free himself from Stanley.

Nick
AFTERNOON

"*Eres bendito, un hijo de Dios, mijo!*"

"What?"

"*Mijo, tu eres el hijo de Dios, un ser sagrado.*"

The woman standing before him was Mexican—something like that—wearing a shawl, black, over her head. The shawl—maybe it was a long black coat—flapped in the wind. It wrapped around her, then unwrapped like dark wings.

Nick recognized the woman he'd seen earlier, in the distance. He was back on his corner after the encounter with the man who had wanted to see his back and then had turned angry, weird, scary. "I don't know what you're sayin', lady."

"You're blessed, a child of God, a sacred soul—and you're my son." She spoke in English now, heavily accented. Her eyes were darkened into black by the shawl shading her face.

Nick started to move away.

The woman reached out for his bare shoulder, restraining him.

Nick twisted away from her. "I ain't your son. Leave me alone, you crazy."

"You *are* my child, among God's children on this street. He's looking for you. Let Him find you!"

"I'm *Methodist*, lady!" He needed to say something, anything, before he pulled away. He crossed the street, looked back.

The woman hurried on, stopping to talk to someone else—another hustler? Then she faded along the street, a dark frightening figure in the wind.

Nick was grateful that a car stopped for him right after that. The woman had spooked him, man. A crazy for sure. Lots of them on the fuckin' streets.

"How much?" the driver asked.

He was no cop, not as out of shape as he was—although some cops were very out of shape. "Fifty bucks, and I don't get fucked."

"You're a cute-looking guy, got a nice body—thirty bucks and you won't get fucked."

"Okay, thirty bucks and *you* blow *me*," he clarified.

"Get in."

Nick hesitated. Too easy? He got in, keeping the door ajar. He was reassured when the man felt his cock.

"Nice," the man complimented.

"Never had no complaints," Nick said. "You mind turnin' the radio on to the Western station, man? Maybe they're playing 'Cheatin' Heart,'" he thought aloud.

"Not much chance of that happening," the man said.

"I know it," Nick said. Of course, he did, although, one time, hitching a ride with a trucker, he'd got in and it was playing. Right now, he'd just wanted the man to ask him if that was his favorite song, and he would have said, oh, yeah, with Hank Williams singing.

"I don't like hokey-pokey music," the man said, and left the radio off.

They drove to the man's place, a small, not entirely neat apartment a few blocks from Hollywood Boulevard. Nick hated it when the guy paying him didn't have a good place. He liked to go to pretty homes and apartments, liked to feel "rich" by the contact.

"Let's see the rest of that gorgeous body." The man was sitting on his bed, staring at Nick as if at a performance.

Nick had only to lower his pants and he was naked. He wasn't self-conscious about that, proud of his body.

"Everything."

He meant the socks. Some guys wanted him to keep them on—damned if he knew why. Whatever. This was going to be easy.

"*Really* nice," the man said.

Nick wanted to ask for the money first, a lot of times he did, sometimes he didn't—one man he'd gone with said that when a hustler asked for money first, he'd think up an excuse to split, feeling the hustler wasn't going to be any good. This guy was complimenting him, and that felt good.

The guy lowered his own pants, and Nick looked away from the flabby flesh, shut his eyes. He preferred it when old guys didn't even take off their clothes, man.

He felt the man's cock poking at his ass.

Nick's eyes flashed open. He pushed the man away. "What the hell? I told you I don't get fucked."

"What *do* you do?"

"Didn'ya hear me out there? I told you all I do is get blown. Now you go ahead and blow me."

"Shit, and what do *I* get?"

"You get to suck my dick. I told you out there, man. Didn'ya hear me? You can jerk off while you blow me. Go ahead now, blow me— that's all, just fuckin' blow me."

The man's head bent down and sucked Nick's cock. He stopped. "You can't even get hard."

"You fixed that with your bullshit," Nick said.

"Okay, just relax. There. Umm. That's better. Ummm. Yeah, get it hard in my mouth. Ummmm." He stopped again. "Will you fuck me now that I've made you hard?"

Nick began to get soft again. The thought of putting his dick inside the man's saggy ass disgusted him. "I told you out there, man, didn'ya understand?"

"Okay. Come in my mouth."

"Not for thirty bucks. I gotta save up my cum so I can go out and make some *good* bread."

The man sucked him insistently. Closing his eyes, Nick was able to get a semi–hard-on, but that wouldn't last long because the guy didn't suck that good, used his teeth a lot. "You better come soon," Nick said.

"Will you, in my mouth?"

"I told you—"

"Okay." He blew Nick's softening cock some more, jerking himself off, coming loudly, convulsing.

When people came that loud and shaking, it sometimes scared Nick, thinking they might have a heart attack. But the guy was all right now, wiping himself off with a towel. Nick dressed. Held out his hand.

"Here's twenty—you didn't do anything."

"Motherfucker, you give me what I asked for or I'll— Listen, I'm not eighteen yet, did you know that?" he used a lie that had worked other times when things went bad. "You could get busted, man, so you'd better pay me what we agreed."

The man studied him. "Here." He gave him the ten more dollars he had already prepared.

"Now drive me back."

"Get yourself back. Now you get out, you cheating queer punk."

"Queer! Hey, man! *You're* the fuckin' queer, not me."

"Didn'ya hear me? I said get the fuck out, you punk queer."

The man's voice was tough, and he was big. From other hustlers Nick had heard about guys who picked them up, seemed pushovers, and then turned rough. It wasn't far from here to the Boulevard anyway, he estimated. He started to walk out. His anger rose. At the door, he paused, glancing around. Then he kicked over a small table that had a vase of ugly artificial flowers on it. They fell intact to the floor.

He ran until he was back on his corner.

"How big is your dick?" A car paused.

Nobody had ever complained about his cock. Some johns measured it with their hands, length and around, just before going down on it. Still, that question always made Nick nervous. You never knew what people expected.

"At least seven inches?"

"Yeah."

"How much bigger than that?"

"Uh—well—"

"Come over here and let me feel it, press yourself against the car, I'll hold my hand out like this—"

The guy's hand dangled out the window. But where would the other one be? Getting himself ready to pop probably. Then the guy would drive off after copping a good feel. "Uh-uh," Nick rejected.

"How do I know you're not lying? How do I know you haven't got a tiny dick?"

"Cause I haven't, that's how." Shit, no way he'd go with this guy, already acting like he was going to pull something fast. Nick would bet on it. Johns who started out like that ended up feeling you up in the car and then saying you weren't big enough, and they'd say that even if you had a fuckin' foot-long dick, man, just to humiliate you. People sure could get shitty on the streets, like you weren't even a person. Fuck that shit, man. He'd get this motherfucker first. "I got ten hot inches right here, man." He groped his crotch with both hands.

"Get in and we'll go—"

"I ain't ready to go nowhere." Nick walked away. Man, that felt good, to walk away from the son of a bitch—whatever he'd been planning—and leave him behind, thinking he'd let a ten-incher get away from him.

Oh, fuck, that hustler over there—an older guy—still standing waiting to be picked up. He'd been there for hours. Must've been real good-looking when he was young, Nick bet, still was, but you could tell he was way up in his twenties. Some of the hustlers who bragged the most about how much money they always made—you'd see them still hanging around real late, looking scared. Fuck, what would that guy across the street do next year, and the next? Nick looked away from him, touching his own body.

Clint
AFTERNOON

He stood by the window.

Even from here, he could sense the exhilaration the strange day was creating on the street before the coming of this heated night, cars backed up honking, young people gathering before music clubs, their bodies twisting as if rehearsing their moves, pedestrians running against traffic.

He closed his eyes.

NEW YORK
Last Weekend

Within the dirty light of the Anvil, the performance on the platform held, frozen for seconds. The mouth on Clint's cock had been replaced by another.

The leatherman on the improvised stage lowered the lit candle closer to the naked body.

As if responding to a signal, the naked man lying prone before him turned over on the floor, face down, legs parted.

"Do it, do it, do it!" men in the audience chanted at the leatherman.

The leatherman knelt over the naked body.

Growling, the naked man thrust his buttocks up. His cock remained unhardened.

"Do it! Do it! *Do it!*"

The leatherman held the unlit tip of the candle over the opening of the naked man's ass.

Men shoved forth to watch more intently.

As each drop of wax fell on his buttocks, the naked man arched his body and jerked his head back. His mouth remained open, a scream—or harsh laughter—throttled.

"Push it in, push it in!"

The leatherman held the unlit tip of the candle closer to the opening of the man's ass.

"Do it, do it, do it!"

The leatherman inserted the unlit tip into the naked man's ass.

The silent scream, silent laughter, erupted from the naked man as wax melted on his flesh.

The leatherman put out the flame with his spittle and stood up.

The naked man's body crumpled on the floor with an orgasmic gasp—his cock still unaroused.

In the fringe of darkness about to become black, Clint pulled his cock away—just before he would have come—from the mouth that had continued to suck at his groin.

Beyond the window, where smoke had invaded the edge of the sky, the sun glowed deep orange. The only time the sun really looks as if it's on fire, Clint thought. Toppled fronds along the hotel driveway looked like tossed bodies in a mass suicide.

What did that man feel!

Trying to resist the weariness pulling at him, Clint knew that, this time, he had asked that pursuing question about the man lying on the floor as the candle melted on his flesh—no, it was the face of the man in leather. No, the man—

The man who—

A face he did not recognize had pushed away the image of the naked man, of the man in leather.

Ernie

AFTERNOON

Motherfucking black bastard!

He cruised me and then—

Ernie stopped trying to figure out what had happened with the black guy. Sometimes it seemed that cruising was *all* about rejection. But, hey, you still managed to make out over and over, right?

He walked back to the main road, past an unattractive man standing behind his car with his pants down to his knees. The guy had to be fifty years old. Ernie believed in respecting older gay guys, sure—they'd fought a lot of battles, right?—and he always went out of his way to say hello to them during the Gay Pride Parade. But they didn't belong in the park.

"Say, shorty, is it true what they say about muscle queens' dicks? Well, check *this* out."

Can you believe that motherfuckin' old guy yelled that at *him*?—and shook his big thing up and down? Shit—Ernie didn't bother to answer.

THE COMING OF THE NIGHT

He moved on. A good-looking guy walking ahead of him turned back to give him a cruisy look before dodging under an arch of trees off the road.

All *right!* So fuck the black guy—he wouldn't've made it with him anyway, he was sure now. In a cavity of branches, the good-looking guy opened Ernie's fly and pulled out his cock. Ernie always breathed with anxiety when that occurred so quickly. Nothing to worry about, the guy had already slid on his knees and was blowing him. Terrific!—standing out here, pants down, no shirt, even the hot Sant'Ana lickin' at you— and this good-looking guy starin' up at ya an' suckin'.

It was Ernie's turn, right? Fair's fair. He raised the guy and slipped down on his knees, opening the guy's pants. The guy pulled away, but Ernie had already grasped his cock.

Jesus Christ, the guy was *tiny*.

"Footsteps!" Ernie pretended apprehension. "Lots of vice cops in the area. Let's split!" Anything to get away. He didn't feel good about what he'd done, he wasn't cruel. If the guy had been just average size, okay, but, hey, if you didn't feel desire, you didn't feel desire, right?

Back in his car, he drove up and U-turned to park in an island of granulated dirt when he saw, ahead, on a hill, a man in trunks.

Before Ernie could begin the trek toward him, another man who'd been cruising him got out of his car, slipped down a slope, and motioned. Go with him or check out the guy in trunks?

"Hey, muscle guy, cummon down, I'd sure like to spank those cute buns of yours."

Well, there was no decision to be made now.

Ernie proceeded up the hill. Why was everybody into kink nowadays? What was wrong with good old-fashioned body-worship?

Can you believe who that was up there on that hill?

"Hey, Lars! I knew I'd run into you someday."

"Yeah, Ern, I've been hoping—"

"Howya know my name, Lars?"

"Word gets around da park about cute guys, ya know?"

Pulling away from his fantasy, Ernie climbed up craggy rocks until he reached the man there.

Real good-looking. *Not* in trunks. Bare ass naked.

So what? Challenged, Ernie took off his own clothes. His cock was already aroused, and so was the other guy's.

The naked man inhaled eagerly from a vial of Bolt, butyl. He stumbled. The small dark bottle smashed on a rock. The man made an anxious sound, almost a sob. "I got more poppers in my car." He grabbed for his trunks. "Wait here." He rushed down twisted paths.

The guy couldn't make it without poppers! That happened more and more. Some guys stood alone sniffing and jerking off. Not that *he* minded an extra buzz or two from the stuff, who wouldn't? But you were still making it with a guy, not the butyl. Hey, wasn't sex enough anymore? Ernie dressed and walked back to his car.

He'd go home.

He'd try just one more time.

He'd go home.

Soon, he was slipping down a slope off the road. A guy leaned against a tree along the trail. Really sexy, with a denim shirt and Levi's and a cowboy hat and boots. Must be cowboy day in the park!

"Hi, cowboy," the man said to him.

So? "Hi, guy."

"Just in from the roundup?"

"Later, guy." Ernie slipped away from the park cowboy. No telling what *he* was into.

Down the path, a shirtless man motioned him into a branchy cove.

There, the guy blew him. Then Ernie sucked him until the guy pulled away and got on his knees, spreading Ernie's buttocks with his hands, and slipped his tongue into his ass, nestling it in the puckered opening till Ernie was moaning. The guy straightened up, cock probing the saliva-moistened ass. Ernie bent over and took it like a man.

He felt hot spurts of cum shoot into him. "Ahhhh!"

The guy pulled out. Adjusting his clothes, he told Ernie, "Maybe I'll see you later, when I'm ready to get off again, and then I'd love to have that big dick of yours up *my* ass."

Big dick!

Any disappointment Ernie might have felt at not coming—and he had wanted to come, to end this Griffith Park afternoon—was swept away by a surge of joy.

Mitch
AFTERNOON

Mitch walked away from the ocean's edge, letting the hot wind dry his face—moist from the ocean's spray, nothing more.

He got into his Cougar coupe at the parking lot and pulled away to— Wherever.

On the freeway, people were driving erratically, dodging away from swirls of dusty wind, or attempting to avoid a desolate tumbleweed swept in from miles away.

Heather's car was parked in her garage. He waited before he knocked—and immediately wondered whether he might prefer that she not be home.

"Mitch—"

"Can I come in?"

"Of course. I was watching the news."

Mitch was glad the television was on. They sat together, facing it.

On the screen a house raged on fire. Water raining on it from hoses did not daunt it, the flames leaping up as if to stifle it. "—not far away from the mansion of Studio Head Dick Gellman, who was entertaining guests at a swimming party when—" Now the scene of disaster faded off and an announcer informed viewers that in the late news there would be an "in-depth report on male hustlers." "They ply their trade along Santa Monica Boulevard, selling their young bodies to the highest bidder. They can earn hundreds of dollars a night." The screen scanned anxious young men along Santa Monica Boulevard.

Mitch reached for the remote control. He clicked off the television. "We can't pretend there's nothing to talk about."

"No, we can't," Heather said.

Now he would speak words he had rehearsed on the drive here. I'm sorry, Heather, about what I said—that you were responsible for what was happening between us. You were right, it was me. After I left you, I went to the beach, I met this guy, I really wanted him. Instead, I used him to prove I'm not gay—but I am—

"I'm sorry—," he began.

"No, Mitch," she stopped him. "I'm the one who should apologize. I haven't been honest with you. What you said is true." She put her hand on his cheek. "I did want that woman on the beach, and I do. And others, before her."

Mitch wanted to laugh, wanted to hug her, be angry at her, hug her. He kissed his fingers and brought them to her lips.

Dave
AFTERNOON

The little dude would turn back. Watch.

Dave bet himself that as he saw the kid he'd been cruising walk away. A real beauty. Look at those buns. Showing them off in those tight cutoffs. Begging for something up that ass.

The kid slowed down.

All *right*! I told ya.

The kid turned around, waited, took a few steps back, stopped again.

I got 'im. Dave stretched back on his bike. He let the unlit cigarette dangle from his lips. No question about it, that dude'd never been in a leather scene, not even a light one. That aroused Dave even more. Initiation—that was righteous, to introduce gay guys to what they were looking for without even knowing it sometimes, a feeling he still remembered from the time he had entered the leather scene and played bottom, briefly. Even now, when he saw someone who was exactly right—he'd let himself imagine—just imagine—being a bottom again. But the guys he'd consider that with ended up wanting to be bottoms themselves, with him. Dave's hardening cock had shoved against his jeans, right to the edge of the rip he had encouraged near his crotch. He ran his finger along the tear until the head of his cock protruded.

"Hi, I'm Jesse."

Dave placed his gloved fist on the handlebars of his chromy bike, as if he might just rev it up and drive away. He had no intention of doing that. This kid was *right*. He allowed his lips to curve, only on one side, a crooked smile. Cupping it carefully from the wind, he lit the cigarette in his mouth. He squinted as the smoke he counted on smirched his face. He did not hold out his hand. He just tilted his head, retaining his squint even after the wisp of smoke had faded into a violent throb of wind.

"I'm Dave, dude."

Six

As the afternoon declines, most of the frequenters of the park in West Holly-wood, many retired, leave, having perhaps begun to doze on a bench under shady branches. Parents gather their children, going home for evening ac-tivities. Often a lone player will command the basketball court, competing aggressively against an imaginary rival. But it is too windy for that, on Sant'Ana days like today.

Every now and then, toward late afternoon, a man alone may enter the park, looking around as if inspecting the territory.

Jesse
AFTERNOON

What the guy on the bike said after he had mentioned his name—and it seemed that way, that he only mentioned it—Jesse wasn't sure. The wind had whipped up whatever words he said after that. A question? The crooked smile lingered on the biker's rugged face, a scar promi-nent within dark stubble. Even that, the scar, added to his sexiness—and look at how he just lay back as if he didn't realize the tip of his cock was shoving out of the rip in his jeans.

Wild and hot and lusty! That conclusion confused Jesse even more because now he could tell that the guy was older than he had thought, maybe even thirty-five. A real macho guy and yet—get this—so clearly gay. Great! Gay men had become much more masculine than straight men, and they weren't hesitant about parading that gay masculinity, cocky attitude. This guy had all that, and more, and it was his own.

Well, Jesse would throw back some attitude of his own, just as good. He leaned to one side so that the wind would tousle his hair even more, and he parted his feet slightly to call attention to his terrific legs. He lifted his tank top to blow down onto his chest as if to cool himself but, really, to exhibit carved ridges on his slender waist, which he emphasized further by, then, running a finger along the front edge of the cutoffs, hardly lowering them but suggesting that he might. The success of his performance was obvious because now the biker's prick protruded even farther out of the ripped pants—the whole round head. Maybe the tough guy wanted to convey that the bulge in his pants was real—some gay guys stuffed their groins. Stupid. Because what about the crucial time when the bulge wasn't there? Ugh.

"What did you say just now?" He'd stay around for a short while longer, see what this older guy was all about.

"I said, sit on my fuckin' cock, you goddamn tease!"

Wow! Jesse was as excited by the prospect as he was by the commanding tone in the guy's voice. "Out here? On the street? In the afternoon?"

"Yeah, mount the bike backwards and sit on my fuckin' cock." The guy flicked his cigarette at the street, one flick and the wind pulled it away. When he leaned back against the machine's handlebars, more of his cock protruded out of the ripped fabric.

Jesse looked around, people passing by—mostly gay men because of the proximity to the bar. Even without much going on, several guys were staring, looking back intrigued.

If he did what the guy was challenging him to do—and if he did it real quick, for the buzz—it would sure add to the charge he was counting on for tonight.

He jumped on the motorcycle, straddling it backwards. He pressed his hips back. The guy arched his body. Jesse felt the biker's hard cock probing out of his pants and then he felt the guy's fingers lifting up the edge of his cutoffs, attempting to reach the opening. Jesse felt the round, moist head of the cock on his flesh and—

Wild!

Three gay men walking by halted, watching, excited, as the guy on the motorcycle moved his hips up and down against the tight cutoffs.

Now with his finger the biker lifted the cutoffs higher. His cock rubbed Jesse's bare flesh all around, and then it found the parting. The head of the cock held there, only held at the opening. Two more men had stopped to stare at the exhibition.

"Too hot, too soon!" Jesse jumped off the bike, adjusting his cutoffs. He'd walk away.

"Hop on and we'll go for a ride, kid." Pushing his cock back into his pants, the biker shifted his position on the bike. His gloved hand revved it up. He planted a booted foot hard on its side, ready to launch forward.

Why not? Jesse jumped on behind the biker, holding on to him, arms tight about his waist. He moved his elbow higher because the handcuffs the guy had latched to his belt scraped against his skin.

Buzz, Toro, Linda, Boo, and Fredo
AFTERNOON

Linda's crooked smile remained as she faced Buzz, Boo, Fredo inside the abandoned house Toro had led them into. Weeds crept out of cracks in the rotting floor. The stench of cheap wine wafted into the heat. The wind entered in gusts, stirring litter, and then it would retrench, leaving the house quiet, as if it was waiting for sounds of violence.

Toro said to Buzz and the others, "You ain't answered her question. This where you want her to prove she's not a lez?"

Something was off, way off, Buzz knew. They'd talked a lot about banging a bitch together. But was this it? Buzz stared at Toro for a signal. Nothing.

"Whatya intend, Buzz-man?" Linda said.

"Go on, tell her, Buzz," Toro said.

"To fuck your fuckin' ass, bitch," Buzz said.

Boo laughed, a sound in his throat, and spat on the ground. So did Fredo, harsher. Both hopped about Linda, Boo fumbling at his groin.

Buzz's cock was so hard it almost hurt. God*damn*—that fuckin' smile on her face. He wanted her to scream. Now she would! He'd *make* her scream.

He leapt at her.

He staggered back, holding the side of his face, feeling moisture there, seeing it, red, dripping onto the filthy ground. Only then did he realize what was causing the sting on his cheek and remembered Linda slicing at it.

Linda stood before him with a small razor blade, the kind carried in a plastic holder, ready.

Boo and Fredo stared at Buzz's bleeding cheek.

"Who's next?"

Toro had said that. The sting on Buzz's face became pain. He held his hand against the rip. Blood seeped through his fingers. Toro stood next to Linda, and he was holding—

A knife.

Buzz reeled back against Fredo and Boo, who almost fell.

"Fuckin' jokers," Toro said in a calm voice. "That's what you are, fuckin' jokers. You wanted to know what Linda was hiding, right? Fuckin' stupid bastards, she did everything except *show* it to you. Now how much did you get for the shit you grabbed and sold last night?"

"The niggers tried to fake us, didn't they, Boo?" Fredo said.

"We messed them up good," Boo said.

"After you got the shit, maybe. You think I wouldn't know? I never cheated you, motherfuckers. Now fish out whatever you got with you— fish it out, suckers, or I'll get Linda to slit your belts and I'll shake it out of you."

"Let's just do it, Toro, I'd like to see Tiny's prick."

"Who you calling tiny?" Boo's face twisted.

"You, man, she called you tiny," Buzz shouted through blood on his lips. "You gonna let her call you that?"

"Cunt!" Enraged, Boo grabbed his crotch and jumped in front of Linda. "It ain't tiny, bitch!"

Linda slashed her razor blade before his groin. "Come on, I'll make it tinier, motherfucker."

Toro's knife gleamed in a pool of pale sun.

Boo retreated, mouth gaping.

"Jesuschrist!" Fredo dug into his pockets, handing a few crumpled bills to Toro.

Linda collected the money. "Now you, Tiny," she ordered Boo.

With a shrill cry, Boo lunged at her. Toro threw him onto the ground and clamped him down with a foot. "Come on, fucker, dig."

Boo fished in his pockets, bringing out crushed bills. Toro released him. Fredo and Boo ran out of the house, scattering litter.

Linda faced Buzz. She held the razor blade out. "How'd you like *this* up *your* ass?"

Toro laughed and pointed his knife at Buzz's stomach. Buzz staggered back, fell. Squatting, Toro pinned him with his knees. Linda leaned over Buzz, opening his belt. Toro pulled off the loosened pants and stood, shaking out the pockets, turning them inside out, retrieving squashed bills.

"Jesuschrist, the fucker's got a hard-on," Linda laughed. She held the blade at the edge of Buzz's shorts, and she ripped at them, exposing the erect cock.

"Don't!"

Linda made a slicing motion over Buzz's cock, and then again, nearer, again, even nearer.

Buzz screamed and closed his eyes.

He heard garbage crunching. He opened his eyes. Toro and Linda were gone. He heard the motor of Toro's car starting up.

His cheek still bleeding, his pants down to his knees, Buzz rolled over on the ground, onto his erect cock. He pressed his body down, hard, pumping—"Fuck your goddamn ass, fuck your goddamn ass"—until he came.

Father Norris
AFTERNOON

On a side street off Santa Monica Boulevard, Father Norris waited in his car. On the Boulevard a young man had signaled him to park there. That other young man claiming to be Angel earlier had duped him. Simply the ways of the vile streets. But there was no question—no question at all—that the young man now approaching his car—Father Norris's eyes were fixed on his rearview mirror—was Angel. As he had driven by him slowly, and paused, he had seen him and known. He was dark, with longish black hair, about eighteen years old—very handsome, and beautiful, with sad eyes. How accurate the woman's description of her son had been.

"I'm Angel, you're looking for me."

"Yes." Father Norris closed his eyes.

"Why?"

"Because I want to save you."

"Save me?"

"Yes. The fact that you've chosen to have an image of Our Lord Jesus Christ, during his greatest sacrifice, tattooed on your own flesh, your back—that's evidence of your devotion, whether you recognize it yet or not. I'm here to answer your plea for salvation, because there is no substitute. Oh, let me guide you to your mission."

"I accept that, Father."

"How do you know that I'm a priest?"

"Because I've been waiting for you, Father. I knew you'd come looking for me, for the tattoo of Christ, naked—entirely naked, Father—entirely, the way He must have been, exposed, Father—"

"—concealing nothing—nothing, finally!—in His total and passionate sacrifice for us!"

In his car, Father Norris opened his eyes. Where had Angel gone? He had been so immersed in his revery of what their encounter would be like, shutting his eyes to imagine that Angel was already sitting next to him and that they were talking, that he must have missed him as he walked by—or had he walked away before reaching the car? If so, why?

Urgently, he looked back, straining to search the street.

It couldn't be! That woman hurrying along in a long black coat or shawl—she couldn't be the woman who had come to the confessional today about her son. Was she the reason why Angel had fled? Was she searching for him? Father Norris started his car, to follow her, confront her, tell her she must leave this to him, that she must abandon the street, that he must find Angel first. By the time he had maneuvered the car against oncoming traffic, the woman had hurried on along Santa Monica Boulevard, becoming an apparition within swirls of dusty wind, her black shawl whirling insanely.

Something terrifying will happen tonight, Father Norris thought.

Za-Za and the Cast of *Frontal Assault*
AFTERNOON

"That is *not* in Mr. Smythe's script!" Za-Za shouted as Tony Piazza pounded into Rex Steed's big ass.

The winds had calmed down for now—only whistling as if at the *scandale* occurring just ahead—but Mr. Smythe clearly was not calm. He was standing, and Za-Za could only imagine his expression of outrage. From here, he looked frozen, the way he probably intended to be, she thought—if he ever died. She must assure at all costs that before he was frozen, he would have the opportunity to launch her career in *cinema nouveau verité*. The challenge in this "rehearsal" was clear. So she must adjust, adjust, adjust.

How?

Huck Sawyer sidled up to her. Clearly unsettled by startling events. Almost crying, he pled with Za-Za, "What do you want *me* to do, Za-Za!"

"Go fuck yourself!" She had no time for this.

"With what?"

"Find something!" Za-Za pushed him away. She must plan, control, adjust—

How?

Oh, God! Not possible! Jim Bond was advancing with a hard-on toward—

Lars Helmut!

Face down, that mound of muscles had propped his elbows on the ground, his butt as high as it could go, his legs spread as wide as they could be spread, his asshole as eager as—as eager as Jim Bond's cock, which found its way easily into—was welcomed warmly by—former top man and muscular wonder Lars Helmut's ass!

Another top toppled! Za-Za considered drowning herself in the pool. But no one would attempt to save her. Would anyone even notice? Were these sluts aware of the fire in the hills? Jesus Christ, was she imagining all this?

And now *this*?

Sal Domingo was fucking Dak Boxer, all tough tattoos and hairy chest, and his legs split wider than God intended. Yet *another* top brought down!

Only Huck Sawyer was remaining true to his calling as a bottom. Following her earlier barked instructions, he kept poking himself with several fingers and miming ecstasy—"*Ooo-ooooo-eeeee.*"

Za-Za surveyed the vista of upturned macho-bitch asses with cocks grinding away at them. Those were *not* virgin asses. Oh, what that goddamned Rex Steed had started. This was the most depressing part of it all, that if *she* dropped her pants and added her butt to that chorus line, no one would do her the courtesy, especially not the fabulous Tony Piazza—that *ingrat*! Za-Za's anger raged like the distant fire. All those times—when she was grooming him for stardom as the top bottom in the business—all those times that she had harbored him in her own home—feeding him the Tootsie Rolls he said he required for energy while she *begged* him to put it into her ass, all those times that he had said, "I'm a bottom, Za-Za, remember?"

Za-Za touched her darkly outlined eyes, sure that there would be copious tears. Not yet, but soon.

Was it beyond salvaging? Za-Za looked at the pages of Mr. Smythe's script, now crumpled and still wet in spots. Should she grab one of those water hoses and hose those bitches apart? Rush at them and turn them upside down? Lord Jesus, and all His disciples, grant me a miracle, this once, let me think of something.

Too late. Mr. Smythe had descended one step, was descending another—

"Clarence Butte!"

Clarence Butte? Mr. Smythe had shouted that odd name over an invading vortex of wind that had sent the bougainvilleas into a mad dance. Who the hell was Clarence Butte? Oh, God, it was her real name—well, the name she was born with, but how did Mr. Smythe know it?

She kicked off her shoes and walked barefoot toward the veranda, the altar where her career would be sacrificed. "I'm coming, I'm coming," she called out to the looming form on the veranda.

Thomas Watkins
AFTERNOON

He remained looking at himself in the mirror. The longer he looked, the more incongruous his image became in the clothes he had tried on. He discarded the denim shirt, the tight black pants, the hiking boots. He dressed in his *good* clothes—and proud of them! He sipped the last drops of scotch in his glass and sat down facing the vast Canyon, shifting silhouettes. If Herbert laughed at him *now*, it would be because he was envious of him, a man with dignity, a man who didn't lurk in dark tunnels, a man who didn't buy flesh.

Fixing himself one more drink—mostly ice, really—he decided that he would drive down the hill. The friendly handsome young man would be working on his car, although late now, because he had been waiting for the winds to calm down and had given up. The boy would be grateful to see him. He would walk up to the car and introduce himself. Then they would come back here and gaze out together at what would surely be a calm, starry night.

A calm, starry night.

Thomas stood, staring out the window, trying to penetrate the gray slashes of dust. When night came, the wind would have stopped. The sky would be clear. Stars would be visible, stars so rare now in the City. Obsolete.

Orville
AFTERNOON

Maybe the black guy on the path was cruising someone else. Orville scanned the area. No one but them.

"Hi."

The guy had approached. He was tall, very dark. Lots of guys would go with him. But there was something about him that wasn't "right." "Hi."

"Wanna get together?"

No. But why? Oh, *that* was it! The guy had a mustache, that was it. Something about mustaches, though a lot of guys had them, turned Orville off. Too bad, because otherwise—

"Uh—" He looked at his watch. "I'm late, I'm meeting someone."

Orville hurried away, got into his pickup, and proceeded out of Griffith Park.

Paul
AFTERNOON

The garage next to the porch seemed to be waiting for Stanley's car—his new Chrysler. So did his own Alfa Romeo—both waiting for Stanley. But *he* would not be. Paul felt released—yes, really—from all those years of bondage. That's what it had been, bondage.

He showered, dressed in cruising clothes—tight scoop T-shirt, tight faded jeans, short boots. When he considered himself in the mirror, he looked ready for the hunt.

With the mixture of arousal and exaltation he had always felt when he was about to go cruising before he met Stanley, he got into his car, to drive into the City.

Into the sexual arena. Again.

The song on the radio, Gino Vanelli's "Living Inside Myself," and the awareness of his destination, added another sensation to the arousal—terror at reentering the world he had wanted Stanley to save him from.

Nick
AFTERNOON

Just when you thought the fuckin' wind had stopped and only the heat remained, there it came, man, shoving like it was coming right at you, no matter how you dodged. That's what was making the street so crazy today, Nick thought. Now that the strange woman was gone—he'd looked around for her several times—he could stay on his corner—at least near it, where he was now, in front of a shaded gap between two small closed buildings. If the cops cruised by, he could wedge himself into the dark space until they were gone.

"Weird day, huh?" Another hustler had just walked up.

"Sure is," Nick agreed. "Over there, the sky looks like it's burning." He pointed toward the edge of the sky, flushed by fire. Overhead, the sky was clean, brilliant.

The guy was Chicano, or real tanned, like him. Real good-looking, too, like him. Obviously hustling, because this was hustling turf. Along the farther part of Santa Monica Boulevard, gay guys cruised each other, going for sex, not for pay. Nick had found that out when a man who picked him up drove him to an apartment in West Hollywood. Nick had decided to hitchhike back, maybe make a few more bucks. A good-looking young guy had given him a ride, and when Nick mentioned getting paid, the guy braked, opened the door, and almost threw him out. "Fuck yourself," he'd said. Well, hustlers weren't queer, and that was a fact. Still, every now and then when someone good-looking approached him, he'd be wary until he was sure the other guy was hustling, too.

They were both evaluating cars moving by, drivers leaning to study them. "Queers, man—they're weird," Nick said.

"Just people like us," the other guy said.

Oh, oh. Nick was about to split, but the guy said, "I know what you mean about weird on the street. This guy I went with earlier, man, he wanted me to call him 'Uncle.' So I kept saying, 'Suck my cock, Uncle.' A hundred bucks for fifteen minutes."

Shit. More like twenty bucks. Still, Nick fell easily into the familiar street exaggerations. "This one old guy, man, he picked me up, you know what he wanted? He wanted to shave my balls."

"Did you let him?"

"Shit, no. With that knife so near my cock? But he still paid me, hundred bucks for like ten minutes." The man had given him twenty.

"This guy," the other hustler said, "had a collection of hustlers' short hairs, bunched up. Looked like a big spider. Gave me two hundred bucks for mine."

Maybe thirty. "The worst, though, man, is when guys pretend they didn't know you were hustling," Nick said.

"Yeah—just cruising for another guy."

"They just wanna sound you out, man, I guess, cause they know farther up is where that shit happens for free."

"West Hollywood, yeah. Not easy to hustle, but I did, one night, just off Santa Monica, man, in this small park, under some baseball bleachers, right there, man. Even went back."

That's how he knew about it, cause he'd managed to hustle there, Nick figured. He saw the other hustler studying him, looking at his chest, no, down, to where his pants were open one button.

"That's sexy," the other hustler said.

"Gets queers hot," Nick said quickly.

"I think I'll try it."

The guy was just learning the ropes. "Go ahead," Nick said.

The other hustler pulled his jeans about an inch down his lean torso.

"Lower, man. Whoa! That's *too* low."

The other hustler adjusted his pants, just low enough.

"Now open your shirt."

The other hustler did. "You're right—this does feel sexy. Thanks for the tips."

"Sure, man, sure." He didn't often make friends on the street—he was a loner—but he liked this guy. "Hey, I bet you like that song 'Cheatin' Heart,' huh, man?"

"Uh, what?"

"Yeah, 'Cheatin' Heart'—ole Hank Williams sings it."

"Uh, yeah—"

"I knew it. It's my favorite song, too—"

"There's a squad car coming!" the other hustler said, but he didn't move.

Nick pushed himself into the shaded space between the closed buildings.

The guy moved back, against Nick's body.

"I don't see no squad car—" Nick jerked away.

"I guess I was wrong."

What had he meant by that? Oh, shit, what the hell was he making so much out of the guy's thinking he'd seen cops? Playfully, he nudged the other hustler with his elbow. Then he recognized the car that drove by, almost stopping. "Talk about weird," Nick said, "that guy's the weirdest."

"Yeah? I was about to get into his car just a while ago. He was waiting for me. But he didn't look right to me, like a cop. So I split."

"He's no cop, man. Know what he wanted? To see my *back,* man, just to *see* it, that's all—"

"Sure, I *bet* that's all he wanted, yeah," the other hustler laughed.

"—and he wanted me to tell him my name is 'Ain-heel'—something like that."

"Angel?"

"That's it. Ahn-hel. I said I was him, and then he didn't believe it, got real mad."

The car had stopped on a side street.

"What's the matter, man?"

"My name's Angel," the other hustler said.

"Why's he lookin' for you?"

The other hustler shook his head. "Uh, well, we'd better split so we can make out. You'll be around later? Maybe we can hang out after we're through, huh?"

"Yeah." Nick would welcome ending this weird day early. Maybe even now. "Where you goin'?" he questioned.

"To find out what that guy wants."

Nick watched the hustler who said he was Angel walking toward the waiting car. Maybe he wanted to pick up some easy bucks by pretending that *he* was the guy the weird man was looking for. Maybe—

He saw the hustler about to approach the car parked under the dark shifting shadows.

Don't get in! Nick shouted silently.

Clint
AFTERNOON

Even with the air conditioner on, he was increasingly hot. He remained standing naked looking out at the City. In the far distance, streetlights were coming on, confusing smoke from the burning hills with dusk.

NEW YORK
Last Weekend

Pulled back by the dark energy it exuded, Clint returned to the area of the parked meat trucks, wholesale butcher shops, to enter the familiar cavities of the Mineshaft, where he had often thrived and where, earlier, the leatherman who had stopped to stare at him had entered with two chained men.

Clint walked up the same stairs.

Before an American flag and under a rim of light, two rough guards enforced strict rules of entry—rejecting undesirables, the effeminate, those not in masculine gear.

The two men nodded Clint in.

Heat, cold heat—

Clint thought that as he lay back down on the bed in the air-conditioned hotel room, the cool air battling with the day's heat.

What have I left behind? What have I brought with me?

Ernie
AFTERNOON

Big dick!

He kept singing those words in his mind, the words the guy who had fucked him had said so long with. Big dick!

As he walked back to his car, Ernie felt so good that he began looking around, at the park itself, for chrissakes. God, it was beautiful, this great park, miles and miles of it, like a forest smack in the middle of the City. Flowers, purple, orange, sputtered out of the brush.

There was no place like L.A.!

All that sun always here and great beaches.

Never mind these spooky Sant'Anas. Look how they cleaned the sky, so clear, so blue.

If you stood on the crest of that hill over there, you could see right to the ocean, he'd bet.

Hey, what was wrong with feeling so goddamned good?

Now he could go home, watch television, go to bed early, let the coming Sant'Ana night pass by without him.

Mitch
AFTERNOON

Once the exhilaration of their mutual discovery, his and Heather's, had abated—and finally they had only laughed to the point of tears—Mitch felt abandoned in a new world he belonged in but had to still find.

He drove to a section of the beach he remembered, recognized only now. He parked in a lot, and walked onto the sand. Beach crowds had thinned early as the wind whipped up stinging sand. Here, with Heather, Mitch had seen lone men slipping under a discarded pier. Beyond this stretch, the pier waited to be destroyed, crushed by machines or by waves that pounded its rotting props. Jagged shadows created a lingering dusk underneath it, a strip narrowed by a deep inward curve of the ocean.

Mitch walked there now. In one moment he passed from sunlight to dark twilight. The wind jabbed through only in hot humid gasps, allowing pockets of stillness. Men, perhaps a dozen, most in trunks, stood about or drifted as if in a slow dance, or melded, becoming one shadow.

Walking past him, a man in trunks brushed his hand along Mitch's thighs, fingers pausing at his crotch before he moved on, looking back, tilted head beckoning Mitch to follow into a pool of shadows. Mitch felt a clutch of dread. He could not move, as if he was caught in a spell that had been cast over only this portion of the beach. Didn't that man— and the others drifting about—know that he was "new"? But he didn't feel entirely foreign here. It was as if, in a dream, he had explored this world, and that was why he could move, now—finally, and he did— within its flow.

The man who had touched him earlier stood under slashes of darkness. He had removed his trunks. Only when he approached closer did Mitch realize that there was someone else there, a man cramming himself against the naked man. Mitch halted. The naked man pushed away the man behind him, who now squatted before him to take his cock in his mouth, one hand reaching out for Mitch's groin, goading him forward. Parting his own ass with his hands—and staring back at him—the man standing offered himself to Mitch to enter.

Mitch ran along the sand, stumbling out into the eery glow of sunlight and ocean smeared by smoke and orangy reflections of faraway flames.

He stood on the scorched beach. Whorls of wind clutched at him, pushing grains of sand into his eyes, his mouth.

Could he exist in that world?

He wiped perspiration, his head and cock throbbing.

Dave
AFTERNOON

The kid clung to Dave's waist as they rode along the streets of West Hollywood, gathering admiring looks, the kid laughing and clinging tighter, sliding his hands up and down Dave's chest and gathering the sweat there, then rubbing it on his own chest, and then Dave would park near a gay bar to let everyone see them. Like now.

Look at that guy standin' in front of them, staring and workin' himself up through his pants, imagining what he and the kid would be doing later, Dave knew, and what they'd be doing was *everything,* dude! He'd start now—slowly.

Revving the bike, he swerved off into a shadowy alley. He got off, leaving the kid still mounted on the machine. He popped an ampule of amyl—*real* amyl, dude, not butyl. Bolt, Rush, Locker Room, all that shit was okay, but not like *this.* He held the ampule to his own nose, inhaling the vapor, which raced to his head and exploded in his groin—and then he pressed the ampule against the kid's nose, until the kid pulled away, almost reeling for a second, stumbling off the bike. They faced each other within the heated command of the popper. Dave reached roughly for the kid's head, forcing it down onto the leather chaps, toward his crotch but not onto it.

"Smell the leather!"

The kid jerked back. Dave held his head there, just held it—until he felt the kid relax. Then, quickly—for sure on a stronger rush of amyl—the kid burrowed his head against the opening of the leather chaps, his mouth searching for the tear on the Levi's.

"Stay *there*! Smell my crotch, little bastard! Smell the sweaty leather, ya hungry little bastard." The kid's tongue licked past the leather, to the tear, his mouth attempting to pull out the cock straining under it. Dave rubbed the gnawing mouth about his crotch. "Yeah!" Then he released it on the protruding head of his cock, forcing it to stay there until, in one rough movement, he returned the kid's grasping mouth to the edge of the leather chaps. "Didn'ya hear me, ya fuckin' cock-sucker? I said, smell the sweaty fuckin' leather, smell the—"

The kid pulled away and stood up.

Defiantly? The rush of amyl fading or had he moved too fast? "Got you too hot again, huh?"

"No. Maybe. Weird. I don't know."

But you will know. Dave leaned back on the bike, arms behind his head—one of his most commanding poses, he knew. He touched his dark stubble, a finger lingering on the scar. He said lazily, "So what are you really lookin' for, dude? Cummon, tell me, cummon." He allowed himself to entice in a mellower way. "Cummon, kid."

The kid smiled, all that blond hair tossing about his face. "It's a special day for me—like a celebration. I want to just keep getting hotter and hotter and sexier and sexier until it's real late at night. Then I'll have lots and lots of sex, hot sex, with lots of hot guys, *really* hot, not go home to do it, either—stay in one place, because I don't want to waste time, not even come till the last, and that'll be the hottest, and it all has to be the wildest. Really *wild*."

The kid was perfect. "Sounds—hot," he borrowed the kid's word. "Whatya say you and me ride around and find the best place for your celebration?—and we'll round up lots of dudes for later?"

"O-*kay*!"

But now the kid looked almost embarrassed, shy. "And what about you?" he asked.

Dave had known the kid wanted him real bad—and wanted his own hot trip at the same time. Well, *he* wanted the kid—and *his* own trip—and they'd have both. "Me? I'll be the last one, the one you'll *want* to shoot your load with. I'll hold mine, too. We'll get off together. Dude, I'll make fuckin' sure you have a *real* special night. Okay, kid?" He linked the thumb of his black-gloved hand over his thick studded belt, to add a master's authority to his question. "Now I'm gonna do something for you." He held Jesse's arms up, exposing the blond hairs under them. He licked under the kid's arms, one, then the other, around, up, down, in, rough lappings of his tongue. "Now that I've licked off that fuckin' deodorant, you'll smell like a *real* man for a *real* man, dude."

Seven

Scratchy vines—stirred violently today by the Sant'Ana—cling to the high wire fence about the unused field in the park in West Hollywood. A few trees bunch in isolation in one corner of the field. Branches lean over the open passage between it and the brick toolshed. Those branches, and the narrowness of the open space, create a permanent dusk there until night drops its heaviest shadows over it.

Jesse
AFTERNOON

In the alley where they had stopped, Jesse stood before the guy on the bike. It hadn't excited him when the guy made him lick the leather. He'd done it only on his way to suck the guy's cock, a good, thick one. Maybe that's not all that had excited him. He'd sniffed poppers before, but the biker's— Wow! The amyl had jerked him into a furious rush, blood thumped at his temples, hot darkness engulfed him like he might pass out, and he felt so fucking lusty that maybe he'd kinda wanted to try something new. When the pulsing darkness opened, he'd pulled back, angry—and he might have stayed angry, except that it had been wild when the biker licked the deodorant off his armpits.

"Say, dude," the biker had assumed a huskier drawl, "you ever try two cocks up your tight ass? That'd double up on the guys you'd have for your celebration."

The way he was smiling and rubbing his scar—Jesse wasn't sure he was serious. When he'd gone with the two guys who'd taken turns fucking him last week, he'd teased both cocks at the same time. He'd only imagined that he had both in. Another great thing about being gay—allowing everything as long as it stayed fantasy.

A burst of wind dragged some palm fronds into the alley. Suddenly they lay still, before them, abandoned. Ugh. Jesse looked away from them.

"Me and another dude, at the same time, at the last of your celebration—but me at the very last," the biker offered, still smiling. "How about it?"

"If the other guy's as hot as you." Jesse decided to go along with the talk—just fantasy. He knew how turned on the biker was by him. So he would tease, flirt, play with him—the guy was *too* cocky. Jesse knew how to take control of guys who thought they were in charge and were as hot for him as this guy was.

The biker held his gloved hand to his mouth, licking the black leather, once. "Ever had anything bigger than two cocks?"

Buzz, Boo, and Fredo
AFTERNOON

When he heard footsteps on the litter of the abandoned house, Buzz, still on the floor, sat up. His cheek had stopped bleeding, cauterized by the hot concrete.

"Jesus, man, she sure cut you up." Fredo leaned over Buzz. He and Boo were back.

Buzz adjusted his pants, sitting up. "I'll fuckin' catch up with that cunt and fuck her ass till she's fuckin' wasted."

"Hey, Buzz, ain't that a sin?" Fredo asked.

"Only when queers do it." Buzz spat into his hand, rubbing dust off his face.

"That right? The Pope says so?" Fredo asked.

"Yeah."

"Huccome you wanna fuck her ass?" Boo asked Buzz.

"Cause it'll hurt her."

When they emerged out of the house, the wind toppled a garbage can, spilling more garbage in the alley. A woman hidden in rubbish staggered out. Buzz pulled at her rags and shoved her away. They walked along the alley.

"Whose car is that?" Buzz asked. Boo and Fredo were getting into a crudely painted car.

"Fredo hotted it, man."

Buzz jumped into the driver's seat. "Let's go find some rough action." He spat into his hands and wiped blood on his face.

Father Norris
LATE AFTERNOON

Perspiring, feverish despite the air-conditioning he kept on, Father Norris waited in his car for the boy walking toward him—Angel—the boy who had walked away earlier, perhaps because of the woman in black on the street. Just an ordinary woman dodging the wind, he dismissed now.

A squad car drove by, slowed, stopped just ahead.

"Sir, we've been watching you circling the block, and—"

"I'm looking for Angel. Do you know him? A young Mexican boy with amber, almost-yellow eyes, and a tattoo on his back."

"Oh, sure, Father—you are a priest, aren't you?"

"Yes."

"Sure we've seen him, hangs around the street to be picked up, that kid with the sacrilegious tattoo on his back."

"No, no—his tattoo is not sacrilegious."

"You would know, Father."

"You see, he loves Christ with such passion that he wants Him to become part of his own flesh. The tattoo represents his attempt at total communion—"

"We understand, Father. We stopped you because there are a lot of perverts out here, looking for these kids, wanting to sodomize them, and at first we thought that you—"

"That I—you thought that I—?"

"Sorry if I offended you, Father. Good luck in your holy mission, I can tell that you'll accomplish it."

"Yes!"

Father Norris ended the imagined interrogation when the police car drove away after idling a few moments, surely realizing that he was not one of those debauched men out to debase these boys, to, to—

"How're-ya?"

The boy was leaning against his car window. "You're Angel," Father Norris said.

"Yeah."

Father Norris opened the passenger door. Hot wind gasped in. The young man got into the car.

He was more beautiful than the woman had described him. As beautiful as a martyred saint.

"How do you know who I am, man?"

"I've heard about you, Angel." It had to proceed exactly, slowly, step by step.

"Yeah? You guys talk to each other about us?"

The boy's eyes contained a deep sorrow that his pose attempted— unsuccessfully—to hide.

"So what are you looking for, man?"

"Your back—"

"That'll cost you more," the boy said.

Father Norris lowered his head, twice.

"You got a place?" the boy asked.

Za-Za and the Cast of *Frontal Assault*
LATE AFTERNOON

The journey to face Mr. Smythe on his veranda must have taken her ten years, a slow death march. Behind her, everybody was in the wrong ass, and he was about to blame her. But! Hope sprang. What if, before he could accuse her, she blurted out just the *story* of her epic film?— grab him with it, leaving for later the description of the play of light and shadows, the screen split by a bolt of color—*avant*-Bergman. She did have to tell him—a lot of blurting—about the scene that would honor *L'Avventura*, except that her characters would move fast—run— *hop!*—from level to level.

"Za-Za!"

"Please let me explain my—"

"What is there to explain, my dear? Why, this rehearsal is splen-did. Beyond my imagination."

Was she hearing right? "I'm—well—I'm glad you like it." Where had those insipid words come from?

"Like it? It's sublime, my dear, simply sublime, to turn it all around, to have all those inviolate asses violated, to have all those wasted cocks put to use. Why, my dear, it is—it is—inspired. You have inspired your actors—"

Actors! Those whores piled on top of each other? Actors? What a slur on Cary Grant, Gary Cooper, Clark Gable—my goodness, *trésor,* they all had G's and C's in their names. What could she do with *that* in her epic film?

"But how can you possibly bring it"—Mr. Smythe's wrinkles tangled into a smile—"how can you possibly top all this?"

Za-Za tried to assume a mysterious look, to give herself time to think.

"Remember? *Étonnez-moi!* Astonish me! Now run along, my dear, move on to the grand finale you've surely planned!"

My God, the old geezer is cuckoo. If she didn't blurt now about her film that would return grandeur to cinema, another opportunity might not occur. "Sir, I have an idea—"

"But of course you do, my dear, and I have no doubt it will be splendid. Now run along this moment." He walked back to his throne on the veranda, where his guests had not glanced at her.

Za-Za looked disconsolately ahead.

That slut Tony Piazza, that *magnifique ingrat,* that beautiful tramp—look at him spinning like a top in Rex Steed's ass, after he vowed he would be a bottom till the end of time.

"Za-Za?"

"What!" She had no time for Huck Sawyer, lurking around, al-though, Lord love him, he was the only one not mounting anyone.

"What shall *I* do?" Huck Sawyer tugged nervously at his briefs—arousing himself out of sheer anxiety, the dear thing, and— "What is *that?*" Za-Za reeled back.

"What!"

"That! That! Under your shorts!"

"It's my cock, Za-Za, what else?"

"Let me see." She pulled at his trademark Jockeys. She staggered back, almost toppled over. "My *God!*"

"What, what, what!" Huck Sawyer was almost in tears, his hands working furiously at his crotch as if only that might calm his nerves.

Za-Za grabbed his undiscovered cock with her hand, pressed it forcefully down, and let go of it. It sprang against his stomach, vibrated there—stout, assertive—higher than his navel, higher than— "*Trésor!* I am going to make you a *star!*"

Thomas Watkins
LATE AFTERNOON

Thomas drove down Laurel Canyon. He congratulated himself on the fact that after his usual scotches he steered with even greater confidence than otherwise.

He held his breath.

The young man still wasn't there, at his usual place.

Thomas parked across the narrow street, in the shadows of trees, a few feet away from the garage outside of which the boy so endlessly washed his car. In the early afternoon, never this late. When it was fair, not windy. Still, Thomas adjusted his rearview mirror so that he could watch the entrance to the boy's house. He remained there, waiting. Longer. Longer. Almost dozing. Waiting—

The boy!

Thomas saw the familiar car driving up to the house where the young man lived. Oh, God, he didn't even know his name. What would he call out? Boy? Of course not. Young man? Yes. He rolled down the window.

The young man stepped out. He ran to the passenger side of his car and held the door open for—a girl.

Outside the car, they kissed, very long. The girl's neck strained to meet the boy's lips.

What was he doing with that girl? He *had* to let him know he was there. Thomas turned on his headlights, to signal through blades of dust and wind. He started the car, made a difficult turn on the narrow street, and drove slowly alongside the boy and the girl. They blinked at his headlights. Ahead, he braked, turned the inside light off and on, off and on, for the boy to realize that it was he.

The young man ran to Thomas's car. He leaned into the open window. Thomas smiled at him.

"What the fuck are ya starin' at, you fuckin' old faggot?" the young man shouted.

"What?"

"Listen, you queer creep, I've seen you drivin' up and down lookin' at me when I'm working on my car. Didn't you see me laughing at you? Couldn't you take a hint when I flipped you a fuckin' finger?"

"Laughing—? At me?" No, no, he had smiled, waved, Thomas was sure. Why was he lying? Why?

"Now get the fuck away, cocksucker!" The young man banged his fist on the fender of the Cadillac.

"Ignore him, Scotty," the girl's voice called out.

Thomas drove away, down the road, to—

Where?

That bathhouse he'd driven past some time back, in West Hollywood, so popular on weekends even in the afternoon. It would relax him.

A car coming up the hill swerved to avoid him. The driver yelled at him. Let him, *he* had been driving perfectly well, not recklessly like others drove along the canyon.

Those damned palm fronds! One had tangled under his car. He tried to ignore the scratching. It grew louder. He stopped on a side of the road. He looked under his car. A huge frond clung there. He yanked at it. It wouldn't budge. He yanked more. It seemed alive, fighting him. He pulled and pulled. It clung. The wind was aiding it. Was that blood on his hands? He pulled and pulled at the sharp edges of the frond.

He loosed it. The wind swept it away. Who was screaming out like that—with such terrible urgency?

He looked around. There was no one but him.

Orville
LATE AFTERNOON

Orville sat before his large television and sipped a watered bourbon. Driving up to Griffith Park had been a mistake. Had the strange wind made him act like he did with that muscular guy he wanted? It contributed, and it was now blowing harder. The glow of fires in the hills was singeing more of the sky, he could see through his picture window. Even inside, he could smell ashes. He wished the Sant'Ana night had already come and would be over with. But time seemed to be dragging on, as if it was trying to keep the night away.

When he had finished watching a musical with Fred Astaire and Ginger Rogers—no one new could beat them, no one—on the old-movie station, he showered, slowly, the third time today. He was very attentive to never smelling bad. He changed into fresh jeans, fresh tapered shirt, another set of boots, also Tony Lama. He wouldn't wear the hat, though. Too windy.

He would go out, idle some time, and then go dancing at the Studio Club. He was a great dancer. He smiled at that. Maybe tonight he'd meet someone terrific who would be looking for someone terrific, maybe someone on the rebound from a bad affair and looking for a good one—someone special, true love.

He sighed.

The hot night was waiting, and he was resigned to joining it, but only the early part of it.

Before he walked out, he clamped on his cowboy hat.

Paul
EARLY NIGHT

How long had it been since he'd been here to cruise? Paul parked his car in the lot adjoining the beach that turned gay as soon as it was dark. He got out and walked toward the shoreline. Against the wall of a locked rest room, a man blew another while a third masturbated. Paul walked on.

Even before he'd moved in with Stanley, he'd stopped coming to a narrow stretch of beach under a dilapidated pier. Earlier in the day, men made out under shafts of shadows. Toward night, they began to spill beyond the rotting structure. From where he stood, still away from the pier, Paul could make out entangled figures.

He turned back, got into his car, drove away to Venice, to the section where he had been earlier, where he had met that strange guy who'd come home with him. He'd take a walk on the cooling sand, and think.

Christ! It couldn't be. That guy standing by his car parked at the edge of the lot—it couldn't be that son of a bitch with all his bullshit about his lesbian girlfriend. What the hell was he still doing here?

Looking for me? Odd as the thought was, Paul did not reject it. He slowed his car, still a distance away from the man, who stared out at the ocean.

He looks so alone, Paul thought. Maybe it was true he broke up with his girlfriend, maybe he was figuring himself out. He'd seemed nice, except for that moment when— It wasn't easy, despite what everyone said about everything being so different now—not easy to come out when everything resisted. Paul slowed his car. The man was aware of him now, looking in his direction. Paul lowered his window. He'd drive by slowly.

"Aren't you the guy I went home with earlier?"

"Yeah. I thought I recognized you. Mitch, right?"

"Paul—right? Listen, man, I'm sorry about what happened at your place. I was confused, about my girlfriend, but mostly about myself."

"And now?"

"I've cleared my head. Look, man, you think we could get together again, I mean *really* get together and—?"

"Sure. Okay. It's crazy, but, yes—"

Of course, it wasn't the same guy, Paul told himself as he stopped imagining what might have happened if it had been, what might have been said.

He drove out of the lot. He would go to the Studio Club, where he had met Stanley.

Already there was a line to get in.

Ahead of him, a group of pretty young men walked in laughing past a man guarding the door, choosing who might be allowed in. Paul glanced back. A troop of shrieky black men who had joined the line would be kept out, Paul was sure, and so would a heavy young man, sweating profusely from the heat or out of anxiety as he approached the sentry. No one could say the gay world couldn't be brutal. He pushed away that thought when he reached the entrance and the man at the door let him through with a smile.

Inside, strobe lights slashed at beautiful bodies gyrating in sensual motions, touching, arching, miming sexual positions, at times with and then at times against the palpitations of music, which was drenched through with air-conditioned heat and the stench of poppers. Paul looked at the once-familiar vortex of bodies offered, bodies accepted, bodies rejected, bodies offered again— Did he want to pitch his body among them?

"Dance?"

"Oh, Christ, Stanley, you *didn't* leave—?"

"No, babe. I stayed at the airport, thinking about lots of things, about us, and then I drove back. I saw you with that guy—cute, too, good choice—but I saw him leave right away."

"Why didn't you come in then?"

"I wanted you to be sure, too, that you wouldn't follow him, change your mind."

"How can I believe you didn't pretend to leave so you could go out cruising here tonight, and now that you see me here—?"

"I'll prove it to you, babe. I followed you here, where we met, where we first fell in love, and now we'll pretend it's that time again, and then we'll go home, like we did that night, remember?"

"Remember? How could I forget?"

But I *will* forget, Paul thought, drinking from the beer he had ordered during the imaginary encounter he had, even now, conjured up with Stanley. Even if it had happened like that, he would have turned away from him and—

"Dance?"

"Yeah!" he answered the good-looking shirtless man who had asked him twice.

"Poppers?"

"Sure." Paul sniffed the vial extended to him. He didn't use poppers that often, although Stanley insisted when they were together and
sometimes Paul pretended. But on this hot sexy night, he inhaled again
from the vial of butyl or amyl, and within the sudden rush, he heard
the words he was dancing to—The Little River Band's "The Night Owls,"
and he half heard, half felt its refrain, about a restless breed trying to
find its place, doing time—going where?

The man with him opened the top button of his jeans. Paul removed
his own shirt. They whirled together onto the dance floor. His pelvis
arching toward the other's, their bodies drawing closer, groins rubbing
together, both hardening—bodies grinding against each other to the
throbs of music, Paul knew, *I'm back!*

Nick
EVENING

Nick saw the hustler he'd talked to ride away with the weirdo.

Well, fuck that guy if he didn't wanna listen to me that the guy's a
weirdo, man, Nick thought. And fuck him if he thinks *I'm* gonna come
back to get together. He dodged off Santa Monica Boulevard when he
saw a squad car approaching, at the same time, dammit, that a john
was about to stop for him. He tried to deliberate who'd reach him first,
the john or the cops. The john. The cops moved on along the Boulevard.

He went with the man, who at first rejected his price—fifty dollars,
always ask for more—and offered him twenty dollars—"for a quickie, I
come real soon, and all I wanna do is blow you and you don't have to
come. Coupla minutes. I just wanna get off. We'll do it in the car."

"Make it thirty dollars—"

"All right, get in."

In a quiet street of small tree-sheltered houses, the man lowered
his head over Nick's cock. Nick stopped him. "Uh, the money first,
okay?" The man gave him the thirty dollars he had readied in a pocket.
As the man's mouth enclosed his cock, Nick shut his eyes and thought
about—

That was sometimes a problem, finding something to think about. The girl he'd fucked, with three other guys, back in—the girl he'd met on the street one night after hustling, and he and another hustler took her to a room they'd rented and she blew them both and then they fucked her, the girl and the guy who—

The man came. Wordlessly, he drove Nick back to the Boulevard. Things were moving along better, man. Nick felt encouraged, especially when another car stopped quickly for him. He peered in. But he didn't get in—"Catchya later, man"—because, ahead, beyond whorls of debris-laden wind and walking toward him was the kid who said he was Angel. Relieved that the guy was okay after being with that weirdo he'd warned him about, Nick walked across the street to join him.

It wasn't him. Another hustler. Angrily, Nick kicked away a jagged frond the wind had pushed, trembling, against his feet.

Clint
EVENING

His room at the Château Marmont was dark. Darkened by early shadows falling on this side of the building? By ashen clouds sweeping into the City from outlying fires? Or was it later than he thought? As Clint lay on the sweat-moistened bed, time seemed to be in limbo, as if the day had shattered, holding night at bay, time fractured.

NEW YORK
Last Weekend

When Clint walked into the Mineshaft—into a light like cold fire—he surrendered to the excitement of so many other times, an excitement that bludgeoned everything else. The earlier sense of seeing this world as if for the first time—that had been only an impression, a spell broken. But as he moved into the cold, darkened red light, it was as if one spell had replaced another, and the two were at war.

A smoky redness bled into the large room and flowed into smaller rooms, doorless, like gashes. Slabs of decayed wood slanted in fallen

diagonals, as if a mine had collapsed, leaving only ruins. Crumpled
papers, oxidized cans, garbage—debris imported from the piers and
the area of the parked butcher trucks—accumulated throughout. Low
murmurs of music without visible origin panted into air torpid with
the odor of poppers, sweat, dead cum.

Within the reddish murk, dozens of men—more, a hundred,
more—uniformed or in leather, naked or in chain-decorated nudity—
bunched into masses of flesh and leather as muffled sighs, throttled sobs,
faded into strangled moans.

The dark stare of a man in full leather grasped Clint's attention—
the leatherman he had seen enter with two naked, dog-collared men.
The leatherman jerked the chains that restrained the two men. The
naked men opened their mouths. The leatherman spat into the gaping
mouths. Spittle dribbled to the floor. The leatherman wrenched at the
chains. The two men licked the spattered floor. His eyes on Clint, the
leatherman yanked again at the chains of the collared men. The naked
men crawled toward Clint.

Clint's eyes interlocked with the leatherman's. The collared men knelt
before him, offering their mouths. Clint moved away, past locked bodies.

Wrists and ankles bound, a naked man thrust his torso up from
the floor, presenting it to men bending over him—fingers searching,
tongues licking—his mouth open wide to suck cocks wedging in between his lips, cocks offered to other mouths, more mouths, as a man
tossed the naked man over, down, and fucked him while others waited
to follow, and followed while a man inserted the tip of his oiled boot
into the ass of a man squirming on the floor, wrenching to coax the tip
of the boot in deeper, the boot replaced by a cock, another, prodding
together, while nude men handcuffed to army cots lapped at boots and
gloved fists held over their faces by uniformed men and one man ground
his heel into a naked groin as a clot of bodies lined up to share arching
mouths of men sitting on the props of toilets in black cubicles, men
groveling on the floor between their legs sucking and licking the readied organs and within tangles of dark-red light and shadows, leather
straps restrained naked men in anxious surrender, nipples twisted and
bitten, asses invaded by fingers and tongues and cocks—*and one man
shackled to a wall, contorted, alone, in deep pain, without inflictor*—next

to four nude bodies squatting on the floor, faces pressed down to the littered floor by roaming hands while other men fucked them, one then another, taking turns, and within a pool of red shadows bodies crouched to watch a man remaining unmoving inside another, hips locked against bare flesh, until piss flowed out of the naked buttocks, down, onto the floor, to the tip of the boots of a man driving his cock in and out of the ass of a man bent toward a cluster of cocks, while hands slapped his buttocks, and a man in leather mounted a harnessed man, silver bit between his teeth, head swiveling before cocks slapping his face, shoving into his mouth, other mouths joining, other men mounted, and a few feet away, men surrounded a nude man in a tub—and others waiting to replace him mimed his contortions—his mouth gnawing at genitals pushed at him as others spat on him, came on him, pissed on him, his mouth twisting to receive the liquid mixture until hands forced his face down to slurp the stained tub, muted gasps joining those of men strapped in a row of leather slings hanging by chains from the ceiling, feet bound, legs spread open, feet lodged in metal sockets in preparation for cocks to penetrate, mouths to rim them, legs to straddle faces, fingers to probe and squeeze—and then move on to other masses of flesh, other mouths, other cocks, more flesh.

A leathered cowboy held his greased fist against the ass of a naked man lashed into one of the slings before alerted shadows emerging out of pits of darkness to witness the signaled ritual now progressing as men hunched under the slung body, spreading the man's buttocks, moistening the opening with their tongues, preparing him for the leathered cowboy, who, ready, inserted one finger, two, three, deeper into the widening hole of the slung man, sweat like black dye coating the delirious face, cock soft, mouth opening, making no sound, as more spectators leaned closer to watch as the leathered cowboy's fingers eased out to form a fist—

Clint turned away from the rite he had once been eager to perform. He swung about to confront a pursuing presence.

As he had moved through the carnal vista of the Mineshaft—moving as if in a trance awaiting definition—he had felt the presence of the leatherman. Now they faced each other. The leatherman tugged at the collars of the crawling men—and the two naked men sprang up on their knees—and he flung his head back in silent laughter.

Through a wide slash on the floor, a wooden ladder led to a lower depth. Clint descended.

Flesh and leather copulated on imported garbage.

Ahead, a darker silhouette within dark silhouettes, a naked man lay supine on the rancid floor. His outstretched hands and feet were tied by leather straps. Before gathering men, a man in black leather pants and boots held out in both hands a thick black belt, an offering.

Next to Clint, the leatherman jerked the chains of the crawling men. They rose. Now one held a vial of white powder, the other held cracked ampules of amyl. The leatherman snorted from each, deep, over and over, and nodded toward Clint. The chained men crawled toward Clint, rising before him to proffer the powder and the amyl. Clint's eyes steadied on the leatherman's. *He's challenging me to take it and resist its control.*

Clint inhaled from the powder and the amyl, once, again, again.

He felt caught in the same clasp he was sure contained the leatherman, the same violent craving, and he knew that the leatherman had seen him here before, performing like him and with the others, and had recognized him outside, without the full regalia, had sensed in his reaction a wavering of allegiance, and he was now demanding that allegiance back, and as he became certain of all that, rage invaded his senses, time jumped into a darker darkness that enclosed him and the leatherman, and within it he saw the leatherman take the proffered belt and slash over and over—spitting out aroused words, *"Fuckin' cocksuckin' queer!"*—and flailing at the buttocks of the naked man, who groaned—*"More, master, more!"*—at each harsh sting, and within the darkness, which erupted in his head in a burst of cold red light like ice on fire, Clint saw the leatherman hold out the belt to him—*"Take it!"*—and at the same time that he knew he would resist this challenge—*"No, bastard!!"*—he saw himself emerge out of the circle of men watching, and his hand lashed the belt across the bound body, and his mind imploded with rage that had not yet found its object, and he drew the belt back and lashed again across the naked loins of the bound man, who growled in pained ecstasy, and Clint came.

Throttling a scream, as his cum continued to spurt, Clint dropped the belt and faced the triumphant smile of the leatherman, heard his muted laughter.

As he moved out of the bowels of the Mineshaft, Clint saw masses of flesh grinding, throbbing, moaning like a great wounded beast devouring itself or licking its own wounds—coming or dying.

Coming or dying.

In his hotel room as he lay in the sweat-drenched bed, Clint welcomed voices outside in the hall, the sound of the elevator, the hum of the air conditioner, the distant sound of hectic traffic, the panting of wind at the windows. ·

What did that man feel?

Who?

This time he located a face, but it was a face he had never seen except in his mind, a face that dissolved into another, another, others—faces of the men he had encountered that long night, the faces of the collared slaves crawling on garbage, the face of the leatherman, of the man slurping cum and piss and spittle in the filthy tub, of the men spitting on him, of men sitting on the props of toilets, men crammed against their mouths, the face of the man at the piers, his open mouth begging, and of the men straddling him, the face of the man pressing a boot over the face of another, and of the man licking it, the faces of shackled men, faces of men strung up in slings, of the men crouching about them, the face of the man who had yowled as hot wax dripped on him, the face of the man holding the lit candle, the face of the man prepared for the leather cowboy's assault, the face of the leather cowboy, the face of the man mounted like a horse, the face of the man who had held out a belt as an offering and the man stretched out on the floor to be flogged, his face as the whip lashed—*and the face of the shackled man contorting alone in deep pain inflicted by an absent torturer*—all those faces, and now his own joining others rushing across his memory, shaped in his feverish mind into the face he had been trying to locate.

It was the face of a man he had never seen, the man he had heard about when he was leaving Fire Island. It was the face of the man who had been brutalized by a group of straight punks in Sag Harbor. They had called him "faggot, queer, cocksucker!"—kicked him with heavy boots, whipped him, shoved him against garbage, spat on him as he lay on trash, pissed on him.

Ernie
EARLY EVENING

Hey! Nothing wrong with checking out Griffith Park just one more time before he left, right?

And a good thing he did, too, because look at that cowboy along the path—definitely cowboy day. Oh, shit, no. Yeah, it was the same cowboy he'd met earlier who had asked him if he was in town for the "roundup." Ernie proceeded ahead.

The cowboy slipped into a nest of dried twigs and branches.

Nothing wrong with checking him out. Backing up, Ernie could see the cowboy licking his lips, squatting on his haunches, pants down to his ankles, cock aroused—

Ernie walked in.

"You're hot, gotta great bod, hmmmmm," the cowboy said, "glad I saved myself all afternoon for the best, hmmm." He grabbed the cowboy hat off his head, pushed it onto Ernie's—"Yeah, cowboy!"—and pulled Ernie's pants down. "Lemme lick your hot cowboy balls, yeah, turn around so I can rim your cowboy hole—mmmmm. Real hot from the roundup, huh, cowboy?" He licked under Ernie's balls, and pushed his tongue into his ass, probing in and out, around. "Now, cowboy, fuck the beejeezus out of me, you deserve a good fuck after the hard roundup. Yeah! Ride 'em, cowboy!"

Ernie gave it to him like a man, and the guy took it like a cowboy. After only a few strokes Ernie let himself go. "Yeah, comin', cowboy's fuckin' your ass, yeah, ride 'em—ahhhh—"

"Great fuck." The guy removed his hat from Ernie's head.

"Glad I came in from the roundup, guy," Ernie said.

Who said things couldn't stay mellow? Ernie worked his way down along the sloping path. He would definitely leave now.

"Wanna get together, muscleman?" On the fallen trunk of a tree charred by fire sat a guy with longish hair, his hand groping his exposed groin.

Was he ready to, again? Ernie considered. Nothing wrong with finding out, right? Too open here. So he walked ahead toward a cove. When he glanced back, he saw that another man had advanced on the guy on the fallen trunk, and so he proceeded ahead. Then he heard scuffling, agitated voices. He backed up. Can you believe this fuckin' shit? The guy who had sat there working his cock up, the guy who'd admired his muscles—that fucker was a vice cop, and he was handcuffing the man who had approached him. A fat cop was rushing down to join the arrest. The handcuffed man looked—trapped.

Really trapped.

Mitch
EARLY NIGHT

Mitch got back in his car and wondered, Now where? He was parked in a lot in Venice Beach.

After he left the area of the corroded pier, he had driven aimlessly along Pacific Coast Highway, far out along the coastline, where the ocean lapped fiercely at jagged cliffs. Was it possible that the guy he had met earlier, the guy he'd gone home with—was it possible that he would return to the same beach where they'd met? He lived nearby. Not possible. Still, Mitch had driven back and parked in the lot beyond the strip of gaudy stands and shops.

He had been standing by his car when he had noticed a car moving toward him, slowing. Grayish lights had come on in the lot, but whorls of wind obscured everything. So he hadn't been sure—not sure at all, but, Christ, wasn't that the guy, driving by slowly in his car? Jesuschrist, it *was,* it *was* the guy he had met earlier. The car had paused near him—and then driven off.

Mitch had waited a long time afterwards before he had decided to leave the beach.

Of course it hadn't been the same guy, he was sure now, as he joined
the current of cars on the freeway. Where would he go? He exited into
the lower streets of Beverly Hills, drove onto Santa Monica Boulevard.
His radio was turned on to the news station. "—power outages have
occurred throughout the City. Two deaths have been attributed to the
violent Sant'Ana. Winds gusting up to ninety miles an hour in outlying
areas have darkened wide swaths of the City."

In West Hollywood, the hot winds had not diminished the crowds
along the blocks. Mitch had driven through these streets often with
Heather, who had commented on "all the gorgeous men—what a
waste." He saw them now—so many men, so sexual—walking, idling,
alone, in groups, the heat encouraging displays of male flesh, gleaming torsos.

He turned on a side street—no, it was an alley, he realized—to drive
along the busy blocks again. The alley paralleled a small park—he saw
the dusty outline of a merry-go-round. Hearing the urgent roar of a
motorcycle, and wanting it to pass him, he parked against the wire fence
that enclosed the park.

The motorcycle, driven by a rough-looking guy in leather, glided
by, close to him, close to his open window, pausing. Sitting on the back
of the motorcycle, a good-looking kid in cutoffs looked at him and
smiled. What was he doing with that rough-looking guy? The motorcycle pulled ahead, stopped several feet away. The man in leather
pointed to—

A small hut in the park—

A toolshed?

Mitch saw the kid nod, Yes. Then the kid faced his car, faced him—
and then he leaned over and shouted something to the man in leather.
Mitch heard one word clearly—"Him." The man in leather looked back
at his car, and yelled, "Over there, later!" If he spoke more words, they
were swept away by the wind. The motorcycle roared off.

Mitch stared at the shed they had pointed to. He saw nothing but
darkness there. He heard, echoing into the alley from Santa Monica
Boulevard, words tossed off by the sultry wind, distant harsh voices
shouting—

"*Fuckin' faggots!*"

Dave
EARLY NIGHT

The sound of distant harsh voices faded.

"Fuckin' punks!" Dave said, raising his middle finger toward where the shouts had come, from Santa Monica Boulevard.

"Shits," the kid dismissed. After they had driven out of the alley, Dave had squeezed his bike between two cars in a lot bordering one side of the small park.

"Come on, dude." Dave led the kid across lawns, past the baseball field, bleachers. Petals and leaves shaken off by the wind formed jagged patterns at their feet.

He and the kid stood in a playground, a sandlot.

"Over there." Dave pointed to the passageway between the toolshed and the abandoned field. "That's where you'll celebrate."

"Wild!" The kid sat on the merry-go-round. Spinning on it, he reached out for Dave, pulling him to sit next to him.

"Stop flirting, motherfucker, we're scouting for serious stuff." He halted the merry-go-round with his leather-gloved hand.

The kid laughed, throwing his head back as if about to spin again, but Dave's fist kept it steady.

"You think that guy parked in the alley understood?" the kid asked. "I hope he did. He was hot."

"Hotter than me?"

"Now who's flirting?"

"Shit."

"You wanna know something, *dude*?" the kid imitated Dave's voice as they made their way back to the parking lot. "I think that under that black drag, you're just a queen, a leather queen."

Dave grabbed the kid by the shoulders and pulled him roughly to him, face to face. "Don't fuckin' call me that, shit-punk. See this scar on my face? I made it myself. I didn't even wince!"

The kid shook himself away from Dave's grip. "Joking."

"Okay. But remember." To show that the moments of anger were over, Dave extended a fresh ampule of amyl to the kid, even before he sniffed it himself, offering the kid the best rush.

The kid inhaled, deep, several times. "Oh, by the way, what's bigger than two big cocks?" he challenged Dave's earlier remark.

"A fist is bigger. Two fists are even bigger."

The kid was afraid! That could make the action even better. But maybe he'd gone too far, too soon. So Dave shrugged and mounted the bike. "Hop on, kid." He softened his voice.

"I think I'll walk."

Eight

Evening, early night, muted lights about the park in West Hollywood create hazy shadows. During the Sant'Anas, wind whips branches about. Streaks of yellowish light filter through them, shifting like restless ghosts.

Jesse
EARLY NIGHT

Jesse walked a few steps away from the biker. He waited. Sure, the guy was real sexy in a way he'd never encountered before, a weird sexiness. He was also full of shit, mouthing weird stuff about fists. He walked ahead. As fantasy, kinda exciting—maybe. He stopped walking. Throughout the hours he'd spent with the biker—and, jeez, what was taking the night so long to come, real night, late night?—his cock had kept at least a semi–hard-on, and so had the guy's, and that was wild. The biker had certainly helped to prepare his celebration, flushing everything with lust. He'd understood. Look how he'd suggested this park. Jesse looked back. Wild *and* hot!

He waited at the edge of the lot.

"Aw, cummon, kid," the biker said. He was rolling his bike along without starting it up.

He was *something*—acting so tough one moment, and then flirting, however he denied it.

"Cummon over an' suck my dick."

That was more like it. Jesse turned back, knelt before the guy, who swung his legs about, pulled out the guy's cock—no surprise, it was hard—and sucked it deep in one swallow. The biker threw his head back and groaned. A few men leaving their cars halted, to watch. Jesse continued, letting them watch. Then he stood up.

"Sexy motherfucker," the biker complimented. "I'll bet half of West Hollywood is gonna be after ya once we put the word out."

"Yeah, I—" Then Jesse almost reeled. A belated rush of amyl? The heat?—entrenching now that the wind had paused? He wiped his perspiring brow, and shook away a sudden chill, cold sweat. A cool breeze? The disorienting sensation subsided. The guy's cock was still out, waiting. But he wouldn't suck it again now the way the biker expected. His excitement for the coming night was gathering. And damned if the panting heat, and the Sant'Ana moaning again, didn't make it seem as if the night itself was coming.

Buzz, Fredo, and Boo
EARLY NIGHT

"Look at 'em, fags everywhere," Boo said.

"Hey, queers!" Fredo yelled out of the car window at men along Santa Monica Boulevard. "Fuckin' faggots!"

"I'd like to kill 'em all," Buzz said. The heat was intensifying, now that the wind was settling for longer periods. He swerved off the Boulevard, into an alley. He drove through it, slowly.

"Whatcha lookin' for?" Boo asked him.

Buzz drove out of that alley, into another, another—

"Yeah, what?" Fredo asked.

Buzz braked by a garbage bin behind a grocery store. He jumped out, rummaging through discarded boxes.

Boo and Fredo followed him out of the car.

Buzz stomped on a discarded crate until it split into heavy boards. He gave one to Fredo, one to Boo. He kept the heaviest one for himself.

With it, he whacked at the metallic trash bin, denting it.

Father Norris
EARLY NIGHT

He had not answered Angel's question about where they would go, he had just driven on, aware of him beside him. Go to the sacristy? The darkened church? There? "Are you ready, Angel?"

"We gotta get a place, remember? If you don't have one, I know a motel—a block away."

It was right that he would be led by Angel himself to the place of discovery. He nodded. He followed the boy's directions, driving slowly, extending the encounter, giving to it the importance it deserved, the gradual pace of discovery. Even the windy night had achieved an aura, a shiny aura, a glowing night of reflected, purifying fire. Angel was beside him, in his car. Father Norris did not dare look at him now, not yet. But he was aware of his presence, his and that of the naked Christ, violated flesh on violated flesh.

Father Norris parked in a lot in back of the motel.

At one time, two neon lights had formed entwined palm trees to announce the presence of this cheap motel. All that remained lit were pieces of fronds.

"I know the guy at the desk," the boy said when they entered the tired lobby, "so there won't be no hassle. It'll cost you"—he paused—"uh, forty bucks."

Father Norris nodded.

Behind a counter, a gnarled old man glanced up from a small television screen.

"Give me the money for him," the boy said to Father Norris.

Father Norris heard words which he had to react to, steps in this sublime rite. He reached into his wallet.

The boy gave the old man money.

"Ten more," the man said, "I saw what he gave you."

"Oh, fuck, man." The boy handed him more money.

The old man took a key from among those dangling on a board. "Down the hall. Room 8. You know where."

As they walked along the yellowing hall, the boy turned to Father Norris, his hand out. "Me. Remember?"

Father Norris fished more bills, which he put into the boy's hand, not counting the money. The boy did.

They passed a young man leaving with an older man. "Hey, man," the young man winked at the boy.

"Hey, man." They slapped hands.

Father Norris opened the door to the room. He looked in. The room was bare except for a bed, one spindly chair, an opaque mirror reflecting a bare bulb on a shadeless lamp, and a tin can for the remains of cigarettes. The green bedspread was rumpled, made up hurriedly, barely covering a pillow.

Father Norris waited at the open door.

So spare, humble. The room was correct for this glorious ritual of revelation.

Za-Za and the Cast of *Frontal Assault*
THAT AFTERNOON

"What the fuck are you doing, Huck Sawyer?"

"Following Za-Za's directions. Didn't you hear her, Tony Piazza?"

"No. Now get the fuck away from me."

"Za-Za said—"

"Christ. What's *that*?"

"What!"

"Your cock—it's huge! Why've you kept it hidden? Shit, who cares? Go ahead, fuck me."

"That's what I'm *supposed* to do," Huck Sawyer told Tony Piazza, who had been complaining about his pressing against him while he humped Rex Steed. "Then I'm supposed to do it to Sal Domingo, then to Jim Bond, then, if they turn around—and Za-Za says they will—I'll give it to Lars Helmut, and Dak Boxer, and, at the last, Rex Steed. Cummon, Tony Piazza, help me in, I don't know how, and I don't want Za-Za angry at me. Okay?"

"O-*kay*!" Tony Piazza abandoned Rex Steed's ass and braced himself. Rex Steed remained sprawled.

Hearing Huck Sawyer's words over their moans, Jim Bond and Sal Domingo—and, soon, from under them, Dak Boxer and Lars Helmut—looked, astounded, at Huck Sawyer's cock.

"*Jesus*christ," Jim Bond greeted the spectacle, "that's the biggest damn thing I've ever seen."

"*Jesus*christ! Vat da hell is *dat*?" Lars Helmut called, from under Sal Domingo.

Huck Sawyer turned pleadingly to Za-Za. "Za-Za, I don't know how to get in!"

He was excited enough, more from jangled nerves than from his new assignment, Za-Za knew. Whatever the reason for that monumental hard-on, she had to assure that it was used properly to "*étonnez*" Mr. Smythe. She rushed to where Huck Sawyer stood before Tony Piazza's upturned ass, lubed Huck Sawyer's cock with the *équipage* she always carried, with hope, in her pockets, and grabbed him by the hips and pushed and pushed until the head of his cock slipped into Tony Piazza's welcoming ass.

"Oh, my *God*!" Tony Piazza whooped.

"Oh, my *God*!" Huck Sawyer cried out. "It feels *good*!"

A star is born! Za-Za welcomed, glancing over at the spectators on the veranda, one hand holding their binoculars, the other certainly rummaging through their groins. Only Rex Steed had not reacted to the new revelation, had not even opened his eyes. His legs—God, please witness this—must be petrified by now, spread out forever. Well, he could wait, *trésor*, because he would provide the grand finale to this mammoth "*étonnez*ment."

Now Sal Domingo hopped off Dak Boxer, and Jim Bond sprang off Lars Helmut, and all four—yes, all four, look at them, Za-Za congratulated her strategy—thrust their asses up into the smoky wind. Was the fire nearing?

With a start, Za-Za saw that Rex Steed had stood up. *Malheur!* The captain of the topsy-turvy team was taking in the array of perched asses, holding his now-not-quite-extravagant cock as if choosing from among the banquet. Goddammit, if the blond trollop turned top again, he'd ambush her chance to win Mr. Smythe's support for her life in art.

So Za-Za shouted at Huck Sawyer, "Hurry, hurry. Now hump Jim Bond." She pulled him off Tony Piazza, who muttered, "What the fuck?"—and she didn't even have to shove him into Jim Bond, because—look at him, so eager now, a real top man, bless him—Huck Sawyer was already in him. "Just a few strokes each!" she demanded, because that harlot Rex Steed was still studying the alignment of asses. "Hurry, hurry!" She pushed Huck Sawyer into Dak Boxer's ass, in and out, in and out. Out!—and into Lars Helmut. "Just two strokes. Okay, three," she allowed when Lars Helmut reached back and wouldn't let Huck Sawyer pull out. So she grabbed Huck Sawyer by the waist and tugged and tugged until she freed him from Lars Helmut's mighty clasp.

"*Goddamn* look at that fuckin' weapon!" Rex Steed's eyes opened wide, wider. And with that, he fell back and opened his legs and resumed his favorite position, and Huck Sawyer lunged in.

What was that sound? The wind? No, it came over the renewed puffs of air, which were thrashing vines of bougainvillea about. Oh, my God! It was— Applause from the veranda, led by Mr. Smythe!

Caveat emptor! It was time to approach him about her emergence into the ranks of great directors. She rushed forth.

She stood before him.

"Magnificent, my dear! Let me congratulate you."

She couldn't help noticing a moist smudge on his pants—probably the first orgasm he'd had in decades—and *that's* why he had demanded being "*étonnezed*"—astonished, yes, by his own orgasm. He would *certainly* be amenable now.

"I am ready to embark on the creation of a great film," she flung her words out, "in the tradition of D. W. Griffith—remember the Babylonian scene? Well, I'll go for *grandeur moderne,* with a mirror scene that will rival Welles's in *The Lady from Shanghai,* because the mirrors will *already* be broken." Mr. Smythe's mouth was open in new astonishment—at her artistic range. "I'll create a series of huge closeups, like Bergman's, except bigger, bigger—until you don't even know what you're looking at." She was perspiring, but she was fighting for her future, and the future of film—and she, and it, were winning! "Of course there will be a *fromage*—an *hommage?*—to Renoir's *Rules of the Game,*

except that instead of upper class, it'll be *working* class. The great film
noir in Technicolor!" Look at him, transfixed with admiration.

"Let go of my hand! What are you ranting about?"

She hadn't realized she had grasped his hand. "Film. About film,
my debut—"

"Silly queen." Mr. Smythe jerked his hand away. "Mad creature."

Mad creature? Silly queen? *She?* A mad creature, a silly queen?
Za-Za adjusted her wig, puffing it up for even greater stature as she tried
to comprehend what had happened—which was clearly that this
fucking psychopath Smythe, who, thanks to her, had managed his first
orgasm in the two centuries of his life, was shoving her away, just like
that, tomorrow's master of cinema.

Raising her chin, she remained standing proudly before the degen-
erate, so he would remember the exact moment during which he had
dismissed the great *auteur* of modern times—and, to assure that, she
would be certain to mention it in her first major interview in *Cahiers du
Cinema*—conducted, of course, by none other than Marsha Kinder, only
she—and when Smythe pled with her, *la Grande Za-Za*—yes, and *begged*
her—to join his studio—

"Please, come back, Za-Za! I'll double today's fee for the splendid
performance that gave me my first orgasm in decades! Come back! I *must*,
this instant, discuss the brilliant film you were kind enough to offer me
first! Come back, Za-Za! Come back, Za-Za!"

"No, I shall not come back. You called me a mad—you called me
a silly—"

"Oh, Za-Za, my dear, it is *I* who am a mad queen, it is *I* who am a
silly queen—"

And an ancient one, to boot! Za-Za added to her fantasy that would
come true when Smythe implored her to return. It wasn't happening
now, but it *would*.

The mansion was flooded with light—orange light. Flamy reflections glowed in the swimming pool. The drone of helicopters penetrated
the wind, helicopters splashing water over the hills. A voice from a
loudspeaker was booming, "Evacuate—fire threatening—take only
essentials."

Flames reached toward Smythe's hill.

As Za-Za dashed away from Smythe's perch—he remained un-budging while his guests scattered—she looked at the cast of *Frontal Assault* running wildly about in search of their clothes, some abandoning their search. I hope the fire singes their asses, she thought, especially that heartbreaker Tony Piazza, who had, this fiery afternoon of devil winds, squandered—yes, *squandered*—what he had denied her. Now she would walk regally away from the mansion—and then she would run away screaming to her car.

Thomas Watkins
EARLY NIGHT

He stood with the others, leaning against the wall to avoid being shoved by the wind, and he waited to be allowed to enter the popular bath-house. He felt confident—nicely warmed by the extra scotch he'd allowed himself before coming here—that he would soon be inside the famous emporium. Perhaps he didn't look quite as young as some of the other men in line, but young enough, as his expertly altered—adjusted—identification would verify. Even if he was dressed a tad less informally than the others, he *had* removed his tie and opened an extra button on his shirt. The line moved slowly.

Thomas's eyes focused on a young man ahead. He wasn't attracted to muscular men, no—often they repelled him—but this young man, with dark hair—and he was quite short—looked highly sensitive, for all his muscularity. Thomas closed his eyes and imagined him inside the bathhouse. The sensitive muscular young man would be lying on a small cot, and he would be covered only by a white towel. His body would not be hairy. He would have rejected three people in a row just as he, Thomas Watkins, paused at the door of his room. There would be an immediate synapse. The young man would sit up, letting the towel drop to his feet, and he would stand there, his body glistening from steam. His penis would be semi-hard, in anticipation. It wouldn't be a large penis—that had never mattered. "Hello," the young man would say. "Hello, young man." Once he was inside the cubicle, as others drifted by envying him, envying them together, the young man would close the door, and he and Thomas Watkins would—

"I.D."

The line had moved fast these last few moments. "What?"

"Your, I.D. I gotta see I.D."

Thomas Watkins fished in his pocket, for his license.

"This yours?"

"Do I look that much younger?" Thomas Watkins was flirting with the man, who clearly wanted him to linger. What were those men behind him giggling at?

The man threw Thomas's identification back to him. "Look, sir, I don't want to be nasty or anything, but you see over there—"

Sir! How odd. Thomas Watkins looked to where the man at the door was pointing—a posted sign, vague letters. He hadn't brought his reading glasses, and so his vision was blurred.

"It says that we reserve the right to—"

"—refuse entry!" a giddy young man chortled.

"Why!" Thomas heard a pleading voice.

"Look, sir. We're not issuing new membership cards now."

"Membership cards?"

"Oh, move the line," someone behind Thomas ordered.

"Yeah, you gotta apply for membership." The man at the door pushed a card toward him.

"I'll fill it out, now." Thomas Watkins could hardly hear his own voice. "Let me have a pen."

"It takes longer than that to become a member," the man said through tightening lips. "Now why don't you go to the baths on Melrose?"

"Go to the baths on Melrose!" the giddy young man shrieked. "That's for oldies, grandpa."

"Stop holding up the line!" another young man shouted.

"I demand that you look at my license." Thomas kept his dignity.

The man at the door said, "Listen, buddy—I tried to be nice. Now get the hell out of here."

Thomas Watkins saw a burly man approaching them from inside the bathhouse. "Trouble?"

"No, he's just drunk, he's going."

Drunk! How dare they, how—? Thomas Watkins walked back down the stairs. Was he imagining laughter? He stumbled on the last step and fell. Someone in line helped him up.

"Are you okay, sir? Can I walk you to your car?"

Thomas Watkins pushed at the hands helping him up. "I don't need help, I'm not feeble, I'm—"

Orville
EARLY NIGHT

He'd go to the Barnaby Coast before he went dancing. He didn't like gay bars, and he suspected that many others didn't. You didn't say so because then why were you here? Still, he might get lucky and find someone early at this bar.

The Barnaby Coast was so crowded that he had to wait in line. That was uncomfortable because you couldn't help evaluating the people going in but you didn't want to convey that you were already cruising, before entering. So you tried to pretend you didn't see anyone and no one saw you.

The resurging wind blew his cowboy hat off. He ran after it. An old woman walking along the block with her husband bent down, grabbed it, and put it on her husband. "Now *he's* a cowboy, everyone's a cowboy," she said in a heavy accent. The old man imitated a bow-legged cowboy. Guys in line laughed and applauded. The old man removed the hat and extended it back to Orville. Orville let the wind carry it away along the street. He considered going to another bar after that. But someone in line called out that he'd reserved his place for him and so he went back.

He didn't have to wait long to get in, because a group of men left the bar, laughing loudly as they walked out. Christ, that goddamn laughter that some queens assumed. Orville always winced at it. It started like ordinary laughter and then it just looped back into a goddamned giddy shriek, not even like laughter anymore.

Inside, Orville made his way to the oval bar in the middle of large room surrounded by tinted windows. Men stood about, in groups or alone.

The bar was dim, the air thick with cigarette smoke. The music was loud, as if to keep you from thinking too much other than about silent cruising, Orville always thought. He asked for beer. In this bar he'd look less masculine drinking bourbon.

He stood apart, casing the room. Oh, no, over there, a type of crew that annoyed Orville. They'd come in all giggly and giddy, like they were just slumming because they weren't here to make out as long as they were in a group. They'd camp it up, looking at everyone "to die for," pretending to swoon, and calling each other "girl." If you saw them, later, alone and cruising, they would have turned macho— or tried to—their hands clenched to their sides, hips stiff to avoid swinging. Oh, hell, that guy coming over to him, not attractive. Orville walked away.

And everyone was looking for sex, heads swiveling, laughter erupting over constant music, cigarette smoke stinging your eyes, guys talking to guys staring at someone else, no one connecting, everyone laughing, looking for sex, and no one coming over except wrong guys, music pounding but not as loud as the laughter, and you moved and stood and caught someone staring at you and you stared back but someone came and talked to him or to you, the wrong person, and broke up the connection that lasted only for moments and wouldn't have survived anyway and you noticed two guys leaving, to make out, and you thought, I'll stick around, and you saw a guy you'd go with but damned if you'd let him know it with his attitude and damned if he'd let you know it with yours and so you walked by and ignored him, and he ignored you, and you pretended you'd been going to the bar for another beer, and you got one, and there was more laughter and people looking for sex and shouting to be heard over the music and laughter and the giddy squeals going up from tight little groups getting drunk and screaming, "Oh, girl, really!" and now here was another wrong person and you walked away and someone walked away from you and it made you mad because you weren't even interested and then someone you wanted came and stood near you and you stood next to each other, both looking for sex, and stood and

stood waiting for the other one to talk first until you knew it wasn't
going to happen and so it was a contest about who would reject first and
then another wrong guy came up and you moved away looking for sex
and hoping for a lover.

Look who was here—Danny, who'd agreed to come over for dinner and then called back because he'd lined up a trick.

When Danny saw him, he tried to retreat.

"I thought you had a hot date," Orville called out.

"Uh, well, you know, I did, but he—"

"Stood you up?" He wasn't mean, but this guy could've come over
and neither one of them would have to be here.

"No—uh—he had to—uh—go to San Francisco."

"Right. Ciao." Orville made his way along the crunch of bodies,
listening to Billy Squiers and "Don't Say No." Why did every song in a
gay bar seem to be telling you something?

"Buy you a drink?"

Christ, it was Bruce, coming over—the guy he'd made out with
earlier. He wouldn't mind making it again—and this time the guy would
stay over, whatever his plans had been earlier about more cruising.
Maybe he'd had enough. "Hi."

"Oh, my God. Orville! For a moment I thought, Who's that hot man?
Yum-*mee*. Well, I'll sure call you again, okay? Good to see you." He groped
him as he walked away to talk to someone else standing alone.

Son of a bitch.

A desolate unattractive man stood next to him against the railing
along the walls. Orville moved away.

"Fuckin' faggots! Queers!"

A car driving by braked right outside, men in it shouting.

In the bar, motions slowed. Everyone listened. Did the punks have
weapons? Guns? The car screeched away.

Slowly, it would all resume, the laughing, the talking, the cruising—
just another bad incident, not rare. Orville had been in a bar in Westlake
one night when a squadron of punks in motorcycles—about ten of them—
lined up outside when it was almost last call. They had thrown bottles at
the bar, shouting, "Faggots!"—daring anyone to come out and be gunned
down. The bartender had called the police. They hadn't come— not rare,

either. The motorcyclists had roared off after hurling cans of garbage into the bar and firing one shot into the air.

There was no one Orville hated more than punks like those. Often he imagined that he confronted one, smashed his face. Just thinking that made his fist clench.

"Fuckin' faggots!"

The punks had come back, braking again.

"Fuckin' queers!"

"—a new song, not out yet—," the DJ hurried to identify his next record, his voice prodding the men away from the shouts. "We got a peek"—often records were tried out in gay bars, versions not yet released. "It's sure to be next year's biggest hit."

"Fuckin' faggot queers!"

The car roared away.

The DJ's exuberant voice rejected the tense moments that continued to hover over the bar. "And here's the song"—he waited, to allow the songs edgy synthesized sounds to assert their urgency before he finished—"and it's called, 'Tainted Love.'"

Before Orville walked out, he checked the street. Punks like those yelling were known to lurk around, rush anyone leaving a gay bar. The street was bustling just as before.

The man at the door of the Studio Club was checking I.D. He had just rejected a chubby young man. When he saw Orville, the man at the door started to ask him for I.D., the first signal of rejection. "We require—" Then he stopped, looking admiringly at him, and allowed him in.

His looks always allowed him entry into dance clubs, bathhouses, orgy rooms that questioned black people. When he saw one or another turned away, he considered leaving in protest, but every step forward had to be taken. That's how you broke barriers.

He walked into the swirling pit of sweating bodies, smoke, poppers. Multi-hued strobe lights illuminated bared torsos revolving in the large arena.

By the long bar, Orville took off his shirt, knowing that the lights would linger on the sinews of his dark-brown body.

"Dance?"

"Yeah."

A blond guy, good-looking. If it all worked out, would he go home
with him? Yes. The guy held a small vial to Orville's nose. Amyl? He
snorted, powder. Cocaine. The rush accelerated his dance movements.
Someone held an ampule of amyl to him and his partner, and they
breathed it in. His body pulsed with desire. As he continued to writhe
before the other's body, becoming part of this terrific spectacle of gorgeous bodies curving, melding into one churning mass—in contortions
of intercourse or torture—

What?

The unwelcome impression was gone after the initial rush of coke
and amyl.

"Want to get together? I mean, go home with me?" Orville decided
to risk it.

"Ah, jeez, yeah, I'd love to, but later—huh?—the night's still young."
The blond guy looked around at available sensual flesh everywhere.
"Let's just dance now, okay?"

Orville turned away from him, to leave, walk away from the shim-
mering bodies. That was it for tonight. This disturbing night was taking
its own bad direction. He paused. He had seen a handsome guy—
shirtless like so many others with terrific bodies. The guy had broken
away from the man he'd been dancing with, and his eyes were scanning the room, toward him.

He'd stay a short while longer, Orville decided.

Paul
EARLY NIGHT

Oh, yes, he was back, like a repentant lover. Scanning the room after
he'd danced with a guy he hadn't finally been all that attracted to, Paul
saw a terrific black man, who seemed, like him, isolated. The black
man was looking at him. Paul walked up to him.

"My name's Orville. Want to dance?" the black man said quickly.

"Yeah—and my name's Paul." How remarkable, to give even first
names so soon, to push away anonymity, often retained after the most
intimate sex.

They danced, moving together, kissing as Queen lamented a final
dance, a final chance.

Their torsos pressed against each other, glued by perspiration, hardening cock on hardening cock, they held on to each other and laughed. They stopped, went to the bar for drinks—and then, in the soft light of a corridor farther in, they talked.

"You want to come home with me?" Paul rushed his words. His throat tightened, girding for rejection.

"Yeah, sure. Yes!"

Paul leaned over and kissed the guy gratefully, and the guy kissed him back just as eagerly. The thought of Stanley intruded only for moments—but now it did so like a shadow, receding. *If he does come back early, let him find me with this great-looking guy.* When he thought that, Paul knew, with certainty, that he was through with Stanley, that nothing Stanley could do or say would ever change that certainty.

"Okay, let's go," Paul said. The night would end as he had wanted it to, softly, throughout this strange day.

Nick
EARLY NIGHT

"How much for a fuck?"

"I don't fuck."

"I know, I meant how much to fuck you?"

Nick walked away furiously from the car that had stopped for him. What the hell! So many guys wanted to fuck you. Didn't they know hustlers were *straight,* man? Maybe others got fucked and didn't admit it. Maybe—

Nick stood at his corner. The winds had stopped! No—here came gusts of dust right at his face.

Did guys on the street get fucked? The fems, man, sure, the wispy boys who acted like girls and flirted with masculine hustlers. *They'd* get fucked. Drag queens and transsexuals, almost women—natural that they'd get fucked. But straight-looking guys, man—straight guys, like him and that Mexican kid, the guy who said he was Angel—real masculine, good-looking, too, like *guys,* good body and everything— Would Angel—if that was really his name—did he take it up the ass? Angel— if they did meet up later—and maybe they would, huh?—maybe he'd ask him. No—the guy might misunderstand, get mad, or—What would it feel like, to put it in a guy's ass, a tight ass, not like that fat old guy earlier. Tighter than a cunt? What would it feel like to have it in your own ass? Well, he'd never find out any of it because that stuff wasn't for him. Whatever other guys on the street did, *he* was straight, and that meant—

"*Fuckin' queer!*"

A twisted face had leaned out of a car and screamed that.

"*Fuckin' cocksucker!*" another voice yelled. The car attempted to stop. A door almost opened.

Honks, and shouts from behind it, demanded that the car move on. It proceeded, slowly because of crammed traffic. A hand threw something out.

"*Faggot queer!*"

Grimy pieces of oily food splashed on Nick's bare chest. "I ain't no faggot, motherfuckers," he shouted at the car. He bent down for a bottle on the curb and flung it. It hit the car's tires and smashed on the street.

The car braked again, cars in back forced it on.

Nick wanted to wait, face the punks down, man, but there were three of them, mean-looking, one had a shaved head. So he walked in the opposite direction. The street could turn dangerous—cops, punks, psychos like that guy who'd wanted to see his back. Was that kid he'd warned about the weirdo okay? On these streets you were the only one who knew who you were, and that meant bad things could happen to you and no one would know or care. Fuck, you could fuckin' die, man, and nobody would know.

Clint

EARLY NIGHT

He tossed on the bed. If I could get up, place a towel on my face, to cool— He fell into deep, dark sleep.

The phone rang. "Norman?" His closest friend, the only one who knew he was in Los Angeles.

"I've worried about you, Clint. You seemed troubled when you left. You're all right?"

"Yes, of course. Yes." He was cool again. He felt resurrected after the deep sleep he'd fallen into. "Your voice sounds strange, Norman."

"—terrible news. His sister called me just before I dialed you—"

"What?" Clint tried to register the words Norman had spoken.

"—Troy Lawrence, yes. He died—"

Troy—dead? One of the most vibrant presences on the scene, one of the handsomest, in discos, bars, orgy rooms, Fire Island in summer. "An accident?"

"No. A strange kind of cancer—pneumonia first. His sister wasn't entirely clear. Apparently he was sick a long time and stayed away so no one could see him because he lost so much weight. I keep remembering how proud he was of his beautiful body. Remember?"

"Yes." Clint remembered the time they had been together after seasons of silent courtship. "Troy? Dead?"

"Yes. Dead. At thirty-five."

NEW YORK
A Year Ago

Clint met him in Fire Island.

Like so many others populating the gay horizon, Troy was very handsome, lean, hard-muscled—the "great beauty" everyone desired and talked about. He conveyed a sense of contagious sexual delirium, augmented by his constant use of uppers—the best coke, the strongest amyl—and downers, when sleep was demanded.

That year, Clint and Troy kept running into each other in New York. Both attractive and desirable, they began a silent game to see who would approach first—at the usual places. Studio 54 was for dancing, doing drugs, arranging late-night liaisons, with several, or making out briefly, there, among glamorous bodies in decorated nudity. St. Mark's Baths was for private encounters in rented cubicles, or for orgies. The Penitent was for exotic parties—all black leather, all white costumes, fore-play for orgies scattering into the night.

And the two men ran into each other, that same year, at the Museum of Modern Art. It was at the Picasso retrospective. Clint stood staring at the artist's "Guernica" when he noticed that, among others there, Troy, too, was gazing at the same mural of anguished bodies. As if they had caught each other in an unwelcome interlude, they turned away without even cursory acknowledgement.

That season in Fire Island, two summers ago, Clint had gone to cruise the stretch of sand and foliage known as the Meat Rack. Troy was emerging from a sexual encounter with several men—all now moving on to others. This time, Clint and Troy nodded to each other. At the Ice Palace, the late-night emporium, they maneuvered to dance near each other but with different partners throughout the late night.

On the beach the next day, Clint saw Troy appear over a crest of sand. Facing the strip of beach claimed by gay men and a few women, Troy stood there, tall, tanned, aware of the admiring, desiring, and envying looks he always collected. Having gathered them, he removed his trunks, tossed his towel over his shoulders, and walked naked up to Clint.

"When are we going to fuck?" he asked him.

Clint said, "Now. Here?"

"Yes."

They did, but in Clint's rented bungalow. Troy preferred to be fucked, and Clint preferred to fuck—but the frenzy that withheld desire had aroused demanded no qualification of roles. Breathing coke, inhaling poppers, they kissed, blew each other. Clint fucked Troy, then Troy fucked Clint, and then they changed positions again, and then again. They alternated all afternoon, resting in between.

As Clint began to doze, Troy sat up, staring in the direction of the ocean on this pristine day. "This is all there is, love—just sex and more sex and still more sex. That's all God gave only us—and to no one else—to compensate for all the shit they keep throwing at us. It's the only thing that blocks it all out, isn't it?" He touched his beautiful body, and then Clint's, as if to assert the reality of flesh. "That's all some of us have," he said to himself. "When that's gone—for some of us, there will be nothing."

No, that isn't all we have. It *can't* be, Clint thought, but didn't speak that aloud because Troy had become moodily silent.

"At times," Troy continued after staring into a vague distance, "I think cruising—sex—saves some of us from despair."

"Would you die for it, for sex?" Clint asked him, smiling to soften the edge of his words.

Troy said, "If you asked me that when I had a cock in my mouth and a cock up my ass, I would know that, yes, I would. If you asked me afterwards, I might reconsider." He laughed, erasing seriousness.

That night they ran into each other at the Ice Palace. As if there had been no intimacy between them, they looked away, thwarting any further intimacy—the silent courtship had been too long, the sexual encounter had been complete, and an unexpected vulnerability had been exposed.

The next season, earlier this summer, Troy did not appear in Fire Island. Clint heard rumors—that he had settled down with a French lover—no, an Italian—that he had moved back home to South Dakota—no, to Utah—"some odd place like that—imagine?" Someone said he had retired to write "a slim—*very* slim—pamphlet about the handsome men he *hasn't* slept with—yet."

Now Troy was dead.

In his hotel room in Los Angeles, Clint felt a surge of sexual desire. He drew from his unpacked suitcase a fresh bag of cocaine he had brought with him, carried always in reserve. He snorted from it, again, more. The sexual urgency increased, an urgency to push away death—and to expiate the judgment of the face of the man in Sag Harbor—and to do both with an assertive act of *living,* with sex—lust and desire, yes—but not what it had twisted into, what he had seen that long night in New York, punishment for desire, sex that was no longer sex.

He forced himself to get up. He showered, did not shave, touching the stubble that framed his face. He breathed more of the coke, more, until he felt his body jolt into bold alertness. He dressed in jeans, shirt open over a white sleeveless undershirt, low boots, a uniform suited for the hunt without signaling any faction. He had brought no leather garments with him.

At a chic, loud restaurant near the hotel, he couldn't eat.

He drove the rented Mustang to Santa Monica Boulevard. He parked on a side street. He walked long blocks. The Sant'Ana wind hushed eerily, then resurged with new power.

Hundreds of men were out on this sweaty night. So many men, so many beautiful the way only gay men could be, men who emphasized their sensuality. Many shirtless—flaunting defiant, defined bodies, some posing as cowboys, bikers—they strutted by, displaying the new masculinity that was entirely gay. Everyone seemed happy, euphoric, laughing, sitting in outdoor restaurants, standing outside bars, laughing, walking or standing along streets, laughing—laughing that laughter that he had located last week in New York, mirthless laughter veering toward hysteria, and he understood it, and the look that went with it, that reflected a sad frantic weariness even when the face smiled, an inherited weariness that came from the knowledge of a troubled journey ahead—"all the shit they keep throwing at us," Troy had said—a journey already charted, but not by them.

The sexual urgency he felt wouldn't be fulfilled in crowded bars.

Removing his shirt, leaving on the undershirt to cling to his body, Clint prepared to cruise the alleys of West Hollywood that thrived, especially on weekends, even before the bars closed.

Men flowed along a row of dark garages. A good-looking man passed Clint, stared back, moved into a garage. Pants lowered, cock hard, the man squatted against the garage. Clint stood before him. The man pulled Clint's cock out, licked his balls, under his balls, then sucked him. Clint felt his urgent cum shoot into the other's throat, deep down.

The other man stood up. At other times, Clint would have walked away—he had come—and that would be understood. Now he lowered himself before the other man, whose pants remained opened, and he sucked the still hard cock. He needed to feel life surging into him. Moaning softly, arching his body, the man came in Clint's throat, warm cum coursing into the depths of his body.

Ernie
EARLY NIGHT

The arrest he had seen had sent his mood crashing. He had left Griffith Park immediately, and knew he would *definitely* not go out tonight. The hot day had turned bad.

In his apartment he watched television, looked through a porn magazine, ate a tuna sandwich, took a shower, had some potato chips, and made a firm decision.

Hey! He'd call friends to come over!

He had lots of friends. Sometimes they went out together to a gay Mexican restaurant—why did gay guys like Mexican food so much?—and commented on cute waiters or customers. *They* did, he didn't. He didn't like too much idle cruising when he went out. He wasn't a swivel head like some guys who *never* stopped cruising, right?—like one friend of his, who'd whistle out loud if any attractive guy came in.

Sure, that was it. He'd call a few friends, he'd go out and buy some dips 'n' chips and a few cold ones. Sure. The guys'd be over in *no* time.

In no time—

"Ernie! Great idea! How many did you invite? Seven's an orgy. More than that is a mess."

"Jeezus, Sam, I didn't call you over to have a goddamn orgy. Hey, we're all just friends, right?"

"Which means we don't fuck each other. I know. Here's James. Hi, sweetie. I heard you broke up with Milo. Sor-ree."

"Milo? I broke up with him ages ago, and you know that, Sam. I just broke up with Tony."

"Oops!"

"Put on a little weight, huh, Ern?"

"Yeah—five pounds, all muscle, James."

"Hmmmm. Anything wrong with your teeth, Sam? You keep picking at them. Got something caught there? A hair?"

Just imagining how it would go made Ernie say, Fuck it, especially since, afterwards, they'd want to go out cruising and leave him with all the paper plates and soggy dips. For sure they wouldn't want to waste this hot night on friends. Oh, no, all they wanted was to go out and fuck their brains out—and so did he.

Mitch
EARLY NIGHT

Mitch remained parked where the motorcyclist and that handsome kid had spoken to him, in the alley and against the wire fence bordering a section of the small park there. Had he imagined that the kid had been referring to him when he shouted, "Him!" to the motorcyclist?—if that's what he had said. What had the motorcyclist meant when he called back—and Mitch was sure of this—"Over there, later!"—pointing to the shed they had gone to in the park?—as if they were scouting—
   For what?
   Mitch saw figures disappearing into mesmerized shadows. They moved as if in some entranced dance, gliding, pausing, all men—like at the darkened beach earlier.
   Leaving his car parked against the wire fence, he got out. He walked along, trying to locate the entrance to the park. No entrance here? Where? Not here either. Where! He clenched the wire fence, shaking it, as if to tear it open.

Dave
EARLY NIGHT

"Cummon, dude, we're wasting time."
   The kid stood by the side of the motorcycle. He bent over and leaned his head on Dave's shoulder,
   "What the fuck you doin'?" Dave turned his voice gruff.
   The kid nuzzled on the bare shoulder.
   Dave dropped his hand before it would touch the blond head. He revved the bike. "Now stop fuckin' around and hop on, we gotta go

choose some more hot dudes for your celebration, and then you and me've got a hot date at the last."

The kid hopped on. "Yes, *sir*!"

Sir? Yeah! Mocking? Learning?

Learning.

Nine

Into the small park in West Hollywood a hushed incursion begins, increasing as night deepens. Men sit alone within shadows, on benches, on the bleachers facing the darkened fields. They roam about paths, lawns, in and out of patchy gray light, shadows shifting within the Sant'Ana night.

The open space between the toolshed and the wired field is so hidden by then that if a police car flashes bright lights into the park, the glare will not stir the darkness there.

Jesse
EARLY NIGHT

Spooky, Jesse thought, the way the Sant'Ana stopped, just stopped, leaving all this heat. He mopped his chest with his tank top and remained shirtless as he leaned against the motorcycle he had ridden on all day. The biker, seated on it, had parked near several bars and a cruisy alley. He and Jesse were reviewing the parade of men to choose from for this night's celebration. They had already selected a few from among the hot men spilling out of nearby bars, bared flesh exposed to dark heat.

"Him," Jesse chose a young guy in shorts—jockstrap peeking out—cap cocked. "And him." A guy in tight jeans—big bulge—striped tank top.

As the two men Jesse had chosen passed by, the biker called out now-memorized lines, "*Real* hot time—that park"—pointing—"late night, tonight."

Like others, the invited men looked from the biker to Jesse, who confirmed the invitation with a great smile and a nod. He and the biker had refined the approach, the doubled attraction.

"*That* guy."

Jesse looked at the man, the first the biker had chosen by himself. He had emerged out of one of the garages. Wearing jeans and a white sleeveless undershirt, he wasn't dressed like the biker, but he looked like he belonged to the same breed, maybe even about the same age, too. The two resembled each other—no, not at all. Yeah, in an odd kind of way. For sure both were *really* hot.

"Yes, him," Jesse approved.

"Hey!" the biker called out to the man leaving the alley across the street.

The man turned, stopped, stared, as if deciding whether to walk away. Then he did.

The biker revved his bike angrily for attention.

The man turned around.

Did they know each other? Jesse wondered. Was the guy in the undershirt avoiding the biker?

The man across the street walked on to Santa Monica Boulevard.

"Hop on, dude," the biker told Jesse.

Jesse jumped on. Something between those two guys—

They caught up with the man who had emerged from the alley. The biker rode by slowly, parallel to him. "*Real* hot night—over there." This time, he had spoken those words in a kind of quiet way, almost timid, Jesse thought, and as if he really wanted to say more to him.

The man looked away from the biker and looked at Jesse.

Jesse smiled, his most irresistible smile.

The biker revved up the bike, and they drove off.

"I know a coupla places we can go scout for some tough dudes," he said.

As they drove past men lingering along the street, Jesse wasn't sure how many guys they'd already invited to his celebration. Some would tell others.

Buzz, Fredo, and Boo
EARLY NIGHT

"Whatya doin'?'" Boo asked.

"Christ!" Fredo said.

Buzz was trying to make a U-turn in the middle of Santa Monica Boulevard. "That queer threw a bottle at us and I'm gonna go back and kill 'im." He thrust his upraised finger at cars honking.

"Traffic's too tight," Boo said. "The fag'll be gone by the time you turn."

"That shit queer," Fredo said. "Did you see him—standing there almost naked? That's a fuckin' sin." He crossed himself.

"The fag'd be gone if we went back," Buzz agreed. He steered back onto the Boulevard. "Fuckin' car you hotted don't have air-conditioning, and it's fuckin' hot. When'd the wind stop?" He held his hand out the window.

The wind had stopped. Trees along the Boulevard and beyond braced, upright, for its possible return. The ring of fire about the City settled there, an unmoving dark glow.

"If we stay away for a while, that guy at the corner'll come back," Fredo said, "cause he was hustling. Some of them ain't queer, go for bread. I know a guy did that kinda shit, and he ain't queer, just gets picked up and robs the fags."

"They're *all* fags," Buzz dismissed. They rode along the upper part of the Boulevard, West Hollywood, where they had driven earlier, up and down, braking before gay bars to shout and threaten.

"You know where lots of them go late at night?" Fredo asked.

"Where?" Buzz demanded.

"A small park." Fredo rubbed his shaved head excitedly. "The guy I told you about, who robs queers—he goes there."

"Where is it?" Buzz clutched the board from the crate he had smashed.

Father Norris
EARLY NIGHT

"Your mother—," Father Norris said to the young man, who sat on the bed in the rented room.

The boy removed his shoes, which, Father Norris noticed, were worn. "I don't have no mother." The boy did not look up.

Father Norris understood. The boy had to deny connections in the world in which he was now existing.

His socks in his hands, the boy looked up at Father Norris. "Naked—?"

Father Norris nodded.

The boy took off his pants, he wore no shorts. He reached for his shirt, began slipping it off—

Father Norris closed his eyes. He did not want to see yet. Not yet. Not too soon. He allowed moments to pass.

When he opened his eyes, Father Norris saw the boy lying on the rumpled green bedspread, naked, one leg propped up, the other dangling on the floor, his hand cupping his groin.

"Now what do you want me to do?" the boy asked.

So innocent, so eager to surrender to salvation. Father Norris clasped his hands before him, touching his lips in the attitude of prayer. "Your back, Ahn-hel."

The room was silent. Had the wind stopped? Yes, as if everything was now entranced.

The boy started to twist over on the bed. He paused. "You'll have to go easy, man. Put it in slow and use a lot of spit if you don't have lube with you. If I say stop, stop till I say okay, and then go slow." He turned over, parting his buttocks with his hands.

Father Norris did not hear the boy's words—just sounds. He had closed his eyes, had clasped his hands before him as if in prayer. Prepared to gasp, he opened his eyes now.

There was nothing on the boy's back! No tattoo—nothing!

Father Norris reared back fiercely from the boy.

"What's the matter, man?" The boy sat up, facing him.

Father Norris gasped. His voice turned into choked groans. "The naked Christ—*where*? *Where!*" The groan of anger became a sustained sob. His eyes blurred with perspiration or tears. His hands tore apart from their prayerful position. He advanced on the boy. "*Where!*"

The boy backed away, slipping off the bed, pulling back. "If you try any shit, motherfucker, I'll shout and the guy downstairs'll be up in no time."

"You deceived me!" Father Norris wailed into the room, beyond the room. "You deceived me!" He sat on the bed, rubbing his face. "You deceived me," he whispered.

He was alone. The boy had run out of the room, his shoes and socks left behind.

Father Norris remained motionless on the bed. Who was that woman who had come to the confessional this morning?—so commanding, so ominous. Had he imagined her? A vision of doom, of something terrible approaching—

Whatever he had to do, wherever he had to go, whomever he had to ask, follow, track, pursue, whatever he had to do within this charged territory he had entered, he would find the naked Christ tonight.

Za-Za and the Cast of *Frontal Assault*
THAT AFTERNOON AND EARLY NIGHT

As she joined the others rushing away from the threat of fire, Za-Za heard a booming voice and turned back to see Smythe on his veranda, refusing to move, challenging *anything* to burn his mansion, and shouting—

"The flames *will* shift, they always do."

"Silly queen, mad queen!" Za-Za shouted back. She forced her full attention on reaching her car.

Ah-ha! Tony Piazza, clutching pants and shoes, was running past her. She grabbed him. "You little slut, I should leave you here to burn, but you're coming with me."

"Let go of me, you fat queen!"

That did it! Za-Za clasped his shorts even more tightly and shoved him ahead of her. "Into the car! I drove you here, and I'm driving you away."

"You didn't drive me here, I came with Jim Bond—"

"—who's already gone, in case you didn't notice." They were outside the gate. Cars driven by naked and only partially clothed performers were almost running into each other, skidding back, dashing into the road. Za-Za pushed Tony Piazza into her car.

"Ouch!" He grabbed for the door.

"You get out and you'll have to walk through flames," she warned him. He sat back, sulking.

Minutes later they were at a standstill. Cars crept down the hill, an exodus from other nearby homes. Fire engines cluttered lanes. Water spouted out of giant hoses held by men in yellow uniforms. Police guided vehicles down the hills, motioned directions to television crews.

Like a giant premiere, Za-Za thought as she reached over with her arm—and left it there—to assert that Tony Piazza remained in place. "You jump out, Tony Piazza, and I swear I'll run over you," she promised.

It took forever to maneuver out of the bottleneck and onto the blocked highway. Once they did—and the sky had darkened—they were stuck again near the freeway, cars unmoving. When disaster struck, the whole City, connected by freeways, was ambushed. Za-Za turned on the radio. Clyde Barnes, the station's "Rhymin' Weatherman," always inebriated, had been enlisted to report on this emergency. "—has burned two homes in one of the wealthiest sections of the City. Spared, however, when flames shifted to another property, was Studio Mogul Dick Gellman's mansion. 'I knew the flames would not touch my estate,' Gellman, who had been entertaining, was quoted. In another—"

Za-Za turned off the radio. That mad old queen had been spared, along with her mansion. Where was the justice? Never mind, now the silly old queen would be around to see her soar to the top of the heap of *auteurs,* and be so regretful she'd *wish* she had vanished in flames.

It was dark when they reached their destination, Za-Za's small, smart house located in the cul-de-sac up from Beachwood Drive in Hollywood— a house where, the Realtor had sworn, Greta Garbo's personal lighting man had once lived and the great aloof star had stayed over frequently.

Za-Za prodded Tony Piazza up to the entrance. "Run off and you'll be miles away from where you want to go." She knew he loved to make "personal appearances" in the many cruising areas of the City.

She paused. The hot wind had stopped. The only evidence that it had raged was the stifled heat left behind, and torn palm fronds piling, criss-crossed, not even quivering now, dead.

With her urging him on, Tony Piazza walked in petulantly, and sat down in her favorite chair, a giant puffed mushroom that seemed to embrace him—the way she would like to, dammit, but mustn't, although, God, she longed to. Look at him still in his briefs, deliberately not bothering to dress.

She sat before him on a *moderne antiquité,* a sofa striped black and white. She tried to drape one arm over the chair's jutting angles, but it slipped, snaring her pose. She'd make do. She held her hand lightly to a brow she hoped had remained arched.

"What happened at Smythe's mansion—," she began.

"I was performing. I'm a star."

"A star! You are *not* a star. Garbo was a star, Bogart was a star, Hedy Lamarr was a star, Gable was a star, and Bacall and Elizabeth Taylor are the *only* stars left. *You* are *not* a star."

"Yes, I am," Tony Piazza said.

"You're a piece of trash I tried to salvage!"

"I'm a star," Tony Piazza insisted.

Za-Za relented, somewhat. "Whatever you are, who made you?" The way Welles reshaped Rita Hayworth, and Norma Jeane created Monroe.

"Me."

"Why, you thankless little sow—"

"Huh? What the hell is a—?"

"—sow! A sow!" Sow? Where did that word come from? Oh, yes, in *The Exorcist,* that's how Satan, the voice of the great Mercedes McCambridge, referred to the possessed girl, that unforgettable line. "The sow is my-iiiine." Why had she thought of that? Whatever. "Ungrateful sow!" she reiterated.

"Okay, okay, so you helped me along."

"Helped you along? I *sponsored* you, changed your gaudy look, made you shed your baby flesh, weaned you off Tootsie Rolls, encouraged you to work out. I took you to Bob of Transcend—in Los Feliz!—where *real* movie stars go to get their hair done."

"Hey, that's where Rex Steed says he goes. You *never* took me there, Za-Za. I begged you to take me to Bob of Transcend, remember?"

"I gave you a gorgeous place to stay—here, where Garbo once lived. Herman Marcus, I even renamed you."

"Huh?"

The dumb, divinely gorgeous slut probably didn't even remember his true name. Or had that been somebody else's name? "I took you away from the streets, where you would have disappeared like all the others after one summer."

"Oh, yeah? Yeah?"

Obviously he was struggling to think of something to say. "Yes—and I put you in my erotic films, turned you into a star"—oops—"into a *performer*—"

"See, you said I was a star, and you don't make erotic films, Za-Za, you make porn—and I made money for you, and I bet you'll get paid much more than I will for today—"

True.

"—and, Za-Za, you're just a pimp, ya know?"

Hmmmmm. "And you're just a whore."

"Right. I'm a whore and you're a pimp who sells *our* flesh."

How to argue? "Yes! As long as your flesh stays young, trollop, and then you'll be through while I go on—grandly!"

"Right again, Za-Za. You think I don't know that?"

"What?" He had startled her.

"Think I don't know that everything'll end for me in a few years? Fuck, I'll be around only as long as people want my ass. You'll go on, Za-Za, there'll always be young guys to use in your porn. Think I don't worry about what's gonna happen to me?"

"What?" He had startled her again.

"Shit, Za-Za, sometimes I think about suicide, y'know?"

What! "You—?" No, she would not listen, not allow her heart-strings to be tugged. True, there were always newer bodies. But didn't she always introduce the ones on the way out to rich fans who had desired them for ages and might still see them as they had been—for a while? Of course she felt sorry for the ones who were out, like Wes Young, and those—most of them—that she never saw again. They were all self-destructive anyway. Whose fault was that? Not hers. It wasn't as if she didn't have compassion. She always kept a white baggy in reserve for those who came to her in need, to get them through. Obviously, she couldn't lend them money or they'd keep coming back demanding it. So who could blame her? Who? No one! "I provided you the best coke."

"You got some?"

Greedy harlot. "No! I opened doors for you—"

"—you got me johns, yeah. But you always got a big cut, Za-Za, don't forget that. You make money from us, and you don't have to do anything. *We* do."

The sow was gaining *some* ground. Za-Za snorted a pinch of coke, spooning it carefully with a tiny silver spoon—from India?—out of a little crystal *affaire* shaped like a hand and kept on a plastic table like a twisted tube.

"Cummon, Za-Za, let me have a taste."

"No." She deliberated. "All right."

He snorted, twice in each nostril. Then again.

Like a sow. "I had bigger plans for you. When I become a big Hollywood director—you may have seen me and Mr. Smythe discoursing about this—"

"Yeah?"

Oh, *that* interested him. "*Then* I intended to make you a *real* star, like—uh—" Whom would he know, the stupid magnificent shit? "—like—James Dean!"

"Dean!" He slouched on the couch. "Yeah, I—"

"But now—"

"Listen, Za-Za, let's make up, okay?"

He stood up, his briefs bulging at the groin.

Hypnotized, Za-Za's eyes didn't budge from there for long seconds. She forced herself to look away. Then back. Had he fingered her stash box in that brief moment? Impossible.

"I don't even know why you're so pissed at me, Za-Za."

He just stood there, enticing, the dazzling slut.

"You don't? Because all these months I've—" Longed for you, dreamt about you, imagined you, every time I saw someone fucking you, I wished that *you* were fucking *me*—and—because—I've—come—to—love—you—have I, *really*? "Because all these months I've groomed you as the best-known bottom in erotic films, and then all Rex Steed had to do was open his fucking big legs, and you—"

"I wanted to expand my horizons."

Expand his horizons? Where had he heard that? "Expand your fuckin' asshole!" she yelled at him.

"You're pissed because I never fucked you."

What to answer?

"Za-Za—" He walked over to her, putting his hand on her shoulder. "Za-Za, I do have feelings for you."

"You do? Really?" She hadn't intended to answer so quickly, certainly not to sound pleading, eager. But she had, oh, she had.

"A lot."

"Really?" She had to stop saying that.

"A real lot."

"Really?" Oh, this would make a bad script. She didn't care, didn't care at all. Of course it was true. In his own way he had loved her all along—loved, truly, for the first time in his desolate life, and now it would all come out. She reached over to touch him, to touch the maddeningly desirable crotch.

"Za-Za," he whispered into her ear, nibbling on it.

"Yes?"

"I love you, Za-Za, I've loved you from the first. It hurt me when you put me in porn, because the only person I wanted was you, and I wanted to hurt you back because I thought *you* were keeping *me* away, and I didn't know what to do. Za-Za, would you really make me a *real* star like James Dean? I'll even try to fuck you, I swear I'll try."

"You sow!"

"What the hell *is* that?"

"You fuckin *sow!*" There was no other word. She stood, shaking. "Get your stupid ass out of here now—and you can walk to wherever the hell you're going. And you're through in porn!"

He stood defiantly before her.

Oh, he looked so beautiful.

"No, I'm not through, I can always go to Alfred Chester, be one of her stars, you're not the only porn maker, not even the best. I heard someone say your closeups of asses look like hairy cunts."

"Oh, oh, you despicable—strumpet! Get out!"

Clutching his clothes, he stood at the door pondering how to resurrect it all, pondering how to make it all right, Zaza was sure.

"I *will* get out—and fuck you, you ugly fat bitch!" He opened the door. "I'll tell you where I'm going, I'm gonna find the hottest place in the City,

John Rechy

wherever that is, and I'm just gonna fuck up a storm, and it won't be you, I'll just go out and hump and hump and hump—everyone but you."

"Sow, sow, *sow!*" Za-Za screamed, and like Vivien Leigh in *Gone With the Wind* she threw a vase at him—rejecting the first one she had grasped, a favorite *cher objet*—but he dodged before he fled in his shorts. "And don't you come back when everyone's through with you, Tony Piazza, because then *I* won't want you either!"

Then Za-Za realized that her feet hurt. Where were her shoes? She'd kicked them off, left them at Smythe's, walked through the scorched earth without feeling anything—nothing!—and those shoes had been favorites. Probably drowned in hosed water by now along with—she hoped—that silly, mad queen Smythe—she'd forgotten his real name. Well, thank God's infinite wisdom for allowing her a closet full of other wonderful shoes, just as grand. What better—more than enough!—to assuage whatever she had *ever* felt for that little sow?

Dabbing at her cheeks—where she was disappointed to find no tears—she walked to her shoe closet, an interplay of mirrored slabs slashed silver at the edges. She pushed the panels open onto a dazzling array of shoes. Before she bent down to choose among them, she thrust her head back, the way the heroic Ida Lupino did in *Hard, Fast, and Beautiful* to indicate that nothing—nothing—daunted her.

Thomas Watkins
EARLY NIGHT

He couldn't find a parking space after he'd driven away from that infernal bathhouse. He hadn't realized—until he saw men gathering, most dressed in leather, others as "cowboys," God knew what else—that there was some kind of gay place nearby.

He found a parking space and walked hurriedly. So quiet suddenly, so hot. His feet ground on dry palm fronds, like scattered bodies—he pulled away from the dreadful image and walked on. He had to see it at night, just see it.

At the mouth of the street tunnel he had fled from this afternoon, a tall man leaned against the wall, his hand over his groin. Another man walked past him, paused, touched the other's crotch, and walked up the darkened stairs. Forms entered the tunnel.

Thomas remained at its mouth. He was numb. All his feelings had been disconnected at the bathhouse. He stood waiting, for—what?

An older man, older than him, out of shape, matted black hairs clinging to his exposed oiled chest and protruding stomach, stopped near him. Thomas retreated in disgust. The man moved toward someone else pressed against the graffiti-smeared wall.

When had he taken the first step up into the tunnel? Thomas waited for his eyes to adjust to the blackness. When they did, he saw, at the top, shadows. His eyes penetrated the darkness, stabbed by shafts of street light. He could see three—no, four—four men, more, standing before a squatting form. Trying to hold his breath to avoid the stench in the tunnel, a mixture of urine and those filthy chemicals everyone carried, Thomas moved up, steadying himself.

The kneeling man was sucking several standing forms, head arcing from one penis to another, sucking, withdrawing, swallowing another. A fourth man moved down from the stairs above, his penis out. As the squatting form shifted toward the new body in the stained light, Thomas saw the face of the man kneeling.

He ran down the stairs, past other figures ready to join the bunched forms. Had he imagined it? Had he really seen the man kneeling before all those bodies, shadows, just shadows, erections, just erections, any erection?

Had he really recognized Herbert?

Orville
EARLY NIGHT

The night was calmed. The Sant'Ana had abandoned its heat, stagnant heat.

Orville and the man he had agreed to go home with, the real good-looking guy he had danced with all night, stood outside the Studio Club. The two faced each other under a streetlight. Nearby, a group of three men whispered among themselves, looked at them. Orville stared back.

The guy with him followed his stare, then turned to Orville and shook his head. "I just remembered—," he started, t   hat I have to meet someone else, that I have to get up early, that my roommate is using my apartment tonight, that I have to pick up my lover at the airport, that I promised to drive my best friend home. Orville didn't have to hear any more to know what words would follow, words of rejection that always began, "I just remembered—" He knew what had happened. The guy had recognized those three guys staring at them and that made him uneasy about being seen going off with a black guy.

Orville stalked away.

Paul
EARLY NIGHT

What the hell was wrong with that guy? They'd been together all night, danced, kissed, even talked—and then he'd just walked away like he was angry. He hadn't even let him finish telling him to wait there, follow his car—that he'd just remembered where he'd parked it. The sudden thought of Stanley angered Paul even more now. On this first night of his freedom from him—and he had gotten even harder thinking about making it with someone else on the bed he and Stanley had shared for so long—this had happened, whatever the hell had happened. He saw the guy turn, as if to come back. No, he had already crossed the street.

Some kind of misunderstanding, Paul was sure. That happened so often in cruising, signals misread, usually as some kind of rejection—so you rejected first. There hadn't been any rejection. It might still work out.

Paul walked after the black guy, who was moving ahead.

Nick
THAT NIGHT

A man stopped for him.

Nick rushed over.

"How much? All I want is to blow you and get off real quick. Twenty bucks? Short time. We'll find a street off the Boulevard."

"Yeah, sure." Nick had shouted those two words into the car, and then realized how still it was all around. The Sant'Ana had stopped, just like that. Only heat remained, unbudging.

They drove a few blocks along Santa Monica Boulevard. The man began to turn.

"Not here. I know a better place. Ahead."

They were out of hustling turf, in West Hollywood. "There's a small park somewhere around here," Nick said. "A guy told me about it earlier. It's got a baseball field, bleachers."

"I think I know where." The man drove on, turned off the Boulevard. Nick saw it, the small park.

The man was about to stop. "Looks sheltered enough."

"No, not here," Nick said. "Drive a couple more blocks. Yeah. Here. Let's do it here."

The man parked under an arcade of trees. He opened Nick's pants, lowered them, bent down, sucked his cock while jerking himself off.

"Here's the money, I'll drive you back."

"I'll just hang around here."

Clint
EARLY NIGHT

That exultant day with Troy was transformed now, the memory of desire linked with death. Had the man beaten in Sag Harbor survived? Clint felt the presence of death within the night as he walked back into the darkened strip of alleys and garages. More men—dozens, more—were joining the cruising dance, men melding into crushed shadows.

The wind had stopped. Dark heat remained, so hot it seemed to pulse, as if the night itself was coming.

This is all there is—just sex and more sex and still more sex—

No, that wasn't all, but it was what you attempted to stop terror with, and Clint felt it now, terror, a desperate, mournful yearning aroused by the specter of death, a rage to live during the short time allotted.

A man motioned with his head toward a garage. Inside, he blew Clint. Clint coaxed him up, knelt before him, and sucked him until he drew

cum into his mouth. Moans floated over the muffled night. Two men
fucked within deeper shadows in the same garage. Out of a car paused
in the alley, a head protruded toward a body pressed against an open
window. Materializing out of shadows, another mouth took Clint's cock.
Clint came as the man jerked himself off. Still coming—urgent desire
unabated—Clint bent to take the other's jetting cum into his mouth.

—the only thing that blocks it all out—

Sudden motion. People walked away, cars drove off. Two squad
cars, lights flashing, entered the cruising strip from opposite ends. One
car stopped before a garage. Two cops, one a woman, jumped out. They
rushed into the garage. They emerged with two handcuffed men.

Desire growing, Clint drove away.

Where had the motorcyclist pointed to earlier? That park? He saw
men moving into its shadows. When he had first noticed the biker
earlier, Clint had thought he was the man who had followed him
throughout the night in the Mineshaft last weekend. But he wasn't. What
had that beautiful kid been doing with him? So incongruous, those two
together—and so sensual in their disparity.

Clint made a U-turn and parked.

With his undershirt, he wiped perspiration streaming down his
chest as he made his way into the small park in West Hollywood.

Ernie
EARLY NIGHT

Ernie walked to a private cubicle he'd rented at the baths. He left his
clothes in the locker room by the entrance to the popular bathhouse.
He wrapped a towel about his waist, not too high. Getting lots of looks
already. It would be a good night at the baths.

Too bad about that old guy trying to get in earlier. He hated to see
people hurt. But, hey, didn't old guys like him know this place let in
only hunky young guys? When *he* got old—which was years and years
away—and maybe by then they'd have a pill or something—he wouldn't
want to bust in where he wasn't wanted, right?

Gorgeous bodies, stripped and almost stripped—everywhere. The
odor of amyl and butyl wafted, steam coiled about halls, into cubicles.

Ernie peered into the steam room, a dark red light allowing only silhouettes within the vapor. Arched bodies, bent heads, the usual sucking and fucking, shifting partners. Ernie didn't want to join that mess, not now, although he had once or twice.

He left the door to his cubicle open. He lay on a white sheet over the small cot, towel bunched over his cock. He put his arms back, stretched his body. He imagined how he would look to someone passing by—and stopping. Wide lats tapering, pecs outlined, round biceps, flaring thighs, full calves—

He was already hard.

Good as he looked, he hoped he wouldn't have to wait long for someone terrific. You never could tell. Sometimes you just lay there and lay there, even working yourself up, and people you would've made it with would pass by, look, move on—only God knew why—and sometimes people you didn't want came in, but—

Ernie heard footsteps approaching.

A cute guy walked in. Ernie didn't move, just flexed on the cot. Removing Ernie's towel and letting his own drop, the guy licked Ernie's arms, under them, his pecs, down, around his cock, down, down to his thighs, around his calves—great body-worshiper! Ernie still didn't move, continued to hold his flex. Now the tongue brushed around his cock, then under, licking his ass, staying there—and then the mouth moved to his cock and the lips opened and the mouth sank down—

Ernie eased the head away. He didn't want to come yet. The cute guy understood, reached for his own towel and walked out.

More footsteps.

Hey! He'd try this. Leaving the towel off, he turned over on his stomach. He closed his eyes.

Someone entered the cubicle, waited, waited— Ernie raised his ass. Legs straddled him.

Keeping his eyes shut, he imagined what the guy looked like— great bod, lots of muscles, tousled hair—brown hair—body gleaming with clean sweat—he felt drops of it on his bare buttocks. A big cock lingering over his opening—rubbin', teasin' around—hands spreadin' his ass—large hands. Thighs brushed with hair—he felt the furry flesh—flanking him. Fingers parting his ass, one finger poking in. Now the muscular body—terrific pecs, look at those deltoids, got a small tattoo there?—would be about to enter, the guy staring down at the rounded ass waitin' to be fucked—yeah, and he wore cowboy boots and nothing else. No, a cowboy hat and nothing else. A cowboy hat and boots and nothing else—lookin' great with all those muscles, cowboy! He felt the cock at his opening, and he girded. Go! What was the guy waiting for? Oh, sure, uncircumcised, like him, peeling the skin back from the shaft, head emerging, a dot of moisture at the tip, cock throbbing over puckered asshole—workin' it good for ya—yeah, shove it in—feel it, ya feel it?—hold it—okay, go in. The cock slipped out. Hands—muscular arms, triceps really cut, veins stark—clasped it, aiming in, the guy's butt raised, ready to hump down—ah!—cock buried into hole huggin' it, releasing it, hugging tighter—

Ernie's eyes remained closed. The body over him would be preparing to arch, long leg muscles stretched, feet clamped down to push in harder—in!—up, down, up, down, bare butt hunched over bare butt—fuck me, fuck me—cowboy with boots comin'—head flung back, great ass, great fuck, hold it, go—Ernie heard a groan, and felt hot cum filling him, way in.

Then the guy walked away—Ernie heard the muffle of bare feet—no boots?—but the sculpted torso—wearing boots—would pause to look back at the great ass he'd just fucked, ass shiny with clean male sweat, a dot of cum squeezing out.

Someone else came in.

Ernie did not turn around—did not open his eyes—lay there.

The new guy would be *real* handsome, dark hair barely receding, that studdy macho look that went with his square jaw, didn't smile big, only sideways. Hairy guy, a dark T on his chest trickling down to his crotch, heavy triangle there. Ernie felt matted body hairs sliding back and forth. What was—? Oh, yeah, the guy was wearing a jockstrap—snap it, jock—round beer-can cock poking out of the pouch to probe the hole, entering—I wanya to feel it, ya feel it?—yeah, jam it in—one heavy ball popping out of the strap. Fuck me, fucker, fuck me deep—

Feet. Someone else entering the cubicle. Ernie shut his eyes tighter and raised his head, mouth open, over the edge of the cot. A cock brushed his lips, college-wrestler's cock. Bulky guy, great neck, butch haircut, like that since high school. Cock teasin' open mouth—wrestle ya for a blow

job—slapping around his face—ya wannit, ya wannit?—while the guy
with the hairy chest and the jockstrap just barely on fucked the hell out
of him, and Ernie clasped his butt, let go, pulled the cock back in, and
the hairy guy put his hands behind his neck, showing dark pits, smudges
of hair—lick 'em—a trickle of sweat running down his chest—follow it
with your tongue, lickit—while the wrestler's cock poked about his face,
thick thighs against his head—muscular thighs, almost too big—headlock, headlock, whoa—wrestler's hands guiding his mouth to heavy
balls—great balls, round balls, bounce them in your hand, stud, got one
in my mouth, gimme the other one. His tongue flitted out where it was
moved by the tattooed arm—got a panther there?—moved under his legs,
to his ass, a brush of hair along the parting—rim my hole—yeah, lickin'
the champ's ass—whoa!—champ turning around to shove his cock into
my mouth, one stroke, in, in—choke on it—whoa, buddy—gag—shove
it in all the way in, deep throat, deep throat.

The hairy guy with the jockstrap—he tore it off before he came—
spurted inside his ass just as the wrestler's cock—he lit a cigarette at
that moment and let it dangle from his lips real tough—jetted into his
throat, and—

Hey, Lars!

Ernie lay there until he heard feet moving out. He didn't open his
eyes for long seconds.

When he did, he sat up. Great! Three—four!—ideal guys! Perfect.
He dressed, walked back into the night.

Christ, it was hotter now that the weird Sant'Ana had stopped.

Damn! *He* hadn't come.

Mitch
EARLY NIGHT

Mitch looked at his bruised hand. In his urgency to find the entrance
to the park, he had clenched the bordering wire so tight that a piece of
his skin had torn off. He'd returned to his car by the wired fence. He'd
pressed his palms against his handkerchief. Now the handkerchief lay,
bloodied, next to him as he waited. Did he *want* to join the shadows in
that park?

No.

He started his car.

Yes.

He turned off the motor. He got out. When had the Sant'Ana blown over, leaving the night drenched in heat?

This time he found an entrance easily. Of course, it faced the street. He moved in. There were even more men cruising the shadow-splotched park than he had determined from the alley. It was suddenly familiar, this new world, as if he had walked through it in a dream, along these paths, or others like them, had seen these strangers, or others like them, and, like in a dream, everything, even what he saw move, seemed to have halted. The Sant'Ana had left not even an echo of its fading howls.

Dave
NIGHT

"Him!"

"That's enough," Dave told the kid as they rode back onto Santa Monica Boulevard. "We gotta start, dude."

"Wild!"

Dave could *feel* the kid's excitement, could feel his stiff cock behind him—and the kid had a real good one—and his own cock hardened, even more, if possible, considering that it had remained at least semi-hard throughout the hours he and this goddamned sexy dude had driven around the City collecting guys for his celebration. Crazy, yeah! Oh, man, *real* crazy!

In minutes, they were back at the park in West Hollywood, in the lot adjacent to it. In one parked car—Dave rode right beside it—there were three young dudes. With the kid holding on to his waist, Dave paused his bike beside them. The three guys were tense—maybe here for the first time, waiting to join. That excited Dave, and this did, too, that the dudes in the car were already trying to appear tough, to assume the kind of look that took years to perfect, a look like his. They stared at him from within the shadows of the car. Admiring him, yeah—*and* intimidated. Yeah!

Dave found a space a few cars away and parked his bike.

The kid hopped off. "Comin' with me?"

"Sure, kid." Dave dismounted.

They made their way across the small park—past men already cruising around—past the bleachers, the baseball field, along shadowy paths, past the basketball court.

The kid stopped before the merry-go-round. No one else there yet. He put his hand on its railing, as if to spin it about and hop on it.

"Don't fuck around!" Dave warned.

The kid smiled at him, and they moved toward the toolshed.

Removing his shoes, the kid almost ran to the mouth of the open corridor between the squat building and the wire enclosing the adjacent field. There, he stood under a shaft of light, darkness pushing at its edges.

"Remember, dude," Dave whispered into his ear—not wanting to incite anyone yet—and he heard his own heart pounding, "*I'll* be the last."

"O-*kay*! Hot and wild and lust-*ee*!" the kid said.

The kid faced the wall and leaned his body, hands out, against the bricks of the toolshed. Dave took the tank top the kid had carried draped over his shoulders. Reaching in front of him, he unbuttoned the kid's cutoffs. He could feel the kid's perspiration and stiff cock against the cool brick wall as he slipped the cutoffs down, exposing the kid's bare buttocks. The kid raised one foot, then the other, and Dave flung the cutoffs aside on the dirt. Cracking an ampule of amyl, which in the stilled night snapped like a tiny bullet, Dave held it in the kid's nostrils. The kid inhaled, inhaled.

Dave shoved the ampule into his own nose. Keeping it there, he bent down before the kid's buttocks. Then he pushed his tongue deep into the hole, moistening it in round, jabbing licks, his mouth adding spittle.

"You're ready," he said to the kid, and stood up. "Now you'll have some of me in you all night."

"*Wild!*" the kid said, excited.

Before he moved away, as they had planned—he would return only for the last of the celebration, the best, him and the kid—Dave looked back.

Under the wedge of light abandoned there, the kid's naked body—beautiful, Dave thought, Jesus, what a beautiful kid he is—leaned at a slant against the wall, and waited.

Ten

Everything—palm trees, distant pines, litter—was locked in the stilled night. Discarded by the Sant'Ana, dark heat lay on the streets like a festering corpse.

He was alone now. Jesse's throat tightened with anticipation. Leaning against the wall of the toolshed, he felt hotter than the night, hotter than desire, hotter than lust, as if it was all one. He was aware—because his ears strained to hear every sound—that forms were beginning to stir, footsteps closer. Once they moved past the knot of darkness, seeping light would reveal him, and his celebration would begin.

Mitch passed cruising shadows in the park. His steps slowed to meld with the stirred silence. He felt eyes on him. He made his way toward the merry-go-round, a slide, swings—idle props that deepened his sense of waking into a dream.

A patch of dirt, a bench under a hovering tree—

The toolshed a few feet away—

The place the biker had indicated—

But where was—? Mitch heard breathing from a hollow of darkness. He moved in closer.

Jesuschrist!

Within a smear of light, a naked young man faced the wall, hands against the toolshed. Mitch gasped, but he heard no sound.

The naked body turned.

The handsome kid he'd seen with the biker, the kid he'd been looking for.

Jesse saw the man he'd chosen in the alley next to the abandoned field. The guy looked hot but unsure. His first time at wild stuff? Great! Just right to begin the celebration with. Jesse reached back with his hands and parted his own buttocks.

Footsteps! Mitch turned toward the sound. A shirtless, muscular man had emerged out of encircling darkness. Mitch ran—no, felt himself running out of the park, but he had not moved, was stalled within a real dream—in which he moved now—felt himself move—saw himself ap-proach—knew he had approached—the naked body, close, closer—

Jesse guided the hard cock into him.

Mitch felt himself enter the young man.

Ernie watched as the clean-cut guy fucked the kid against the wall.

Mitch jerked, spurting inside the young man.

Jesse held him, tightly, to draw out fully the night's first burst of cum.

Mitch withdrew, feeling a surge of exhilaration, as if this orgasm had been accumulating for years.

His celebration had begun! Jesse looked back. The shirtless mus-cular guy was readying his cock, spitting on it. Him, yes. Wild!

Ernie approached the naked body. A few drops of the other guy's cum had moistened the crack, but there was much more inside, hot cum. That aroused him more. Damn, this was a *real* fantasy! But was it enough yet?

Mitch hurried along shaded paths. Exhilaration was punctured by panic, which grew into greater exhilaration, greater panic, greater ex-citement— So many men here, all available, so many men, but would there be enough time to make up for all those years before? So many men, so much desire— He fused into other shadows roaming the park.

Ernie saw two hunky guys watching him and the naked kid. If those guys—look at their mean cocks ready—if they fucked the kid first, there'd be even more cum in him to mix with his. Nothing wrong with helping a fantasy along when what was going on wasn't enough. He spread the kid's ass, inviting one of the two aroused guys to enter the kid. One did—in one sure jab—while the other bent down and blew Ernie, and he let him for a while.

When the first guy gasped and pulled out of the kid, Ernie eased away the guy blowing him, raised him up by the shoulders, bent down and sucked his cock a few strokes, then stood up and turned him around, leading the stiff cock to the kid's ass.

Jesse reached back and took the other guy inside. Great—even the night was contributing its heat. At the end of it, he'd be ready for the biker, the wildest!

Ernie stood next to the guy fucking the kid, stood there prodding him forward and back, adding to the awareness he needed for his fantasy, lots of fuckin', lots of cum. The guy bolted, came, pulled out, still spilling. Ernie fingered a few drops of cum that had remained on the kid's ass, and he wiped them onto his own cock. All those cocks shootin' jiz into the ass he was gonna fuck, all that cum in there waiting for his— He'd get this fantasy goin' even better. He looked around—two other guys there. He'd let them shoot before he went in. His cock brushed the kid's flesh, and he spouted clumsily all over.

Jesse reached back, pushing the cum into himself. He coaxed another cock in—

Shit. Ernie wiped cum off his pants, wasted cum. His terrific fantasy had been ruined before it had shaped. He wouldn't let it be ruined. He'd hang around, get hot again, come back—mix even more cum. Fantasy gettin' better all the time.

Two tough-looking guys—them, Jesse chose—pulled away the man who was still inside the naked body. They turned the kid around roughly. They licked his body, up, down, took turns blowing him, blew each other, rimmed the kid together—wild, wild—probed his ass with fingers—hot, lusty—rubbed saliva in to prepare him for the cock piercing him, and then there was another, two cocks alternating every few strokes. A third?— the guy he had just nodded to? Wilder than he had anticipated. More!

A tall man advanced from the periphery of the toolshed.

Him, Jesse chose.

The tall man held a vial of amyl to his own nose, then to the kid's. Jesse inhaled. Not enough. He inhaled again. Not enough. More— The gasps of amyl ganged up in a series of heated throbs.

The man fucked the kid, keeping the bottle of amyl stuffed into his own nose—cock in, out, in, deep in—

"Fuck me!"

"I'll fuck the hell outta ya, ya teasin' motherfucker!" the tall man said as he came.

All *right*! A little rough talk. O-*kay*! More!

Before he moved away, the tall man spat on the kid's ass.

Orville made his way into the park from a street. He walked across, heading toward his car in the farther lot. He slowed, he looked back. He thought he saw the guy he had wanted to go home with earlier. Following him here? No, couldn't be. He saw only shadows. What was happening over there by that toolshed?

Three men—Jesse recognized two from outside one of the bars where he and the biker had recruited—enclosed the naked body. Bare flesh clustered within stabs of amyl and heat, popped ampules passed around, mouths on mouths, mouths on cocks, cocks, hands, mouths— Jesse guided a cock into him, bent to suck another—felt cum spurting inside his ass, in his mouth, on his thighs— "Fuck me!" he breathed, and he felt the night cloak him in heat.

In the parking lot on the far end of the small park, Buzz opened the door of the stolen car and stepped out with his club. Boo and Fredo followed with theirs.

By the toolshed, three men grappled over the kid. One spun him around, they fell, and he forced the kid's head down on his cock, another cock joining, both cocks crammed into the kid's mouth—

Jesse inhaled amyl-drenched heat, and with his hand led one of the cocks in his mouth to his ass— A night worth waiting for! Would the biker be watching, getting hotter for him?

Groaning with desire, a heavy man shoved aside two men groping the naked body.

Jesse twisted away from the man he hadn't chosen, didn't want.

One powerful hand keeping away the men he had tossed aside, the heavy man clasped the naked body and pulled it out of deep shadows, into a larger area, against a side wall.

Jesse tried to pull away from the fierce grip.

The man fought him as he undid his belt.

Jesse tumbled to the ground, felt a foot pinion his shoulder, and then he was aware of moisture spattering his body. He rolled over on the patchy grass, kicking hard at the groin of the man urinating on him. The man flailed with his belt at the naked skin—

Orville yanked the man away from the kid. "Dirty pig!" he yelled at him.

With a whine, his mouth trying to connect with the black man's groin, the man staggered back, stumbled, fell moaning on the merry-go-round, which spun slowly about as he tried to jerk himself off.

"You all right?" Orville bent over the kid. Even while wrestling that filthy son of a bitch away, he had become aroused—had pulled his own cock out.

"Yes." Jesse wiped dirt from his body, raising himself. Nothing to be afraid of, nothing to stop his great celebration, which would continue, must continue—

"What the hell are you doing here like that?" Orville felt sad for this kid, felt hot for him, felt rage, felt desire—

"Fuck me!" Jesse chose the black man and braced against the wall.

Orville shook his head, sadness deepening, desire growing, demanding. He lunged into the naked body.

Jesse threw his hips back to receive him.

Turning the kid's head, to face him, keeping himself inside, deep, Orville whispered, "Feel my nigger cock in your goddamned white ass, boy!"—and he came in violent spasms.

Jesse's body trembled. He felt— Wild! More!

At the merry-go-round the heavy man came into his hand.

The words he had spoken resounding in his mind, Orville hurried away to leave behind the unwelcome reality of what he'd said and done. Almost halfway out of the park, he saw the man he had danced with all night at the Studio Club.

They turned away from each other.

Soggy heat clamped Jesse's flesh. In this less sheltered area, he saw himself naked in the dim light. No, he didn't feel afraid, why should he? He felt hot, hotter—

More—

Hands—he had not seen whose, had not had a chance to choose, could not tell how many—flung him back down on the ground. Mouths licked his body, his balls, his cock. A tongue jabbed into his ass. Cocks slapped his face, stinging his flesh. Hands spread his legs open, wide, wider, hurting, wider. A hand held a cracked ampule of amyl to his nose, cupping it there to enclose the rush until—

Jesse almost blacked out, as if the night had invaded him. Circles of darkness spun out, then enclosed, narrowed, and opened when he gasped. Cum squirted inside his mouth, on his face, on his ass. Shadows fled, discarding him on the dirt, a foot rolled him over. He heard a sound that was like crying. Who? A howl? *He* had not howled. He reached for someone's hand held out to him, lifting him.

"Are you okay?" Paul asked the kid.

"Yes." Jesse touched his own face, a bruise there. He felt the burn of the belt that had struck at him. He looked at the guy who had helped him up. More. Him. The celebration—

"Can I drive you home?" Paul asked.

The kid shook his head urgently.

Paul retreated from the naked body, turning away, because he had understood this kid, had seen himself there, had felt a violent craving to squash him*self* against the wall, to be entered the way this kid was being entered, over and over, to take one cock after another, up his ass, in his mouth, to block out the desolation he felt, to make up for all the years away from this exciting terrifying world— No.

He would not return. With his handkerchief, he wiped perspiration from the kid's face. Then he hurried past two men rushing toward the kid's body, hurried away through unmoving heat, to his car.

At the entrance to the park, Nick stared ahead. He had walked here after the man who had picked him up on the Boulevard had blown him in the car. He moved behind bleachers, past men inviting him with stares. What was he doing here? All these guys cruising— queers looking for each other, not hustlers. Over there on that bench, a guy blowing another, and two guys jerking each other off against that tree. Why was *he* here? He walked across lawns, farther in, toward— Looking for—

He stopped. Had a man just fucked that naked guy against a brick wall? The guy was young, good-looking, coulda been a hustler himself—tanned—no, dark—light hair—? No, dark—the street light made it look light— No— Yes. It was— Yes, it was— When had he opened his fly? He was holding his cock, and it was hard—and pressed against the naked body. He was aware of smooth, moist flesh enclosing his cock. He heard a sigh, a sob—his own—whispering, "Angel!"—and he came.

He walked, slowly, along the grass, out of the park.

Alone, Jesse felt a longing for—even more! Yes, him—

Near the merry-go-round, Tony Piazza stared at the naked guy who'd just been fucked, and there was another guy about to go at him. He snorted several pinches of coke from the bag he'd stolen earlier. All that fucking and sucking at that bullshit mansion earlier, that fuckin' script—a goddamned *script*—all that bullshit— Hardcore? Shit! *This is the real thing—over there, that kid, those guys. For as long or as short as it lasts, this is the real thing,* he knew, as he jostled aside the guy about to enter the kid—cum spattered on the bare ass—and he rammed himself in until he came.

Buzz, Fredo, and Boo invaded the park, Buzz running ahead.

Jesse heard discordant sounds. Cops? Bashers!

Alerted by a different rhythm, the sounds of invasion, men about the toolshed scattered.

Jesse remained against the wall, did not dare move.

Ernie made his way past the bleachers, going back to where that kid was getting fucked. By now, there'd be lots more cum in him, and he'd jam his own in—a *real* fantasy, all that male cum in that beautiful ass— Wait! That cocky guy strutting toward him, tryin' to look rough, pretending he was a real redneck. Nothing wrong with pretendin', right? He'd check him out before that other man cruising did. He'd swagger right up to the tough-lookin' guy and— Wait, there were two other guys with him—

Driving by, Thomas Watkins had seen men entering a small park, and he had followed them. Now on a tree-flanked path, he heard shouts, saw tangling shadows. He heard curses, the thud of clubs or bats. He moved toward the struggling figures. Thugs were pummeling two prone forms with wooden boards!

Ernie crouched as blows beat down on him and the other man on the ground.

"Fuckin' faggot queers!" The words shattered the silent heat.

Ernie tried to twist away from the motherfuckin' bashers, but he was trapped, and so he lay very still with his eyes closed, pretending he'd passed out so the fists and kicks would stop, pretending this wasn't happening, pretending—

"Stop it! Stop! Help, help!"

Who had shouted that? He had, Thomas realized when he repeated the cry into the night.

Startled, Fredo and Boo turned toward the old fag who had shouted. The two assaulted men staggered away. One fell face down.

Raising himself forcefully, willing his body forward, attempting to pitch himself out of this sweating, bleeding nightmare, Ernie ran out of the park.

Against the wall, Jesse heard footsteps approach closer, stop. He did not dare look back. The biker? No. Whoever was there remained. Jesse heard only harsh breathing.

Orville heard shouts as he was about to enter his car.

Board raised, Boo rushed to beat the shit out of the old faggot who'd yelled for help.

Thomas faced the menacing form about to spring on him.

"Hey, faggot, you want this?" Boo taunted, hitting his own palm loudly with his board. "Ya wannit?"

Thomas did not move. If he could only reach out, wrest the club away. If he could only move—

"Well, you got it, queer!" Boo flailed the board before him, with each step moving closer to the old faggot. He felt hands clutch his shoulders, twisting him away from the old queer. Clint smashed his fist against the punk's surprised face and seized the club, striking at the punk, forcing him down.

Fredo rushed with his board to charge the fag wrestling Boo to the ground. Hands wrenched him back, down.

Dave planted a boot on the fuckin' punk's chest and, leaning over, punched the contorted face. "Fuckin' shit punk!"

Fredo grasped the biker's boot, sending him reeling back. Fumbling for his club, Fredo raised himself.

Clint pinned the punk's arms back.

Dave's fist crashed into the punk's face.

Boo and Fredo slipped, fell, stood, ran. Now two other fags were chasing them, pummeling them. Bleeding, startled, reeling, running,

Fredo and Boo reached the stolen car in the parking lot. Fredo tried to
open the motherfuckin' door—locked. Boo shook it, cursing, Motherfucker, motherfucker—

A hand spun him around.

Orville's fist struck at the punk's face.

Boo dropped to the ground, and Fredo fled into the street. Boo remained bleeding on the concrete. He did not move until he was sure
the nigger queer was gone, and then he ran out of the park in the direction where Fredo had disappeared, and he shouted back, "Fuckin'
faggot queers!"

Orville waited by his car until he saw the punk disappear. He was
about to get in and drive away when— *Was* it him? Yes. He saw, looking at him and waiting by his own car, the man he had danced with
earlier. Was it possible they might still connect? He'd wait, only a few
minutes—a minute— Was it still possible?

When Paul saw the man he'd danced with all night hit the punk, he
felt good, and then he felt even more regret that he and the man had not
connected. Was it still possible?—the black man was staring back at him.
Sometimes it worked out after all kinds of misunderstood signals. He'd
wait by his car, a few minutes, wait for a signal— Was it still possible?

In the park, Clint faced the man in leather who had joined him in
stopping the assault. The older man who had intercepted the mugging
watched them a few feet away. Clint sat on a bench. The man in leather
sat next to him. Cruising shadows reconvened about the park. How
quickly the sex-hunt survived everything, Clint thought.

"We showed those punks," Dave said.

"There's many more," Clint said. They talked in hushed voices, not
to disturb the night. "A friend of mine died," Clint spoke words his
mind had been repeating.

"Older guy?"

"Young."

"Accident."

"He died from a strange illness. Something mysterious, something
new, something terrible—"

"That bullshit some guys are talkin' about?" Dave lowered his voice
more.

"If it's not bullshit—" Clint looked about at the cruising forms. He wiped cold sweat from his face.

"There's one sure way to push all that crap away," Dave said.

With sex, Clint's mind echoed Troy's distant words.

"Wanna get into some heavy stuff with me, dude?" Dave tried to sound as if that had only now occurred to him, had not occurred the moment he had seen this moody, sensual man leaving the alley, the moment when he had felt an allegiance between them, a common bond, the moment when he had known that they were of the same breed. "Share a sex slave? Do everything? That kid I was with—"

The real bashing, the invitation to mimed violence—that paradox had eluded him, too. And yet— Both of them fucking that beautiful kid, telling him what to do, ordering him into humiliation, desiring him and desiring each other, and— Clint's cock hardened.

What the fuck was wrong with this guy? Dave knew he was interested, *way* interested. So what was bothering him? This? "Nobody's gonna force anything, the kid wants it, a kind of celebration, gettin' fucked over and over, but I know he'll want more, wants it wild and hot, wants the wildest at the end of the night, and I know how."

From the distance, Thomas still stared at the two desirable men. He wished he had wrested the clubs away from the thugs. Still, he had summoned help, and he and those two men had joined for moments against the invaders. Now the two men would go off together, and he would be alone.

"Whaddaya say, dude, share a sex slave?" Dave rubbed his fist.

Clint stood, staring down at the biker's black-gloved hand. "No," he said, and he walked away.

Thomas moved toward an exit near a desolate merry-go-round. He would now retreat to his haven in the Canyon.

Alone, Jesse waited for fear to allow him to breathe freely. The silent presence had remained there—Jesse saw a black shadow against the wall, a shadow growing, nearing. Jesse saw the shadow raise a club—

"Fuckin' faggot," Buzz barely whispered as he moved toward the naked queer.

Jesse saw the shadow of the club rise higher, ready to crash down on him. He closed his eyes.

Buzz still waited before the naked body he had been staring at since he had run away from the old fag who had shouted for help. He listened to the naked queer's frightened breathing, and that excited him. He pulled the board back, to crush with more force when he dashed at the queer. Now!

Jesse felt a body hurl itself against him.

Buzz's cock pulsed inside the naked body—*"This is what you want, isn't it, ya fuckin' queer!"*—and then, coming—*"and this is what you're gonna get!"*—he swung the board down with all his force—

Thomas Watkins grabbed the raised club, beating the thug away with it, driving him down to the ground, beating—

Buzz reached for the old faggot's legs.

Thomas kicked at the thug.

Buzz tried to pull the fag down.

Thomas kicked at him, harder.

Buzz squirmed, covering his head.

Thomas kicked again at the twisting body, kicked harder each time, and with each kick he uttered fierce words. "For! All! The! Cruel! Names! For! Every! Ugly! Thing!"

Thrashing with his hands—his face and body hurting, bleeding— Buzz fled out of the park.

Jesse's body felt— Felt—

With a gasp, Thomas stared at the beautiful naked boy, the glistening body against the wall. The frustration, anger, yearning of this long, endless day tangled into desire, only desire. The boy would reject him, but he could overcome him, he was strong, he had just proved it. He staggered forward.

He stopped.

Oh, no, he would never force himself on anyone, much less a beautiful and vulnerable young man.

As he walked to his car, Thomas passed a handsome man he recognized.

Clint made a loose salute toward the man who had stopped the bashers earlier.

Thomas Watkins nodded to him in mutual acknowledgement. Tonight, he thought, I have surrendered the impossible.

Against the wall, Jesse felt captured by the heat, the darkness, felt throttled by the night, the heat, felt abandoned by the dead wind— He was—

Afraid.

He was—

Soon there would be others here. The terror in the park would fade, his own terror would fade— It was already being pushed back by a demand for—

More.

Clint saw against the brick wall of the toolshed the beautiful kid who had smiled at him outside the alleys.

Jesse looked back and recognized the man the biker had recruited. He nodded.

The naked body was shivering within the unbudging heat. Clint held the young man in his arms, close to him, sheltering him from the night, felt the young man's trembling— Should he try to talk him away from whatever it was that was driving him to this? Yes—

No.

Clint felt a respect for fate, and this beautiful young man was pursuing a sort of destiny he had clearly chosen for himself tonight— perhaps only thought he had chosen it—and that must be allowed, wherever it led him beyond the choice.

He turned the kid's face toward his, licked the perspiration there, cooling the heated face, licked the lips—

"Fuck me," Jesse whimpered.

This is all there is—just sex and more sex and still more sex. That's all God gave only us—and to no one else—to compensate for all the shit they keep throwing at us. It's the only thing that blocks it all out. That's all some of us have. When that's gone—for some of us, there will be nothing.

In a rage at death—in a rage at the world that in countless ways exiled this young man from everything except this and then would condemn him for it—Clint thrust himself into the naked body. He held himself there, kissing the young man on the lips, and came.

Jesse kissed the man back.

Clint released the beautiful body.

Jesse leaned back against the wall.

Clint moved away from the night.

And yet, as he walked toward where the sky would eventually dawn, he had the impression that he was walking into deeper darkness, deepest night, and in those uncertain moments, he saw a stark form, a gaunt, terrified man—was he really there?—standing at the edge of the park shouting—was he really shouting?—no, whispering, but it was as if he was shouting each gasped word—

"Plague— Plague is coming. Plague—"

Clint shook his head—no—and walked away.

Shadows stirred about the toolshed.

Jesse waited.

There had been three punks! Dave remembered. Only two of them had been chased out. Where was the third? He ran to the toolshed.

The kid was all right! Dave saw, and he shoved aside two men advancing. The wooden board the punk had carried lay on the ground. Dave touched the kid's shoulder, turning him around. "Did that punk hurt you, kid?"

"No." Jesse laid his head on Dave's shoulder.

Dave took off his leather glove and stroked the kid's hair with his fingers, calming him, stroking. "I won't let anyone harm you, dude." Christ, he had beautiful hair. He felt the kid's skin—so smooth!—against his own bare chest. He ran his fingers down the naked body—so beautiful. He held the kid's face in both his hands, close to his own. Christ, even all shaken up like this, he was beautiful. The kid edged his face closer, opening his lips. With a finger Dave touched them, the parted lips, touched them, his face only an inch away from them, touched them, and he opened his own mouth and leaned forward, to—

"Do you love me?" the kid whispered.

"What!" Dave halted his movements.

The kid did not repeat his words.

Dave eased the kid away from him. He turned him around, to face the wall.

"More," Jesse said.

Yeah! The dude was tough, ready for anything, not scared, *real* tough. Everything would proceed like they'd planned. He'd promised

the kid a wild celebration, the two of them together at the end of the
night, and that was now.

A shadow joined two already watching.

Dave clenched his hand into a fist, holding it, hard, against the kid's
ass.

The kid did not move.

More shadows huddled.

Dave brought out a small bottle, an oily mixture. He rubbed his
fist with it. He cracked an ampule of amyl and held it to the kid's nose.
He cracked another and held it to his own. He rubbed his greased fingers on the boy's ass and held his hand there, fingers tightening.

Gathered shadows watched.

Dave released one finger into the kid, then another—and he
waited—three fingers—and he waited—another finger—four—deep
in—

The kid wrenched.

Dave's hand clenched into a fist and pushed.

Jesse exhaled, a smothered moan.

Dave twisted his wrist, slowly, and pushed again.

Cold perspiration draped Jesse. He wanted to shout, scream, protest, wanted—

"More."

Yeah! Ultimate trust, closer than brothers, the strongest bond
among tough men, real men, all willing, no sissies, nothing questioned,
all allowed!

Dave held his fist inside the kid. Yeah—and after this, he would
fuck him, spill his cum in him—jet loads of cum into the tough dude—
and the kid would come, they'd come together— He held the fist in,
in—

Jesse pressed his mouth against the wall, gnawing at brick. He
screamed—no sound.

Dave withdrew his fist—slowly, slowly, inch by inch, finger by finger before the congregation of men staring in silent awe. He faced them
and held his clenched fist up.

Blood flowed down it, down his elbow, down to the ground.

Dave retreated in horror. He staggered from the sight, fell back. "*No, kid! No!*" he shouted into the stagnant night.

Jesse's body tried to cling to the wall.

Father Norris stood before the toolshed. He saw men kneeling beside the beautiful naked body. With a moan he threw himself into it. When he pulled out, the naked Christ crumbled, shaking, bleeding, outstretched hands reaching.